# MEMORIES OF YOU

MEMORIES
of You

Calypso Key
SERIES

# MEMORIES OF YOU
## Calypso Key Series

ERIN BROCKUS

GREEN SAGE PRESS

# Chapter One

## Stella

EVERY STEP WAS A JOURNEY, from the past to the future. That was never truer than this morning. Sunlight glinted on the gentle waves, making me squint. The path under my running shoes was a familiar one, winding like a lazy river around the perimeter of Calypso Key as I ran. The late-morning sun was going from warm to hot against my exposed shoulders, but the breeze cooled me slightly as I kept a steady pace. My muscles complained from last night's final shift at Blue Nirvana, but I pushed on, the burn a welcome distraction from the whirlwind of thoughts in my head.

*New day, new start.*

A grin tugged at my lips, the kind of smile that comes when you stand on the edge of a precipice. Thrilling and terrifying all at once. Today marked the beginning of my official role as the head chef at Orchid, our family's crown jewel of a restaurant nestled right here on the resort island. My title was more than just a job description—it was the mantle of a dream I'd cradled since I could reach the kitchen counter on tiptoes.

The path wound past the beach barbecue area and onto a trimmed green lawn, the morning's serenity broken only by the rhythmic scrape of a rake over the ground. Peter, a landscaper I'd known since I was a teenager, was raking old leaves and blossoms from the flat expanse of green, his signature straw hat bobbing in time with his movements. He stopped as my brother, Evan, who was Calypso Key Resort's general manager, approached him with a slight hitch in his gait. Halting, the two men spoke.

I detoured to join them. "Morning, guys."

Peter looked up. "Good morning, Stella!" His tone was cheery as he waved a weathered hand. Evan tipped a friendly nod toward me.

I returned the greeting with a smile. "Hey, Peter. How's life treating you today?"

"Can't complain." He leaned on his rake like it was an old friend. His wrinkled face was ruddy and tan from a lifetime of tropical weather. "Welcome back, by the way. Are you done down in Key West yet?"

My eyes met Evan's, the weight of my new title pressing down for a moment. He shot me a sheepish smile and rubbed his clean-shaven jaw. He'd recently shaved off the beard he'd had for years, and I couldn't help smirking that his nervous habit still remained. Despite Orchid being my dream, taking this position hadn't been an easy decision. Less than a month ago, our brother, Gabe, had appeared in the middle of my shift at Blue Nirvana to tell me Orchid had just lost its celebrity chef and was in desperate need of my services.

As in *now*.

I'd stared at him, dumbfounded, as he explained that

Evan had fired their temperamental chef. I couldn't quit my job with no notice, especially since Blue Nirvana was one of the most celebrated restaurants in Key West and had served as my culinary apprenticeship.

"Yes, and I've cleared out my place in Key West," I said to Peter, my running shoes sinking slightly into the soft grass. "I've been juggling the two jobs for several weeks. It's been wild, but it's over now. I'm officially back at Calypso Key as of today."

"And she's already won everyone over," Evan said.

Peter nodded, a knowing glint in his eyes. "Well, if anyone can make Orchid shine, it's you, Stella." A slight grimace crossed his face as he glanced back at his rake and the long stretch of lawn still ahead of him. "I should let you get on with your run and get back to work. See you around."

After he moved away to resume raking, I turned to my brother. "Everything ready for the new landscaping project?"

Evan's evaluating eyes took in the area. "As ready as possible. It's going to be a big job, so get ready to have some disruptions for a few months."

That made me laugh. "I'm an expert at that. I'd better get back to it." With a wave, I stepped back onto the path.

"Thanks for stepping up, Stella. We're glad you're back!" he called after me, his assurance a gentle push against the small knot of anxiety in my chest. I picked up my pace again and soon the winding path opened up to a view of the restaurant.

My restaurant.

Orchid's pale pink walls gleamed against the backdrop of turquoise sea, and warm timber eaves supported the roof. My heart thudded with something more like stage fright than exertion. Instinctively, my pace slowed as I neared the arched live trellis leading to the entrance, my shoes padding softly against the gravel. A delighted smile rose on my face as I stopped to inspect the tropical ground cover that served as a carpet for the structure beneath. There they were—my orchids—nestled among the lush foliage framing the entrance.

"Morning, beauties," I greeted them, bending to inspect a particularly stunning Cattleya. Its petals were a vivid fuchsia, and I marveled at how something so delicate could thrive here. But they did.

I loved cooking with a passion that was almost sacred—the way flavors could weave together to tell a story that ended with the satisfaction of a dessert's flawless presentation. But orchids... they were my secret retreat, my silent partners in the art of creation. I had missed them while living in Key West. But now that I was home again, tending to them would be more than a duty. It would be a privilege, an act of love mirroring the care I poured into every dish. But as I stood there, the weight of my new title pressed upon me with an intensity that tightened my lungs.

"Can I really do this?" The whispered question escaped my lips unbidden, carried away on the breeze before I could snatch it back. Doubt crept in, and I sought to dispel it by moving on. I straightened and stepped to the next bloom, a lacy white Phreatia. Of course I would be a success. I'd spent my life building toward this very moment.

*But is that enough?*

Wiping the sweat from my brow, I returned to the path and my run. I'd dreamed of running a kitchen, yet dreaming and doing were very different things. And I wasn't just stepping into any kitchen—I was stepping into *the* kitchen. The one that represented my family's legacy.

The specter of failure terrified me.

Tightening the elastic band containing my dark hair, I pushed away the nerves, the fear. I focused on keeping a steady pace as I wound through the mangroves fringing the northwest section of the Key. A new wooden boardwalk had been built over the boggy areas, an idea Gabe had implemented. He also loved to run along the perimeter of the island.

As I emerged back into the tropical heat, our ancestral residence appeared in the distance. The Big House, a six-bedroom, three-story home, had weathered over a century of storms and stood firm for generations of Markhams, including my own. To the south of the house, three smaller cottages stood along the bluff that rose steadily northward. My sister, Maia, the baby of the family who now had her own daughter, lived in one with her husband, Wyatt.

The salt-touched breeze still clung to my skin as I pushed open the kitchen door and entered the Big House. The large room was empty, and I continued through it and down the hall to the soaring entry foyer. A grand staircase greeted me, rising three flights. A bedroom on the second floor was my sanctuary—close enough to feel the pulse of family life and high enough to gaze upon the sea's expanse. I tossed my sweaty baseball hat on the familiar dresser, its surface a collage of seashells and photographs.

After showering and changing into crisp black pants and a plain white T-shirt, I reached for my phone. My thumb found my brother's name with practiced ease, and the ringing tone filled the space between anticipation and apprehension.

"Hey, Stella," came Hunter's deep voice.

"Hello yourself," I replied, sitting on my bed. "Just wanted to hear your voice. How's the big city treating you?"

"Same old concrete jungle, but different palm trees," he

replied, but I could hear the tightness behind his words—the distance he felt from the sun-soaked shores of home. South Beach was less than four hours away, but more than distance separated him from us. My little brother was anything but little. At thirty-one, he was four years younger than me and a veritable granite mountain of a man. A mountain of many dark shades.

"Listen, I'm tossing around the idea of a casual family lunch," I said, my words dancing around the suggestion. "Thought maybe you'd want to come down? Nothing fancy, just... us family."

There was a brief silence, the kind that spoke volumes. I imagined him on the other end, weighing the simplicity of the offer against the complexities of our family. "Stell, you know I'd love to see you," he began, and I could picture him shifting in his chair. "But are you just talking sandwiches on the patio?"

"Okay, so maybe there's a slight chance of Dad wanting to eat whatever he catches that morning," I conceded with a laugh, trying to keep the mood light. "And sure, Evan might be there, but..."

"But we have to start somewhere, right?" Hunter's tone warmed despite his caution. "You've always been the heart of this family. Trying to keep us together, even the ones hell-bent on being islands unto ourselves."

"Someone has to, right?" I joked, though my chest tightened at his words. A reunion, even a strained one, was a step toward mending the deep crack between him and Evan. And this time I'd be right there in the middle to keep my brothers from tearing each other apart.

"All right, I'll think about it."

The silence lingered in the air after Hunter's tentative promise, and I could almost picture his lowered brow through the phone, the way he'd rake a hand through his hair when a conversation treaded too close to rough waters.

"I know it's not easy." My voice softened automatically. "After the accident... Just remember—there were two victims that day. Not just one."

Hunter let out a sigh, a sound that seemed to travel across miles of ocean and memory, settling heavily on my heart. "No. Only one victim—Evan. And two brothers who don't speak anymore."

"But you're both trying now. We're family. And everyone's agreed too much time has passed. Even Evan. He knows damn well he was out of line at Gabe's wedding." I pushed the image out of my head. Even though I'd been in the kitchen that evening—when Evan and Hunter had gotten into it at Gabe and April's wedding reception—I could picture the scene all too clearly. A determined spark ignited within me. "It's time to try to repair this leaky old boat. And I'm here to help. We're supposed to get through storms together, right?"

"Sometimes it feels more like a hurricane," Hunter replied, but the ice was breaking, bit by bit.

"Even hurricanes pass. And then we rebuild."

"Idiot brothers and all, huh?"

"Especially the idiot brothers." I couldn't help but laugh, shaking my head. "You guys are a handful, but I wouldn't trade you for the world. All three of you. You can bring a date if you want to."

He groaned. "God, no. I don't have time to date. Besides, the old homestead seems to be the place sending out love waves these days. Which means you're next for Cupid's arrow."

I wrinkled my nose and tried not to shudder. "Absolutely not. You think you don't have time to date? Welcome to my world. No men for me—except for family, of course. I'll make sure the lunch is casual and low key, I promise."

"All right, Stel." His voice, a blend of resignation and affection, came through the phone. "Let me know when you get it set up."

"Promise me you'll give it a chance." I consciously relaxed my hand clenching the phone.

"I already did, remember? Evan was the one who pushed us into the pool, not me." He paused again, then his voice lightened. "But I'll do my best to keep us dry this time. How's that?"

I could hear the half-smile tugging at his lips, a rare expression on Hunter's face. I was one of the few who got to see this sweet, funny side of him. We talked a while longer, discussing his job in private security for an agency in South Beach. He didn't sound happy, though he'd never come right out and say that. He never did.

Finally, we said goodbye, and the click of the call ending was louder than I expected. My fingers lingered on the black surface of my phone, tracing the edges while my mind traced possibilities. My chest filled with a cocktail of emotions—pride for stepping into my new role at Orchid, weariness from the transition, and a tremulous hope for healing between Hunter and Evan.

Returning to my closet, I luxuriated in pulling on my crisp white chef's coat. Dad had presented me with the coat a few days ago. My fingers found the embroidered words on my left breast.

"Stella Markham, Head Chef," I murmured to myself, testing out the title. It had a nice ring to it, even if the echo of responsibility was intimidating. Orchid was part of my heritage, a legacy entwined with the blooms I adored so much. Several of them flourished on a stand near the door to my deck.

My laughter burst out unexpectedly, breaking the silence of the room. With three brothers who each harbored their own brand of chaos, my life was already a whirlwind of love, frustration, and unspoken bonds. Three men who, despite their flaws, were the pillars of my tumultuous world. Along with a fourth pillar we all leaned on—Dad.

Four men in my life. Four men who had a tendency to stir up enough drama to last a lifetime. I hadn't been on a date in several years, but I didn't mind. I lived for two things, career and family. Both kept me plenty busy and very fulfilled.

I trotted down the steps and back out the door, a routine so familiar I didn't need to think about it. With every step toward Orchid, where my day would truly begin, the weight of responsibility grew heavier. But it was no match for the fluttering hope in my chest. The hope for reconciled brothers, for laughter around the dinner table, for days when the worst we had to worry about was who ate the last slice of key lime pie.

Romance? I scoffed as I reached for an apron hanging by the door and smiled at the happy chatter of my fellow workers.

*The only fire I'll be kindling is under the stove.*

And after tying the strings behind my back and stepping into the familiar embrace of Orchid's kitchen, I was ready to turn the page to the next chapter of my life.

# Chapter Two

## Aiden

THE STERILE SCENT of antiseptic hung in the air, but I enjoyed its sharpness. Besides, I wanted my patients to understand I took cleanliness seriously. I tapped away at my laptop, inputting notes into the electronic charting system that was fully modern despite the quaintness of my small-town practice. Then I looked up to meet the steely hazel eyes across from me.

I tried to mask my trepidation with a confident smile. "Ralph, I appreciate you coming in today. I know it's not the most fun thing in the world."

Ralph Porter sat on the exam table, his bare legs dangling over the side like a boy's, though his frame was anything but boyish. His ruddy cheeks ballooned out, partly from years of indulgence and partly from the exertion of climbing onto the table.

"Sure, Doc," Ralph grumbled, eyes narrowed under bushy gray brows. "Or maybe that's too informal for you? Son, I helped you adjust your jock strap, and now you want to tell me I'm fat?" His voice held a gruff edge, a defensive tone that hinted at the complexity of reversing roles from coach to patient. And from hometown boy to physician. It was a tone I'd come to recognize over the past month.

"Things have changed since high school." I maintained eye contact even as the irony of the situation gnawed at me. "We're here to talk about your health now, not football stats."

"Damn straight things have changed," he muttered, folding his arms across his chest.

I suppressed a sigh, the weight of his skepticism an almost physical thing. Ralph's sentiment was common around Dove Key, where familiarity bred a strange blend of fondness and resistance to change. And me—well, I was the boy who had left town, then come back years later a doctor. Some folks found it hard to reconcile the two.

As I set the laptop aside, I moved my rolling stool closer to Ralph, hoping proximity would bridge the gap between past and present. "I know it's weird, seeing me in this role, but I promise you, I take your health seriously."

"Serious as a heart attack, huh?" He tried to laugh, but it came out strained.

"Let's aim to avoid those," I quipped, though my stomach knotted at the mention. Heart attacks were no joke, not here in my exam room, not with the memories of failure shadowing my every decision.

"All right, then," Ralph conceded, a flicker of trust passing through his eyes. "What's the verdict?"

I picked up my laptop again, running through the data we'd collected. "Your blood pressure is still elevated, even after Dr. Nelson increased your amlodipine dose. I gather you'd prefer not to add another medication." I glanced up to catch his firm, exaggerated nod. "Well, let's start by talking about your diet…"

The conversation unfolded, my rhythms of medical advice interspersed with Ralph's objections, then reluctant acceptance. As he lumbered off the table, I allowed myself a hint of victory.

"Thanks… Dr. Mitchell," he said, patting my shoulder on his way out. "I guess I can lay off the beers and burgers at Conch Republic Brewpub a little. Maybe you've got some sense after all."

"Take care, Coach," I called after him, the title slipping out with an ease that surprised me. Maybe some things never changed, even if we did.

After Ralph left, the quiet hum of the clinic settled back around me. Drawn by the irresistible scent of coffee, I decided to take fifteen and headed for the staff break room. Susan, one of my receptionists with a penchant for floral muumuus, was sorting patient pamphlets on the countertop as I poured a cup.

"Hey, Dr. Aiden," she greeted without looking up, her tone casual but friendly. "How are you settling in?"

I leaned against the counter, watching her with a small smile. "Well, I can't complain about the commute anymore." The cheery light-green cottage that housed my clinic was only blocks from where I lived. "Every day's a new adventure. But it feels right, you know? Though Dr. Nelson left some big shoes to fill."

"Big flip-flops, more like." As Maria, a medical assistant, walked in, her dark curls bounced with each step. "The man never wore real shoes unless he had to."

Their laughter was easy and warm, reminding me that despite the occasional old-timer like Ralph who struggled to see me as a doctor rather than the kid who once mowed their lawns, I was welcomed here.

"Speaking of big shoes," Susan said, turning toward me. "You've been doing an amazing job. I hear nothing but praise from patients."

At least what happened between my patients and I stayed in the exam room. "Thanks, Susan. I'm trying." I accepted the compliment, a result of trying to find my medical path. A path that had unexpectedly led me back here.

"More than trying," Maria chimed in, nudging me playfully. "You've won over several hard-liners in less than a month. *And* installed a much better coffee machine. We're glad to have you here. And who else would put up with our terrible jokes?"

I laughed. "I guess I'd miss the terrible jokes too."

"See? It's fate." Maria grinned, and I was thankful for their presence, for this moment of camaraderie amidst the lingering shadows of my past. Of a residency rotation that had gone terribly wrong and changed the trajectory of my career. Even though that had been over six years ago, and I'd been a successful physician for four years, the failure still haunted me.

We spent a few more minutes chatting, discussing upcoming appointments and community events before we left the staff room for our various parts of my homey clinic. The two women dispersed, returning to their tasks with smiles and easy banter. I leaned against the counter, my heart lighter. While I may not have taken the path I had originally planned, this journey—my practice here in Dove Key —was shaping up to be something pretty fantastic after all.

I settled into the rhythm of the afternoon appointments,

and with each diagnosis explained, each listening ear offered, trust was being built. This small town, with its tangled webs of relationships, was starting to accept me not just as the kid who left during his senior year of high school, but as Dr. Aiden Mitchell.

By the time the sun dipped toward the horizon, signaling the end of clinic hours, I had managed to convince Mr. Jenkins to take his diabetes more seriously and Mrs. Henderson to consider physical therapy for her chronic back pain. The sense of accomplishment was a soft glow in my chest as I got in my Tacoma pickup and headed east on Main Street toward home. Salty air drifted through the open driver's window, increasing in pungency as I neared the marina.

Sailing had always been my escape, the rush of wind and the snap of canvas like a balm to my soul. An escape that I'd had to forgo for many years, but which I had enthusiastically embraced as soon as I moved back. After walking down the wooden dock, I sighed with satisfaction as I boarded my sailboat. Trotting down the stairwell led me into the cabin, where I passed through the galley and dinette into my bedroom. It wasn't huge but still held a queen-sized bed. I changed out of my slacks and dress shirt, loving the freedom of a T-shirt and cargo shorts. Back on deck, I grabbed a nearby bucket and was transported from the confines of my medical practice to the freedom of the open sea. Well, the potential of open sea. We weren't quite there yet.

I grabbed a hand sander and attached a fresh sheet of sandpaper before hunkering down on my hands and knees. The hull, once battered by time and neglect, was slowly taking shape under my attentive care. I moved with precision, sanding the rough edges and ensuring every inch of wood became smooth. The work was meticulous, but it gave me purpose—a quiet satisfaction that balanced the demands of my new life.

I paused to run a hand along the smooth grain and could feel the history within the fibers. The boat had seen better days, yet here she was, being restored to her former glory. The stern was so worn that whatever name she'd originally been called was lost to the wind. I needed to christen her, but something as significant as naming a boat took careful consideration. No names had struck me yet, so I was content to wait for inspiration.

Without meaning to, my eyes lifted to study Calypso Key across the narrow channel of water separating the two islands. Every time I came out here, I thought about driving over that bridge and seeing what changes time had brought to Dove Key's illustrious neighbor.

But I always chickened out. Wasn't sure I wanted to know.

The marina was calm at this hour. The only sounds were the gentle lapping of water against the docks and the distant call of seabirds. Standing to give my knees a break, I leaned against the mast. Loneliness had been an unexpected companion since moving back to Dove Key. I hadn't dated anyone in a while, and the quiet nights sometimes weighed on me. My head turned once more to Calypso Key and its sheer bluff on the northeastern edge. Toward all those memories.

Memories of Stella Markham, who had dared me to dream bigger. Her laughter had been the soundtrack of our high school years, her fiery spirit the counterbalance to my cautious nature. Had it really been over fifteen years? She had been my first love—and lover—as I'd been hers. We'd also shared our first heartbreaks when our paths diverged.

Which had been my fault. Unresolved feelings for her surged like the tide, unpredictable and powerful.

Where was she now? Did she ever think of me, of us, or was I just a bitter memory? Stella had always been destined for great things. Surely, she had found them. Lowering once more to the deck, my hands returned to their steady pace. Each stroke was an effort to carve out my place here, where my roots ran deeper than I cared to admit.

The western horizon barely held a hint of orange when I set down my tools. The sailboat's deck creaked gently underfoot, a familiar sound that spoke of progress and patience. After stretching my tight back and giving in to a luxurious groan, I cracked open a cold beer I stored in a nearby cooler. The hiss of escaping bubbles cut through the quiet air. I took a long sip, the chill of the drink a stark contrast to the warmth of the air on my face.

"Here's to small victories." I toasted the empty air, my voice blending with the soft lapping of water against the hull. My sailboat was thirty-seven feet long, and the cabin was in pretty decent shape. Too bad the engine didn't work —I'd had her towed here from where I bought her in Key West. My gaze drifted to the deck panel that covered the engine, where I worked on repairing the motor when sanding and varnishing got to be too tedious.

I leaned against the wheel. It wasn't just the boat that was being restored. I was too, piece by piece. A part of me wondered if this was all an attempt at rebuilding the life that could have been. The life where I had stayed with Stella.

The thought of her was like a ghostly breeze, cooling yet unsettling. I closed my eyes, picturing her dark hair wild in the wind, eyes bright with mischief. We'd been kids then, fearless and foolish, believing we could conquer the world together.

Vivid memories of her wove through my mind. Her smile, the curve of her lips, the intensity of her dark eyes. They all felt so tangible, as if she might appear if I wished hard enough. But wishes weren't reality. Reality was this boat, this town, my practice.

I turned to look at the water, imagining a silhouette beside me and sharing in the quiet beauty of the moment. I pictured Stella as she had been—young, vibrant, full of dreams. But we were both thirty-five now. Time had shaped us into adults with lines of experience etched upon our faces.

What might she look like now? Had life been kind to her?

The light faded completely, leaving only the soft illumination of the boat's cabin and the glow of lights along the marina boardwalk. For a fleeting moment, I had to wonder if Stella was still in the area. My next thought was automatic. If she was, in this small town where everyone knew everyone, might we cross paths again?

# Chapter Three

## Stella

THE CLATTER of pans and the sizzle of searing onions formed a song in Orchid's kitchen, where I stood at the helm, orchestrating the afternoon preparations for dinner service. Our new prep worker, Matt, sliced a cucumber under the watchful eye of Tomas, who had been working for us for years. Tomas and I exchanged friendly nods, then he returned his attention to his apprentice, who was concentrating on his slices with his tongue parked in the corner of his mouth. My sous chef, Rea, with her pixie-like brown hair neatly tamped down, was a blur of movement beside me. After whisking up a passion fruit compote that smelled like tropical rain, she turned to a sprig of chives and took her knife to them with slow but steady precision.

"Stella, these chives okay for garnish?" she asked, holding up a bundle so fresh they could have still been nestled in the soil outside.

"Perfect." Nodding, I stirred a large stock pot of crab bisque. I added a slice of lime, and the scent of buttery seafood mingled with the tang of citrus, anchoring me to the moment. After grabbing a squeeze bottle of olive oil, I arced a line directly into the pot from several feet away, a skill honed by years of practice, and something I barely noticed.

Rea laughed, even as her eyes became round. "Show-off."

I froze in mid-motion. Flaunting my skills had been the last thing on my mind. Being in a kitchen was almost unconscious for me. After a moment's thought, I made light of it. "Learn from the best, right?" I winked at her, but the reminder of a belated phone call I needed to make nagged at the back of my mind, a dull thud against the rhythm of our bustling kitchen. I sighed, ready to slay this dragon at last. "Keep an eye on things, okay? I need to make a call." I peeled off my apron as I headed to my cramped office tucked away in a corner.

"Got it, boss!"

The room was a tiny cubicle that doubled as overstock for pantry supplies, but it was my sliver of quiet amidst the storm of stainless steel and shouting. I dialed the number, the phone pressed against my shoulder as I started to sort through paperwork.

"Dove Key Clinic, how can I assist you?" The receptionist's voice buzzed through the line, professional yet warm.

"Hi, this is Stella Markham. I need to schedule a pap smear. It's been a while—I've been meaning to do it for a while now." I eyed our produce order absentmindedly, sure they wouldn't have an opening for weeks. So I had plenty of time to work up to the horrible, awkward ordeal.

"Of course, Ms. Markham. Let me see when we can fit you in."

As I waited, the sound of something hitting the floor in

the kitchen punched through the thin walls, followed by a muffled curse. "Everything okay out there?" I called out as I wrapped my hand over the phone's speaker, half-standing as if I could see through the wall.

"Damn spuds slipped! I'm on it!" Rea's voice carried back to me, edged with frustration.

"All right, we have an opening—" As the receptionist started, another clatter sounded. This crash was louder, pulling my attention once more.

"Rea?" Anxiety pitched my voice higher as scenarios raced through my head—burns, cuts, scalds...

"Sorry! Butterfingers today, but nothing's on fire, promise!"

"Okay, noted." I forced a laugh, though my heart hadn't quite received the memo to calm down.

"Ms. Markham, are you still there?" The receptionist's voice pulled me back to the call.

"Uh, yes. Sorry about that. Kitchen chaos." I rubbed my forehead.

"Understood. We all have our days. The good news is we just had a cancellation. Can you come in at nine fifty tomorrow morning?"

"Tomorrow morning?" I squeaked, glancing at my calendar. I winced at the blank square, knowing procrastination just went out the window. Maybe it was better to get the damn thing over with. "Yes, that should work. I'll take it." The crashing sound of glass breaking had me spinning toward the door.

"Great," the receptionist chirped. "Dr. Nelson has retired, and the new—"

"Sorry, I need to go," I interrupted. "The new doctor will be fine. See you tomorrow morning." I tapped the end call button before she could finish and set the appointment in my phone. "Everything under control?" I asked as I hurried back into the kitchen.

"Sorry! The potatoes took a dive," Rea admitted, wiping her hands with a towel as a stainless-steel container of them rinsed in the sink. "Then when I gathered them back up, I dropped the bowl again."

"Don't worry, potatoes are resilient." I smiled and examined the brightly colored baby vegetables. Though thin-skinned, I doubted they suffered any real damage. Just to be sure, I picked up one of the fallen tubers and inspected it for bruises. "You know how it goes—one potato, two potato..."

"Three potato—floor." Rea grinned and we shared a short laugh that cut the tension. She picked up a chef's knife and placed the brown vegetable on a cutting board, peering at it. With a sigh, she started cutting it, her hand moving with slow, unsteady motions.

"Let me give you a hand," I offered, grabbing my knife. The familiar weight of the handle brought a comforting sense of order. I sliced the potato into even medallions, falling into a satisfying, peaceful rhythm.

"Damn, Stella. Your knife skills are unreal." The whites around Rea's eyes were obvious as she watched me work. "Think I'll ever get there?"

"Keep at it, and you will," I assured her, tossing the slices into a bowl. "It's all about practice and patience. And being careful. Don't ever rush cutting."

"I do my best not to draw blood." The corners of her lips turned up in a smile.

"Hey." I nodded to her. "You've got the touch. The desserts you whip up? Pure magic."

"Thanks, Stella." Smiling, she started on another potato, while Matt and Tomas gathered several bunches of celery and started to work on them. Matt was slow but focused, exactly what I wanted to see in a new cook.

As I returned to my work, my mind drifted to the upcoming appointment. And the new fact that Dr. Nelson, the familiar face of Dove Key's clinic and practically everyone's childhood, had retired. Change was inevitable, yet it always seemed to come at the most inconvenient times. Instead of having a month to work up to the embarrassment of having my feet in the stirrups, I had to face it in a few hours. Maybe a new doctor would be a good thing. Sometimes it was easier to bare yourself to a stranger.

THE CLINIC WAS a hive of quiet activity, a stark contrast to the morning stillness I'd left behind on Calypso Key. I settled into a corner seat in the waiting room, my gaze flitting over the sea of faces as patients leafed through outdated magazines or tapped on their phones. I fished out my own phone and started scrolling through my favorite cooking blogs. A new post on sous-vide techniques caught my eye, and I lost myself in the culinary possibilities.

"Stella Markham?" a woman's voice cut in.

"Here." I pocketed my phone and followed a pretty, dark-haired medical assistant down the hallway. The scent of antiseptic hung in the air, mingling with the low hum of hushed conversations from behind closed doors.

"Step on the scale for me, please," she said, her tone professional yet friendly. Her nametag read Maria.

I complied, watching the digits flash before stepping off, and was pleased with the number. All that running paid off, keeping me trim despite being a chef. After seeing me into an exam room with white paint and seascapes on the walls, she wrapped the cuff snugly around my arm.

"Blood pressure's good," she noted, tapping the entry into my electronic chart.

"Good to hear." I tried to sound nonchalant as I eyed the exam room, its ominous metal stirrups already out. I felt silly but couldn't help myself. I should be used to this procedure by now, but it always made me anxious and slightly embarrassed.

The medical assistant took my vitals, typing away on her laptop, then closed it with a thump. "Go ahead and change into this, and I'll come back in after the doctor introduces himself." She handed me a paper top and drape with a practiced smile before slipping out.

Alone, I shed my clothes with mechanical movements, draping my T-shirt over the chair. I perched on the edge of the exam table, the paper beneath my naked butt crinkling in a stark reminder of my vulnerability. I folded my hands in my lap over the light-blue paper drape, desperately wishing for the comfort of my chef's coat—anything to shield me from the clinical chill of the room. At least I left my socks on.

Closing my eyes, I envisioned the familiar expanse of Orchid's kitchen, the sizzle of pans, and the whirr of mixers —a controlled chaos that soothed me. But here, in the silence, my thoughts churned like the ocean during a brewing storm.

*Get a grip. You're not a teenager.*

Opening my eyes, the beach scenes on the walls did nothing to ease my nerves. At least Maria would be in the room too. *Routine* was a word that had always suited me. In the kitchen, it translated to perfect slices and satisfied diners. My career was my life. And now, sitting on a vinyl table while shrouded in paper, I braced for the intrusion of cold hands and colder instruments.

The muffled sound of movement outside the door snatched my attention. Then it stopped. A long pause lingered, heavy with anticipation. The door handle turned, almost in slow motion, before the plain brown door swung open.

And time stalled like a caught breath.

I'd thought I was tense before. Now I became brittle. Frozen at the sight of the man before me.

"Good morning." His words were quiet and hesitant as our eyes met. He softly shut the door, leaving his hand pressed against the wood, as if he didn't know what to do with it.

I stared at Aiden.

Aiden Mitchell.

My new doctor was my old boyfriend.

My first.

The one I'd thought was *the one*.

His face, once so familiar, now held the etchings of years gone by, lines carved by laughter or perhaps sorrow. His posture was rigid, the knuckles gripping his laptop bleached white. But it was the flush of color high on his cheekbones that betrayed him most, revealing an emotion he couldn't completely conceal behind his professional façade.

For a moment, neither of us moved. I was a statue locked in a tableau of shock, waves of numbness rolling over me. The soft hum of the fluorescent lights above filled the void between us as I grappled with reality.

"Stella," he finally managed, his voice a low rumble that resonated with memories I thought I'd buried deep. He took a deliberate step into the room. "I didn't know if you were still in the area. And I wasn't sure you'd want to use my practice..."

"Aid... *Aiden?*" I asked, my voice quivering and breathy. I clutched the edges of my paper gown with trembling fingers, suddenly acutely aware of my bare breasts beneath. How utterly exposed I felt—not just in flesh but in history.

He took a deliberate step forward, his forehead deeply lined. "You look surprised to see me."

"How the hell did you think I would feel?" I snarled quickly, erecting walls with my tone. My mind raced, scrambling as each emotion surged before being drowned by something else—embarrassment, anger, confusion.

Now Aiden's expression changed to shock, his eyes opening wide. "You didn't know I was the doctor here?"

"Know? How could I possibly—Get out!" My voice crackled with a mix of vulnerability and wild indignation. Gathering the shreds of my dignity, I vaulted off the exam table, using one hand to keep all my flimsy paper coverings in place. My feet slapped against the cold tile as I pushed past him, shoving the door open wide.

"Stella, wait—"

"Out!" I hissed and let go of the drape to place one hand on his chest. The paper covering my lower body fell to the floor, causing me further mortification. At least Aiden kept his wide, shocked eyes on my face. I shoved hard, doing my best not to notice how firm the muscles under my hand were. He stumbled backward out of the room, and I slammed the door in his stunned, slack face. The thought of Aiden seeing me like this, after all these years, was too much. The heat in my cheeks rivaled the midday sun.

I grabbed my clothes and began pulling them on with frenzied urgency. My heart was a drumline, pounding erratic rhythms against my ribcage, threatening to break free. Fumbling with my shirt, I barely managed to slide it over my head. My fingers shook wildly. I scarcely noticed how my pants twisted as I pulled them up or how my sandal straps tangled around my ankles.

I stormed out of the exam room, eyes rooted firmly on the floor and my face aflame as I ran down the deserted corridor. I didn't look up when I reached the waiting room either. When I finally emerged from the clinic, the bright sunlight outside was disorienting. I blinked rapidly, my mind replaying the awful encounter, each detail etching into my memory.

Aiden Mitchell.

After... I had to count... seventeen years! The boy who stole my heart and dashed it upon the rocks was here. My first love. Now a professional man in a white coat, holding the power to examine me in my most vulnerable state. The irony made my stomach churn.

The drive back to Calypso Key passed in a blur, the scenes around me out of focus. The Big House, with its stone foundation and windows reflecting the light, promised refuge—a fortress against the storm of embarrassment raging within me. After parking, I hurried through the door and ran up the stairs.

"Stella?" Maia's voice cut through my turbulent thoughts as I stepped past the second-floor salon, the space awash in morning light.

I halted, turning toward her. "Hey." The word stuck in my throat like dry dough. Like me, my younger sister had the dark hair and eyes of a classic Markham, and today she wore her long hair in a messy bun on top of her head. "Escaping from mommy duty?" I tried to use ordinary conversation to center myself.

She was lounging on the antique sofa, her feet tucked

beneath her and a paperback in her hand. A smoke-gray cat with bright green eyes was curled up in an armchair next to her. Smiling, Maia put the book face down on her thigh. "Yeah. Wyatt's watching Skye so I could do a little reading. It's so peaceful here in the Big House, especially compared to our cottage."

I tried to listen as I approached, but my mind still whirled.

Maia noticed and sat up straighter, worry etching her features. "You're as white as your shirt. What's going on?"

After picking up the cat, Pilar, I flopped into the armchair opposite her, my knees giving out as the familiar scent of candle wax and aged wood enveloped me. Pilar purred as I stroked her in my arms. "I have no idea. You won't believe who's back in town."

"Who?" Her eyebrows knitted together.

"Aiden." His name felt strange on my tongue, foreign, as if invoking a specter from the past.

Maia's brow knotted further, then went smooth. Her eyes widened. "Your old boyfriend? From high school?"

"*Doctor* Aiden Mitchell," I corrected, the title leaving a bitter taste. "He's the new provider at the Dove Key clinic. And guess who didn't know that until she was sitting mostly naked on the exam table waiting for a pap smear?"

"Shut up!" Maia gasped, her hand flying to her mouth. "Oh, honey, that's just... ugh, I can't even imagine."

"Neither could I," I mumbled, the heat rising to my cheeks again.

Maia leaned forward, her eyes sympathetic. "Are you okay?"

"Not really. I'm embarrassed. Angry. Humiliated." Each word thudded dully in the room. Pilar must have picked up on my mood because she squirmed in my arms until I gently set her on the floor. She padded out of the parlor, presumably to a quieter destination. I turned back to Maia. "It's like I'm eighteen all over again, and he's the center of my universe. Except this time, it's my adult dignity he's trampled on."

She reached out, her hand covering mine. "What are you going to do now?"

Her question hung in the air between us, mingling with the faint sound of waves from outside. I stared at the delicate pattern of the rug underfoot.

"I don't know, but it looks like I'll need to find a new doctor. There's a clinic in Marathon."

"That's certainly understandable." Her delicate eyebrows arched. "I wonder why he came back. Maybe he wants to see you again."

I snorted and rushed a hand through my hair. "He's probably married with three kids by now. Who knows why he returned? And it doesn't matter anyway. Aiden is a chapter I closed long ago."

She nodded slowly, snapping her book shut and setting it on the end table next to her. "But sometimes the past has a way of resurfacing when we least expect it."

"Maybe so." I watched a tern glide effortlessly above the waves. "But that doesn't mean I have to read that awful story again."

"Stella, look at me."

I turned my face toward hers. Maia might be several years younger than me, but she had been through her own romantic travails.

"You're not a teenager anymore. You're a successful chef, a businesswoman, and a force to be reckoned with."

"You're right." I squared my shoulders. "Aiden might have been my first love, but he's not my last. And... well, he can stay a footnote in my history book. An asterisk with *mistake* after it."

"Good." Maia hugged me, her embrace warm and unwavering. I allowed myself a moment, just one, to lean into her support.

"Let's go downstairs," I suggested. "I've got a restaurant to run and a life to live—without any unwanted plot twists."

Maia laughed, looping her arm through mine as we stood and headed for the staircase. "That's the spirit. Besides, Orchid needs its fearless leader."

"Speaking of which," I added, "I think it's time to try out my new seafood medley recipe. What better way to wash away the taste of awkward reunions than with the flavor of success?"

As we stepped into the bustle of the manor's main floor, that sense of dislocation slipped away, and I became filled with a renewed sense of purpose. Aiden Mitchell had once been my everything. But now I was my own anchor, completely focused on the career I had at last achieved.

# Chapter Four

## Aiden

THE NIGHT HAD ALREADY DRAPED its velvet cloak over Dove Key when Luke asked for permission to board, a growler of beer from Conch Republic Brewpub cradled in his arm. The clink of glass hinted at the promise of easing the day's tension and I rose to my feet, more than ready for some distraction.

"Granted," I called out. "You're the one with the beer."

Tall and rangy with a handsome, amenable face, Luke Stallings and I had been friends since we were kids growing up together. We'd kept in touch over the years and renewed our in-person friendship as soon as I'd come back.

"Hope you're ready for a taste of the best brew on the island." With a satisfying clunk, he set the growler down on a rough-hewn table next to the two pint glasses I'd already gathered from the galley.

I smiled somewhat grimly. "I'm more than ready."

Our camping chairs creaked as we settled into them, the canvas seats embracing us. The glow from the lights along the marina's boardwalk cast a warm, inviting ambience that contrasted with the chill in my bones—a coldness that had little to do with the lilting breeze wafting in from the sea.

"Quiet night," I murmured. The marina was a busy hive of charters and fishermen during the day, but at night, the voices gave way to creaking lines and lapping water.

A bartender at Conch Republic for years, Luke popped open the growler like the pro he was. The yeasty scent of hops and malt rose up to meet us. "Yeah. Quiet's good, though. Lets a guy think." He poured golden liquid into the two glasses.

*Or overthink.*

"Cheers. To small-town living and big-time dreams," Luke toasted, raising his glass toward the stars as he drifted a hand through his loose brown locks. "And nights off, unlike some slackers like you who only work the day shift."

"Cheers," I echoed, the beer leaving a bittersweet trail down my throat as I stared into the distance, unseeing.

"Something's eating at you. Dish, man." Luke's voice broke through the silence that had settled between us. He was leaning forward, elbows on his knees.

"Stella came into the clinic today." The words tumbled out before I could stop them.

"Stella Markham?" His eyebrows shot up, a glint of recognition sparking in his eyes. "As in *that* Stella?"

"Yeah, that Stella." I swirled the contents of my glass, watching the liquid spin. "It's been... a lot, seeing her again."

"Did she come in for a check-up or something?"

"Or something," I muttered, not about to discuss particulars about a patient.

Or even a not-patient.

Standing outside the exam room, I'd clicked open the

appointment to see who was on the other side of the door, just like with any other patient. Then I saw that name and stumbled to a complete halt, a wave of freezing, shocked numbness sweeping over me. I'd stared at the closed door, intensely curious to see her. But I never imagined she wasn't expecting to see me.

"Aiden?" Luke pulled me back to the present, and I glanced up to see both brows halfway up his head. "Are you thinking about trying again? With her, I mean?"

"Trying implies there might be success at the end of the effort." My words felt slow and heavy. "I don't know if she'd even entertain the idea. She wasn't excited to see me. She didn't even realize I was the doctor who took over the practice."

"Ouch. So it wasn't a happy reunion."

A bitter laugh tumbled out of my mouth. After Stella slammed the exam-room door in my face, I'd stood there like a statue. A statue with a raging pulse. Fortunately, she'd been in the room at the end of the hall, so no one was near to see me hurry across the carpet to an open exam room and close the door as silently as I could. Then I leaned back against it, resting my head against the wooden surface as my mind whirled and spun in tight little circles. I'd passed the rest of the day in a haze, welcoming the distractions of my patients simply because they kept me from thinking about that shocked, horrified look when she'd recognized me.

I rubbed my gritty eyes. "Not exactly. Seeing her again —It was like a punch to the stomach." The image of Stella as she sat on that exam table flashed vividly in my mind. The tightness in my chest constricted further. "After all this time, thinking of what she might look like now. And she's..." I trailed off, words failing to encapsulate the rush of emotions.

"Aiden. You're not exactly chopped liver, you know. She's what?"

"More beautiful than I ever imagined. And seeing her so... stunned." *And embarrassed. Mortified.* "It caught me off guard."

"Sounds like she still affects you pretty strongly."

"Yeah." I looked away. "I left my senior year and never looked back. She's probably never even thought about me in years. I can patch up any wound, set any bone, but facing her after this? That's a different kind of fear."

"Because you think she'll tell you to go to hell?"

"Because I'm sure she will. She has every right to."

"Stella's visit really did a number on you, huh?"

"Like a wrecking ball to a glass house." With a deep sigh, I leaned back in my chair and stared at the sky, trying to find some solace in the constellations. I could feel Luke's sympathetic eyes on me.

"Look, I get it. She's... she was your world once." He took a slow sip from his beer, thoughtful. "And maybe that's where she should stay."

"Maybe," I replied with a frown, though a part of me knew he had a point. I reached for the growler and poured the final bit into our glasses.

"Look, I'm not saying forget her. That would be impossible. But maybe... don't let the past hold you back from something better."

I ran a hand through my hair, letting out a long breath. "I know. I do. I was settling in here. I was even thinking about looking around for someone to date. But now..."

"Now things got a little cloudier, huh? Like sailing into the deep, murky unknown?"

"Since when did you become a poet?" I teased. Our laughter mingled with the distant sounds of the ocean.

"Since I came over for a beer and instead found you reeling over a woman." Luke's tone might have been light, but his eyes were serious. "You'll have to find out whether Stella is your hurricane or your haven. Or just a part of your past."

"Yeah, that about sums it up."

Except there had been a tightness in my chest at his last sentence. The one about leaving Stella in the past. Was that what I wanted? I settled back in my chair and rubbed my forehead.

The growler sat empty on the table, a testament to the evening's camaraderie and catharsis. I glanced at my watch, the comforting weight of responsibility settling on my shoulders. "I've got to be at the clinic early tomorrow." I stood and stretched the tightness from my limbs.

"Ah, Dr. Mitchell, the respectable professional," Luke teased, tipping an imaginary hat as he stood too. "Gone are the days of closing down bars and waking up on the beach."

The corner of my mouth lifted. "Or slumped in your car. Yeah, I've got an image to portray these days."

He clapped me on the shoulder, his smile softening. "For what it's worth, I'm proud of you, Aiden. Chasing after that dream—a big dream—and making it happen. You've wanted to be a doctor your whole life."

"Thanks, but..." I hesitated, my gaze drifting off to where the dark outline of the sea met the sky. "Following my dream in Michigan somehow led me back here. Funny how life doesn't care much for your plans."

"Life's like that," he agreed, picking up the empty growler. "The best stories are the ones you never see coming. See you later."

"Good night." I waved as he ambled off the boat, though

my thoughts were already chasing the possibility of reconnecting with Stella, of rewriting our story.

In the silence of the marina, I padded down the stairs into the cabin. The boat's soft, soothing creaking filled my bedroom. I sank into my bed, the pillow cool beneath my folded arms as I stared at the ceiling fan swirling lazily above. Stella's face flashed before my eyes—the way her cheeks had flamed, the horrified glint in her eyes.

"Shit," I muttered under my breath, rubbing a hand over my stubble. She was far more stunning than any fantasy I'd conjured up over the years. Those endlessly deep brown eyes, and that perfect oval face. The thought of approaching her, of laying myself bare to the possibility of rejection—it set my heart racing. How could I possibly bridge the gap between us? What words would unravel years of silence and untended wounds?

The empty years I had created, not her.

# Chapter Five

## Stella

THE BELL ABOVE SWEET DREAMS' door chimed as I pushed through the entrance, the rich scents of freshly ground coffee beans and cinnamon wrapping around me like a warm embrace. The bakery was bustling with the morning regulars, the clatter of cups and the murmur of conversation creating a lively atmosphere.

"Stella, over here!" Grace's voice cut through the hum of activity. I spotted her in our usual corner, her smile as big as the blueberry muffin on her plate.

"Hey," I greeted, dropping my bag onto the chair. Grace stood up for a quick hug, her presence a reminder of simpler times. She had ash-blonde hair and bright blue eyes, and maybe the contrast was what had drawn us together all those years ago. We'd been friends as long as either of us could remember, making sure to keep in touch even when we lived on separate keys.

"Long time no see," she teased, though it had only been a couple of weeks since our last coffee date. "So did you run ten miles this morning so you could eat a guilt-free donut?"

"Only two. I wanted some extra time to tend to my orchids." Smiling, I glanced at the counter. Liv was manning the register today, her apron dusted with flour, her long, curly hair pulled back in a no-nonsense ponytail. She caught my eye and waved me over.

"Morning, Stella," Liv said as I approached, her smile easy and genuine. "The usual?"

"Please." I dug for my wallet. "How are the early mornings treating you?"

"Better than your late nights, at least for me." The baker laughed, ringing me up. She lived with my brother, Evan, in a first-floor suite of the Big House. "Though I do like the solitude when I get up so early."

"I know what you mean," I agreed, handing over my card. "I feel the same way when I get off in the wee hours. Hardly a trace of people in the house."

"Speaking of which, Evan's been asking when you'll get together with us. He says he hardly sees you since you've been home. Maybe lunch or dinner?"

I laughed at that. "He's inside Orchid's kitchen almost every day! But we'll figure something out." I gave her a smile as thoughts of Hunter flashed through my mind. A simple invitation was never simple when he was included. And I hated that. "Thanks, Liv."

"Anytime," she replied before attending to the next customer.

Back at our table, Grace sipped her latte, eyes curious. "So how are things at the Big House?"

"Chaotic sometimes and silent others." I stirred the foam on my coffee. "But it's home, you know?"

"Always has been, no matter where you were," she

spoke softly, understanding the unspoken words. The Big House was more than just a structure. It was where my roots dug deepest.

"Enough about me." I refocused on her. "How's school?"

"I love my class this year!" Grace beamed. She was an elementary school teacher here on Dove Key. "If you didn't dislike kids so much, I'd invite you to come see my new decorations."

I shrugged and took a sip of coffee. "I don't hate kids. I love my two nieces. I've just never felt the urge to be around them twenty-four seven." Unbidden, the unrealized future I'd had with Aiden all those years ago filled my mind, and my happy mood dimmed. "Maybe I should come see your cheery classroom. I could use a bit of beauty in my day."

"Why is that?" Grace asked.

With a deep sigh that weighed a thousand pounds, I told her the story of meeting Aiden again. The words started slowly, then picked up steam as they carried every awful detail.

Her eyes got wider with the telling. "Gawd! What an awful way to reunite. I'm sorry." Wincing in sympathy, she reached over and patted my hand. "So you didn't do any type of catching up, I take it?"

"I literally shoved him out the door, then redressed and ran out of the clinic."

"So that's the end? You have no interest in seeing him again? I agree, that wasn't the most auspicious beginning, but a lot of time has passed, Stel. What did he look like?"

My fingers traced the rim of my coffee cup. "He looked... well, he looked gorgeous. Not that it matters," I added quickly, feeling heat rush to my cheeks as my heart fluttered traitorously.

His hair was still dark blond, but now was cut short and professional, and his warm blue eyes hadn't changed either. He had a handsome, ruddy face as if he spent much of his time off outdoors. He'd always loved boats... I swallowed as I remembered the feel of his very firm chest under my palm.

"You sure about that?" Grace asked quietly.

I recalled the restless nights I'd spent since that appointment, tossing and turning with his image haunting me. When he'd first entered my exam room, there had been hesitation in his eyes—as if he was pleased to see me but was afraid of how I'd receive him. But I hadn't glimpsed any shock. Not like what I'd experienced. In hindsight, it made sense since he'd mentioned that he thought I knew he was the new doctor in town. "I'm not sure of anything where he's concerned."

"Hey, it's okay. You're allowed to think he's hot." Grace leaned forward, her tone serious despite the playful twinkle in her eye. "I've heard there's a new doctor everyone's swooning over," she said, trying to sound indifferent. "Now I know who it is."

"Yeah, Aiden Mitchell."

"And the reason they're swooning is because he's Dove Key's most eligible bachelor..." she said with a pointed look.

Which answered my silent question about his marital status. "I'm not planning on seeing him again." A deep, secret part of me protested at the decision.

"Stella, why not? You're both adults now. You've got nothing to lose by talking to him. Is your hesitation because of your appointment?"

I shook my head. "No. As humiliating as that little reunion was, that's not what's stopping me. It's because..." I paused, the words catching in my throat. "I want to know what he's been up to, yes. What kind of man he's become. But it's so difficult and convoluted."

"Life's convoluted," Grace replied softly. "But sometimes it's worth untangling the knots, don't you think?"

"I'm not sure." My gaze drifted back to the street where life in the small town continued, unhurried and peaceful. Yet inside, I felt anything but peace. Aiden's return had stirred my calm waters, and now undercurrents were pulling me in directions I wasn't sure I wanted to go.

"Stella, talk to me," Grace said gently, pulling me back from the scene outside. "You have circles under your eyes. Let me guess—you've been tossing around the last few nights?"

I took a sip of coffee before letting out a shaky breath. "Yeah, I have. Seeing Aiden again stirred up a lot of old feelings."

"Understandable." She leaned back in her chair, her expression open and attentive. "He was your first love, after all."

"More than that." The words spilled out as the dam of my emotions broke. "I thought we had a future together. Senior year was supposed to be our launchpad—not just for college, but for us. Forever."

She nodded, her eyes never leaving mine. "I know. I was there, remember? You had it all planned out. Until he moved away."

"That was bad enough." I didn't care about the bitterness tainting my tone. "But we had it worked out. We'd hold onto our relationship long-distance and see each other whenever we could. Except that's not what happened. He completely ghosted me, Grace!"

"I know how much he hurt you. I'm still not sure you completely got over it."

I scowled at her. "I've had boyfriends."

"True. Casual relationships where you held the guy at arm's length."

"If the disaster with Aiden taught me anything, it's that my career is what matters. Especially now. But I can't deny that I'm reeling. I thought the wound had healed over, but now I'm not so sure. How am I supposed to trust someone who cut me off like I meant nothing?"

"Maybe he had his reasons?" she suggested, but her eyebrows knitted together as she quickly added, "Not that it excuses him."

"Reasons that couldn't include a phone call or a message? His family moved back to Michigan so he could go to college there where they had roots—and in-state tuition costs. I understood that part of it. Hell, I wanted him to chase his dream of becoming a doctor! But the rest? How could he just go radio silent?" I shook my head and laughed without humor. "Now he's back, and part of me wants nothing to do with him. But a different part wants to ask why—why he left, and why he never reached out."

"Are you going to?" Grace tilted her head, studying me.

I sighed, staring into the depths of my coffee as if it might hold answers. "I don't know. Should I really dig up the past when I'm not sure I can forgive what he did?"

"Only you can decide that, Stella. But whatever you choose, I'm here for you."

"Thanks, Grace. I mean it." I managed a half-smile. "It's just hard to forget the dreams I had. All those plans that vanished when he did."

"Sometimes, people come back into our lives for a reason." Grace's gaze drifted out the window. "Maybe this is a chance for closure. Or a new beginning."

"Or a repeat heartbreak," I countered, though her

words ignited a flicker of hope I was afraid to acknowledge. "Even if we did meet up again, which seems likely given how little our two keys are, I couldn't just pounce on him and demand answers. I need to think about this. All of it."

As I DROVE BACK to Calypso Key, Liv's comment about a family meal came back to me, and I placed the call on my Bluetooth.

"Stella." Hunter's deep voice was even yet cautious. "To what do I owe the pleasure?"

I inhaled deeply, letting the cool air fill my lungs before exhaling. "I wanted to get back to you about your visit. How about lunch at the Big House? Like, soon?"

There was a pause, then a long sigh. "You're persistent. I'll give you that."

"Maybe so, but we have to start somewhere, right?" I watched a lone pelican dive into the ocean, resurfacing with its prize. "You and Evan. All of us. We're family."

"All right," he said with quiet resolve in his voice. "I'll come."

"Good. I'll figure out the details and let you know." My heart lifted a fraction as I ended the call. One hurdle crossed.

I sent Evan a quick text next.

> Stella: Dinner tonight during my break?
> Need to talk.

> Evan: Sure. I can meet you at eight.
> Problem?

> Stella: Nope. Just missing my little brother.

> Evan: Okay, now I know there's a problem.

I sent back a poo emoji and laughed. But as I parked in my usual spot in the voluminous garage of the Big House, it faded. Evan had agreed to meet Hunter, but that didn't mean it would be easy. For any of us.

---

"Spit it out, Stel." Evan's impatience was evident as he drummed his fingers on the wooden surface. Despite the private ambiance of a table tucked away from Orchid's main dining room, the tension between us felt thicker than the humid evening air. Now that the moment was here, I'd been hemming and hawing, chatting about nonsense. My brother's handsome, clean-shaven face grew stonier, and finally, I jumped in.

"Hunter's coming home for lunch," I said abruptly, like ripping off a bandage.

Evan stopped drumming and leaned back in his chair, his expression becoming guarded. Unlike the rest of us, Evan took after our deceased mother in looks, with light-brown hair and blue eyes. "When?"

"Sometime next month. He agreed to it." I cradled my iced tea, tracing the condensation on the glass. "We need to mend things, Evan."

He smiled, a more natural expression for him. "Always the peacemaker, aren't you?"

"We can't choose our family. But we can choose to try to fix what's broken."

"Easy for you to say." He glanced away, suddenly finding a gorgeous bright pink cymbidium orchid fascinating.

"I know it's not easy for you," I shot back. Frustration crept into my voice as he darted his eyes back to me. "I did you a favor by taking this position and starting immediately, remember? Now it's your turn to help make this work."

He ran a hand through his hair, the gesture one of exasperation more than concession. "I get it, Stella. You stepped up when I needed to sort out my own mess. It's just..." Evan's voice trailed off, his eyes dropping to the wooden tabletop as his jaw bulged.

"Hey." I reached across, placing my hand over his in an unspoken plea for understanding. "We said we'd support each other, right? Hunter's trying to reach out after all this time. We can't just shut him out. And you need this as much as he does."

Evan sighed heavily, and the fight drained out of him. "I know what I promised. Fine. I'll sit down to a meal with Hunter and anyone else brave enough to come. But if the whole thing goes south, it's on you."

"Fair enough." I nodded, even though my stomach twisted. "Just remember, we're all adults here. We've changed."

"Have we?" he asked pointedly.

"Only one way to find out." I forced a smile, wishing I felt as confident as I sounded. "If things get tense, we'll deal with it as a family."

"Family," he repeated, almost wistfully before giving me a resigned nod.

I withdrew my hand and took a sip of iced tea, the cool liquid doing little to calm my nerves. "There's something else." I glanced toward the window where the ocean brushed against the shore. At the unpleasant surprise that had greeted me upon entering for my shift. The empty spaces had jumped out and practically bitten me. "Two orchids are missing from the outdoor wall display. And Ben Coleridge—"

"Ben?" Evan perked up, his interest piqued. "What about him?"

"He's part of the landscaping company doing the work installing new lines and sprucing up the grounds." I hesitated, piecing together my thoughts. "I can't help wondering if there's a connection."

Evan snorted. "He's a damn Coleridge and the last person we need hanging around here. But we can't tell the landscaping company who to hire, can we? Still, it wouldn't hurt to keep an eye out. Thanks for the heads-up."

The Markhams and Coleridges shared enmity that went back over a century. Hell, Gabe had gotten into a fist fight with Ben the first night he'd returned home to Calypso Key. Having a Coleridge around was never a good thing.

A server approached, refilling our glasses, and the momentary distraction allowed me to collect myself. My gaze lingered on Evan's profile as he thanked her, the lines of worry etched into his forehead now smoothed out.

"Let's just focus on getting through dinner with Hunter." I forced cheerfulness into my tone. "A couple of orchids is no big deal. I'll go to the farmer's market and pick up more."

"Spoken like a true Markham," Evan joked, raising his glass in a mock toast.

"Thanks," I said, grateful for his support. Evan was like the sun, always there and warming everything it touched. Except Hunter, anyway. "I just hate the thought of there being trouble in paradise, you know?"

"Paradise is where trouble often likes to vacation." Evan broke into a broad smile, a gleam entering his eye that warned me something was coming. "Speaking of unexpected visitors, I heard Aiden Mitchell made quite the entrance back into town—and right into your path, no less."

I rolled my eyes, huffing a sigh. "Isn't anything a secret around here?"

"Come on, Stella." His laugh sounded like the breeze whispering through the trees outside. "You know better than that. You told *Maia*. But hey—" Sobering, he leaned forward, his elbows resting on the table. "He's not a high school boy anymore. He's Dr. Aiden Mitchell now, and you're not the same starry-eyed girl either. You going to see him again?"

"Maybe," I conceded, my thoughts drifting to Aiden's hesitant gaze when he walked in, the way my pulse now quickened despite my reservations. "But I'm not sure I want to."

"Time changes people, Stella." Evan's voice softened, that old vulnerability peeking through. "You should give him a chance to explain. Who knows? Things might be very different this time."

"Perhaps," I murmured, then stared straight at Evan. "Just remember that when Hunter comes home. If Aiden deserves a second chance, so does our brother."

Evan took a deep breath and exhaled slowly, his gaze turning toward the horizon where countless stars glittered like jewels. "I'll try," he promised quietly. "For you, I'll try."

"Try for you too." As we raised our glasses, I hoped the tide was turning in our favor—that the storms of the past could give way to calmer waters ahead.

For all of us.

# Chapter Six

## Aiden

THE AIR BUZZED with the energy of Saturday morning commerce, bringing a smile to my face as I strolled along the central walkway of the weekly farmer's market on Dove Key. Locals and tourists alike mingled in the narrow aisles formed by stalls overflowing with vibrant produce, handmade crafts, and fresh seafood straight from the boats moored near mine. May had always been one of my favorite months in the Keys, and today was a chamber of commerce day.

"Morning, Doc Mitchell!" a sun-leathered fisherman I'd seen several times in my clinic called out as he hauled a cooler filled with snapper onto his icy display.

"Looks like a good catch, Tom," I replied, my voice tinged with the warmth this tight-knit community drew out of me. A community I was now a part of in a way I'd never been as a boy.

I moved through the crowd, taking in the scents—the salty brine of the sea mixing with the sweet aroma of ripe strawberries and the sharp tang of freshly baked sourdough from Mrs. Linley's bakery stand. In the background, the sound of a fiddle blended with children's laughter near the playground, crafting a song of simple pleasures.

Then my feet stumbled to a halt. Stella stood not ten feet away. She was at a flower vendor's booth, her fingers delicately tracing the petals of an orchid. I'd seen no hint of her since the debacle in my office two weeks ago, and that only made her appearance before me more striking. Sunlight caught in her dark hair, adding bright highlights, and her smile held the effortless charm that had once undone all my defenses.

"That one is hardy enough for the restaurant," the vendor said to her.

"They're all so beautiful. I can't decide!" Stella laughed, the sound tinkling like wind chimes caught in a gentle breeze.

I hesitated and shifted from foot to foot, torn between the safety of distance and the magnetic pull of her presence. My hands found the pockets of my shorts, seeking something to ground them. There was so much I wanted to say, to ask. *Go on, talk to her*, the little voice in my head urged, but doubt weighed my shoes down.

She was now holding the orchid up to the light, examining its roots as a furrow of concentration etched her brow. The expression was familiar, one that signaled her deep focus and attention to detail. I squared my shoulders and took the first step toward her.

"Morning, Stella," I called out softly as I approached, not wanting to startle her this time.

The plant froze in her hands. She slowly turned, and a hint of pink crept over her cheeks. "Hi, Aiden." Her blush deepened when our eyes met.

"Looks like we both had the same idea this morning."

She licked her lips quickly, her eyes darting around. "This is a great farmer's market."

"I wanted to apologize for the shock back at the clinic," I spoke softly enough that we couldn't be overheard, ever mindful of privacy concerns as I scratched the back of my neck awkwardly. "That wasn't exactly how I imagined we'd... you know, run into each other again. I wasn't sure if you were still around here until I saw your name on my charting system."

She breathed a sigh, but it was softened by a slight twitch of her mouth that made my tight insides unclench a little. "It's okay. That situation wasn't your fault. Or mine, for that matter. It was just a coincidence—a really horrible, embarrassing one. And I should apologize for pushing you out of your own exam room."

"I really am sorry. I'm well aware of how awkward that situation is for women."

She turned to face me fully, her eyes holding mine. "Can we just move on from it? Pretend this is the first time we've seen each other again?"

"I'd like that. You look great."

Her eyes dropped to the pot in her hands. "Thanks." Her mouth remained open for a moment, then she shut it. As if she was going to say more but changed her mind.

I nodded to the flower she held. "Still can't get enough of orchids?"

That brought a genuine smile to her face, and the air suddenly became warmer. "Yes. I still love them. Though this shopping trip is a bit less happy. We had two plants disappear from Orchid and I'm searching for replacements."

"Orchid thief on the loose?"

"Seems so." Stella shrugged, her eyes scanning the array of flowers before us. She picked up an orchid with delicate pink blooms. "I'm just hoping these new ones won't vanish into thin air as well."

Her gaze lingered on the flower in her hand. "This one could be a contender. The orchids that went missing were part of the public display on the wall outside the entrance. So the replacements have to be hearty varieties, since they're out in the weather."

I picked up a yellow and white one that had a sturdy central stem. "What about this guy?"

Her smile made my heart pound. "Oh, Phalaenopsis! I love those! I didn't see it there."

"Sounds like fate, then. There's a second one next to it." I reached out with the flower.

"Thanks," Stella said, accepting the pot. Her fingers brushed against mine, sending an unexpected jolt through me. The connection felt electric, a current that reignited old flames I hadn't been sure were still there.

*Guess that question is answered.*

"Do you think the missing orchids are due to an over-inquisitive guest, or did someone actually steal them?"

She shrugged one shoulder. "Well, there's no proof pointing to anyone specific. But they certainly didn't sprout legs and walk out on their own."

I nodded, but the notion unsettled me. Calypso Key Resort had always been the premier venue in our neck of the woods and a very coveted place to work. Since returning, I'd learned that that hadn't changed, so an employee was unlikely. A guest then? It seemed improbable and yet...

"Dr. Mitchell!" A familiar voice cut through my thoughts. I turned to see Mrs. Landon holding hands with her young daughter, who beamed up at me.

"Hey there." I smiled down at Mandy, who looked much happier than the last time I'd seen her.

Mrs. Landon reached out to pat my shoulder. "I wanted to thank you. Those antibiotics cleared her strep throat right up. It's like night and day!"

Mandy nodded emphatically. The interaction with them was warm and friendly, a reminder of why I'd chosen this path. I said something positive and reassuring before the pair wandered away. When I refocused on Stella, I found her observing me with an intensity that quickened my pulse.

"I'm sure you're a really good doctor, Aiden." Her voice was soft, like a warm blanket wrapping around me.

"Thank you," I replied, tucking my hands into my pockets to keep from fidgeting. Compliments still made me awkward, especially from her. I wanted to tell her about medical school, but the words lodged in my throat.

"I imagine you had some explaining to do after I tore out of your office last week."

In fact, when I'd emerged from the deserted room where I'd recovered from my shock, I'd met with a lot of curious faces. Especially the old timers, who knew my history with Stella. But I only mentioned something vague and noncommittal.

Now I shrugged one shoulder. "I didn't say anything. None of their business." But my firm stance on keeping confidences created a different difficulty. I couldn't very well ask my staff what Stella had been up to over the years. Where did she live? Where did she work?

But now she stood right before me.

My gaze lingered on her, taking in the highlights in her hair and the laugh lines around her eyes. The orchid in her hand paled in comparison. She stared back and the moment between us drew out.

Jerking her head away, Stella blinked. "I'm happy to see you became a doctor. It was what you always wanted."

*Not all that I wanted.*

But I couldn't say that out loud. Not if I didn't want her to run away again. So I smiled instead. "I did. What about you?"

She straightened, a hint of steel in her spine now. "I just became the head chef at Orchid."

My smile broadened, tempered with admiration now. "Congratulations. Looks like I'm not the only one who has realized a dream."

That flush crept across her face again and her shoulders tensed. As if she'd been prepared for me to challenge her qualification to be a head chef. Like I ever would—that position was her destiny if anything was. So many mysteries here. I dropped my eyes to the orchid in her hands. "Now you get to work with food *and* orchids every day. Let's hope that guy stays put."

That earned me another smile. "Well, it better." She bought two of the yellow and white orchids from the vendor. We lingered outside the stall as she adjusted them, cradling them against her body with one arm.

I stuck my hands back in my pockets and gave her a crooked smile. "I'm surprised you didn't replace the missing ones with monkey-face orchids."

Her hand paused mid-air, and she glanced up at me, surprise and delight flickering across her face. "You remember that?"

"That they're your favorites?" I asked, my tone softening. "How could I forget? You gave a whole presentation on them in Mr. Calhoun's biology class, junior year."

Stella's lips parted slightly, as if she was about to say something. But she just shook her head as a smile tugged at the corners of her mouth. Her gaze locked with mine, and for a long moment, neither of us said anything. Memories swirled inside me, carrying whispers of our shared past—the laughter, our first, fumbling attempts at sex together, and the dreams we once dared to dream. Together.

"Monkey-face orchids are incredibly rare." She finally broke the silence, her voice a soft murmur that resonated straight through me. "Not something they have at a farmer's market on a local key."

"Rare but worth searching for," I replied as we faced each other fully, my words holding an undercurrent that went beyond the topic of elusive flowers. The air between us felt heavy with things unsaid, feelings unexplored, and the weight of years spent apart.

"I can't believe you remember those." The crowd gently parted around us, but I couldn't tear my eyes from hers.

"I remember a lot, Stella."

And right there, with wistful longing showing in her eyes, I knew. I wanted to ask her out, to try to reclaim the time we'd lost.

But how?

Stella broke the trance to stare at the orchids cradled in her arms, her expression shifting. "I should get these home." Suddenly flustered, she fiddled with her purse. "I'll see you around."

"Of course." Any further words I wanted to say remained inside as she turned away.

She'd taken a few steps when she paused and looked back over her shoulder. "It was good to see you again, Aiden. Goodbye."

Her voice was soft, carrying a note that made me want

to reach out and press pause on the moment. What was the message she was sending? The part about being happy that we met up again. Or the goodbye?

"Good to see you too."

I watched her walk away, the sway of her hips hypnotic and familiar. As she disappeared into the throng of market-goers, I was left with the scent of flowers and corn dogs, along with the lingering question of what would happen next. At least she hadn't shoved me away this time, though she'd been guarded and tentative. The laughter and chatter of the market resumed its full volume around me, but I still stood there, anchored to the spot by the weight of unspoken words.

# Chapter Seven

## Stella

I LEANED against the wall of the Big House's garage, anxiously scanning the driveway that cut through the lush tropical foliage. With every rustle of leaves in the gentle breeze, I hoped it would be Hunter's car stirring them into motion.

Today was more than just a family lunch—it was a bridge to start healing old wounds. The ache for reconciliation clung to me. Two brothers who had once been inseparable and were now completely at odds.

The purring sound of an engine announced his arrival. A sleek black Range Rover navigated the final bend and came to a smooth stop in front of the garage. My heart skipped a beat, nervous anticipation making me wipe a sweaty palm on my skirt.

Hunter stepped out, clad from head to toe in black. Black jeans molded to his long legs, and a black button-down shirt framed his broad shoulders and bulging arms. No matter how many times I saw him, I had to remind myself that this shadowy apparition with eyes that were always assessing, searching, was the sweet, shy brother I'd grown up with. In some ways, anyway. In others, he couldn't be more different.

"Is black the only color in your wardrobe these days?" I teased lightly, trying to ease the weight of the moment as I approached him.

"Keeps things simple." A ghost of a smile touched his lips. Hunter's eyes, though, held stories that were anything but simple. They were hooded, guarding his thoughts. By far the tallest of the Markham men, Hunter's dark beard was trimmed short and neat. The tips of tattoos snaked toward his elbows beneath his short sleeves. More ink was exposed at his open collar.

"Still the man of mystery, I see." I reached up to wrap my arms around him.

He returned the embrace, his strong arms encircling me. "Good to see you, Stella."

"Good? I was aiming for great." I pulled back to look at him. But beneath the light-hearted banter, I could sense the steel he had honed as a Marine. He might not show it, but coming home to this island, with its tangled roots and complex histories, had to stir him inside.

"Great, then." His voice was deep yet smooth, and a genuine smile reached his eyes now. It transformed him, softening the edges that time and distance had sharpened. Hunter and I had always been close, and I'd taken pains to make sure we stayed that way through his estrangement. He let his guard down with me, and that meant a lot.

"Come on—let's get inside. Everyone's waiting." I slipped my arm around his elbow as we started toward the house.

"Everyone?" he asked, a hint of tension threading his voice.

"Yes. Everyone." I gave his arm a reassuring squeeze. Though I wasn't sure if it helped—his bicep felt like squeezing a lead pipe. "It's time to mend fences and build new memories. Calypso Key is still your home."

He nodded, squaring his shoulders. The bookish little brother I once knew was long gone, replaced by this towering mountain of muscle who had faced down his own abyss. More than one. Yet I could still see glimpses of the boy who used to chuck rocks from the top of the bluff with me.

We walked along the cement walkway to the front of the house. As we approached the landing, the front door swung open, and our grandmother, Nona, emerged. She'd swapped her usual Western wear for a more formal skirt and long-sleeved shirt, her white hair twisted up with a grace that defied her years. Her sharp eyes grew glassy at the sight of Hunter.

"Nona," Hunter breathed out, the single word echoing both joy and regret. He stepped forward and enveloped her petite frame in his expansive arms, dwarfing her. Yet his embrace was gentle, cautious—as if he were holding something precious and fragile.

"Oh, Hunter, my boy..." Nona's usually whip-solid voice wavered. "I missed you at the wedding."

He offered a tight laugh, a shadow flitting across his face. "That's probably for the best. It wasn't my finest moment. Or Evan's."

I watched the exchange, blinking tears back. Then I took a step backward to let them lead the way inside. The threshold of the Big House felt like a border between past and present, and watching Hunter cross it brought a swell of hope to my heart. Maybe this time, things could be different.

We moved down the hall toward the kitchen, the center of our family's universe, where the murmur of voices grew louder with each step. When Hunter appeared at the doorway, the sounds hushed as if the ocean itself had pulled back before building into a wave.

"Son," Dad said, striding forward. His warm, strong voice was the first to break the silence. He wrapped Hunter in an embrace that seemed to pull him back through the years, back to when he eased scraped knees and sunburns. The resemblance between the two men was striking, though Gabe was the dead ringer for Dad. Warren Markham was a fit man in his mid-sixties, his body bearing the evidence of a life lived outdoors, of boat lines pulled and fish wrangled alongside Gabe and me. Pulling back, he clasped Hunter's shoulders, his eyes not shying from the man his son had become. "Welcome home."

Hunter maintained his poker face—one I knew all too well—but the frantic pulse beating at his throat betrayed him. I caught his eye and offered a silent nod of solidarity.

Maia came next, her own hug enveloping Hunter with an affection that seemed to thaw the chill of his absence. Next to her, her husband, Wyatt, shook his hand and shot my brother a somewhat awkward smile. He swept back his trimmed light-brown hair and nodded.

"You and Wyatt didn't get to meet at the wedding," Maia said with a smile. "And Skye's with a babysitter. You'll see her soon." Maia and I had decided it might be better for Skye to stay out of this initial reunion in case things didn't go as we hoped.

Then it was Gabe and April's turn. Hunter stared at

them, his feet rooted to the spot. "I'm... I'm sorry about your wedding,"

April stepped forward and grasped both of his arms. Her eyes were warm and caring as she stared up into his. "You've already told us that, so no more apologizing! You didn't ruin anything, and we're so glad to see you again."

After giving her a shaky smile, Hunter turned his gaze to Gabe, who agreed with his wife and gave Hunter a hug of his own. The two men, so alike, embraced in the reunion that Hunter had undoubtedly wished for at Gabe and April's wedding. His hand lingered on Gabe's back a long moment before he stepped back and let it fall to his side.

At last, Hunter's eyes settled on the far side of the table.

Where Evan stood stiffly with Liv beside him, her hand resting on his tension-wrought shoulder. The tableau was fraught with the weight of unspoken words, and memories best forgotten yet never able to be erased. Evan looked planted on the wooden floor, unable to move, so Hunter walked casually around the table to stop before him.

"Hi, Evan." Hunter's voice was steady, but his weight balanced evenly on the balls of his feet.

"Hey," Evan returned, equally terse. Their gazes locked, a silent conversation in a glance. I held my breath, along with everyone else in the room. Liv slowly moved her hand to press against the small of Evan's back. Then, firmly, deliberately, Evan extended his hand. "Good to see you, Hunter."

As the two brothers shook hands—albeit a stiff, formal handshake—the sharp edge of tension around the room lessened. The air was still quiet, but the invisible currents moved more freely. I watched the two of them, these pillars of my world, each trying to navigate the space between what was and what could be. Hunter exchanged a somewhat shy greeting with Liv, who was sweet and polite, trying to balance being supportive of Evan while welcoming Hunter.

Turning his focus back to Evan, Hunter slid his hands into his back pockets. "You look good."

Evan stiffened even more. "Were you expecting—" He broke off when Liv softly pressed against his side and stroked his arm. "Thanks. So do you."

Hunter's nod was even more rigid, but his expression was cool, unruffled.

"Let's eat," I suggested, rallying my troops with practiced cheerfulness. Raising my head toward the other end of the kitchen, I called out, "Martin? I think we're ready to start."

Martin was a chef at Dorado, one of several who rotated to cook meals at the Big House, and had been with us a long time. He had outdone himself with this family lunch, knowing the weight of the moment. I hadn't discussed the menu with him, trusting his judgment. And I wasn't disappointed.

"All right, everyone," the chef announced in his Caribbean accent as he crossed the room, balancing platters of aromatic food that immediately drew our attention. His white smile lit his face. "Hope you're hungry."

No fancy entrees here. Martin had made comfort food, designed to make eaters feel welcome and relaxed. The smell of rosemary and garlic filled the air as the chef set down dish after dish—roasted chicken glistening under a golden-brown skin, a kaleidoscope of grilled vegetables sizzling in their own juices, and a mountain of fluffy mashed potatoes crowned with melting pats of butter.

"Smells amazing!" My experienced eye favorably evaluated the spread as my stomach seconded the motion with an audible growl.

"Thank you, Stella. Enjoy, everyone." Martin disappeared through the back hallway where we kept the kitchen staples.

I took charge, reaching for serving spoons and passing plates that everyone took generous helpings from. The clinking of silverware and the quiet murmur of appreciation for the food provided a comfortable backdrop to relieve some of the underlying tension.

"Can't beat a home-cooked meal," Dad said, his voice a deep timbre that resonated with authority and warmth. He sat at one head of the table, while Nona graced the other. Evan and Hunter sat as far apart as possible, which was probably a good thing given the circumstances.

"Definitely different than I'm used to," Hunter agreed, digging into his plate as if he hadn't eaten for days. As worried as he'd been about this lunch, maybe he hadn't.

"Everything's delicious." Evan's words carried the weight of effort, like each syllable was a stone he had to lift. "Martin always does a great job."

I watched as Hunter paused in his eating, catching Evan's eye across the table. There was a flicker of something —regret, perhaps, or the beginning of understanding. But it vanished as quickly as it appeared, hidden once again behind his stoic façade.

"Guess we have to thank Stella for bringing you back into town," Maia piped up with a teasing grin, breaking through the momentary stillness.

"She's like that pebble in your shoe," Hunter responded, the barest hint of a smile in his eyes. "As much as you try to ignore it, eventually you can't anymore."

I burst into laughter and punched him in the arm. Pretty sure it hurt my hand more than him.

"Here's to family." Gabe raised his glass, prompting us all to follow suit.

"Family," we echoed, and the word seemed to hang there, full of promise and pain in equal measure.

"Stella, is it nice only having one job again?" Liv asked brightly from Evan's side, clearly attempting to lighten the mood.

"Oh, yes. Driving between here and Key West every day was getting pretty old. And I have to thank Evan for bringing me back home." I held up my glass to him, but in true Evan-like fashion, he just blushed and touched his mouth with his napkin.

"You more than earned the job, Stel," he said quietly.

"And now Calypso Key has the best dive staff *and* the best chef in the keys," Maia chimed in, her eyes meeting mine with an unspoken understanding that we both needed this normalcy—even if it was thin as ice.

But the comfort food could only do so much. Hunter hardly dared to raise his head from his plate. I could feel the tension coiling around us, a silent serpent waiting to strike. Because though several family members had come home once more, Hunter had no place here. Evan coughed, an echo of discomfort that traveled through the room.

"My new orchids are really settling in," I commented hastily, trying to right the sinking ship. "They look like they've been there for years."

"You always had a green thumb," Dad noted, his voice a bridge over troubled water. "You take after your mother that way." But the undercurrents were there, palpable and anxious. He turned to his eldest son and gave Gabe a wide smile. "And now Calypso Key is doing better than ever. I'm sure your mother is smiling down on us. We can all cele-brate right now and next weekend too."

"Oh, that's right!" Maia turned toward me. I knew that look, the one that meant business mixed with a touch of familial duty. "Evan and I have nearly everything ready for the festival, but I need a hand with a few things. Stella, could you help organize coverage for the medical tent? I think you're the right person for that job." She arched an eyebrow at me, and I silently asked myself why I had confided in her after meeting Aiden at his clinic.

"Of course I'd be happy to help." I'd completely forgotten about our annual Sea and Sun Festival, a Calypso Key staple that Maia had taken the reins of. I tried to recon-cile the side of me that wanted to see Aiden again with the one wanting to stay as far away as possible.

"Thanks," Maia replied, lifting her glass in a toast. "We want to make sure everyone stays safe while having fun."

"Always a priority," I agreed.

"Medical tent?" Hunter asked, his brow furrowing slightly. "Have the festivities gotten that wild?"

"No. Sometimes the heat gets to people, or there's too much sun," I explained, brushing off his concern. "It's mostly precautionary."

"Ah," Hunter said as he picked up his fork again. "I know all about precautionary measures."

Several hands paused in mid-motion as we all digested that. Hunter had spent a decade as a Special Forces opera-tive in the Marines. Now he worked in private security, but none of us knew what exactly that meant. The only thing we all knew for sure was that the man sitting next to me was the polar opposite to the devastated, crushed boy who had left. But he wasn't the only one who'd been nearly destroyed, and I tried to walk the fine line of loving both of my brothers.

Evan's face tightened as he stared at Hunter. He took a breath and appeared about to speak when Liv placed a soft hand on his forearm, her headshake almost imperceptible. Evan relaxed. Liv had been instrumental in helping Evan face his own demons, and all of us were glad to welcome her into the family.

Evan met my eyes. "Always better safe than sorry." His smile was brief, but it was there. I took whatever he was willing to give.

"Exactly." I poured all my focus into smoothing the edges of the conversation. The awkward tension. "Now, who's ready for dessert?"

# Chapter Eight

## Stella

THE WARMTH OUTSIDE was a welcome change from the pressure cooker that had been the dining room. As I walked down the hill toward the resort alongside Hunter, the seaside breeze carried the faintest hint of salt and jasmine.

"Well, all things considered, lunch went pretty well. Don't you think?" I asked him softly.

"I guess. With you there filling in all the awkward pauses."

"Evan shook your hand. That's... progress."

"Small victories," he said with a sigh.

I nodded, sensing the layers of complexity that lay beneath Hunter's stoic exterior. There was pain in his eyes, a longing for connection. I was closer to him than any of us, yet I didn't even know if he had a girlfriend. As we strolled along the path that led to the shoreline, I decided to take a chance.

"You know," I said cautiously, "sometimes it's easier to face our demons when we have someone by our side."

"No woman in her right mind wants to get mixed up with me," he replied, his voice hard. "My own family can hardly stand me."

I stopped walking and turned to face him, my heart clenching. "I know you've been through a lot, but you don't have to carry it all on your own. Your family wants to be around you. We love you, and we want to help shoulder that weight with you."

His dark eyes bore into mine, searching for something, maybe a glimmer of hope. "You don't understand, Stella. What I've been through... It's not something to be shared. Only survived."

I reached out and gently placed my hand on his arm, feeling the tension coiled beneath his skin. He'd never opened up this much with me. "Hunter, none of us are perfect. You did what you had to survive. Dammit, that's why we have family. To help."

He stared at the ocean. "Evan barely talked to me at lunch."

"Maybe he didn't know what to say," I said softly, my voice carrying the weight of understanding. "But that doesn't mean he didn't try. Today was a huge step forward for both of you."

Hunter remained silent, his eyes still fixed on the waves. I squeezed his arm gently, hoping to offer a touch of comfort. "You won't know unless you give him a chance. You're not alone in this. I'm here for you."

He finally turned to look at me, his gaze searching mine. I could see the struggle behind his eyes, the desire to be accepted. Then he slid his arm around my shoulders. "You always have been, sis. Let's keep walking."

We strolled past the newly remodeled lobby. Garden cottages were spaced to the west, their clean modern lines contrasting the green foliage, yet bringing the whole tableau together. After a short distance, the pale pink hue of Orchid became visible in the distance.

Hunter paused, peering around with a slightly bewildered look in his eyes. "This place has really changed."

"It sure has. Especially these past few years. The resort's expansions, the remodeling—it's not the sleepy little resort we grew up in."

"Yeah, I see that." He ran a hand through his hair, a familiar gesture of his whenever he processed something. "It's good, though, right? Growth?"

"Absolutely," I said, thinking of the upcoming festival. And Aiden.

"So what was that weird current between you and Maia about the medical tent at the festival? I'm not exactly in the loop anymore, but something was going on there."

I barked a laugh. "Yeah. I'm supposed to ask the new doctor in town if he'll help. The new doctor being Aiden Mitchell."

Hunter's eyebrows shot up. "As in your old high school boyfriend? He's back?"

I fought back the urge to defend that Aiden had been much more than a casual old boyfriend. I forced a smile. "Yep, and he's Dr. Mitchell now. And since it's a medical tent..."

"Right. The doctor thing would come in handy." Hunter nodded thoughtfully. "You two seeing each other again?"

"No. We've hardly talked." I sighed, the weight of mixed emotions anchoring me. "Aiden and I have a lot of history, but the festival is about community, not my personal baggage. So if he can help, I want him there."

"Guess I'm not the only one with complications in Calypso Key, huh?" Hunter arched a brow.

"Yet another reason for you to come down here more often. We can compare miseries." My laugh sounded hollow, even to my own ears.

The salty breeze tangled through my hair as Hunter and I meandered past Orchid and the weekly beach barbecue area. The turquoise sea lapped gently along the white sand, and ten modern cottages stretched along the length of the beach.

Hunter examined the cottages closely, then blew a long whistle. "Wow, look at those. That one even has a private pool!"

"Yeah, Gabe's been busy." My voice carried a note of pride for our brother's work. "The two on the ends are two-bedroom units with pools. He's got a vision for Calypso Key. You can see it coming to life all around us."

"Yeah. Gabe came through, all right."

We turned and made our way back to the green, manicured grounds near the garden cottages. A straight line of turf was torn up to make way for a new irrigation system. This part of the resort was to be a focus of the recently begun landscaping project. As we rounded a corner, an open work shed came into view. It was supposed to be locked, the home to well-maintained equipment that kept the resort's grounds groomed. But the padlock dangled from the latch, useless, and the door stood ajar.

"Wait. That's not right." I quickened my pace. Hunter matched my steps, his strides easily overtaking mine.

Inside, the shed was dim and musty, shafts of light illuminating the dust motes dancing in the air. My eyes scanned the space, taking inventory. Shovels, rakes, and the lawnmower were all accounted for. But there, against the far wall, were empty spaces where three edgers usually sat.

I didn't like the silence around us. "What happened to the lawn edgers?"

"Maybe they're being used?" Hunter asked, his voice low as he scanned the shed.

"I don't hear them, and the breeze would be carrying the sound to us." Then something else occurred to me. "And a couple of my orchids went missing from the restaurant too."

Hunter shook his head, then stepped out of the shed to inspect the broken clasp. His frown deepened as he raised his gaze to meet mine. "This has been forced open. Small items are missing, easy ones to steal. Stella, why isn't there full-time security? With the resort growing, you're going to attract more attention—good and bad."

I bit my lip, considering his words. He had a point, but the idea was so foreign to me. "We've always been a close-knit community, both here and on Dove Key. Everyone looks out for each other. Security hasn't been an issue... until now, apparently."

"Times have changed, sis." Hunter's gaze scanned the resort grounds with the precision of a man who had seen too much to be easily reassured. "You need to talk to Dad about beefing up security."

"Gabe, you mean?" Turning to him with a smile that was tinged with nostalgia, I corrected him gently. "He's the majority owner now. Dad's more retired than not these days."

"Right." Hunter blinked, a brief flicker of surprise crossing his features before he masked it. "Another thing I need to get used to."

Hunter closed the two doors and replaced the clasp as best he could. We walked back toward the Big House, the sound of our footsteps mingling with the swishing of the leaves in the trees. I glanced at him, noting his neatly trimmed short beard and the way his black shirt clung to his broad shoulders. He seemed so rugged, so unfamiliar, yet beneath it all, he was still my little brother.

"Look," I said. "Forget about the thefts—they're minor. You're working your way back into the *family*. That's what's important."

He regarded me with those hooded, mysterious eyes. "It feels like I'm trying to fit puzzle pieces together, but some of them are from different boxes."

"I know it does." I gave his arm a solid pat, trying to impart some reassurance. "But we can figure out where they go. Maybe you can come down more often. We'll all go fishing or something." I offered him a hopeful look. "Or maybe you can come down for the festival next Saturday."

Hunter's lips twitched into a semblance of a smile, a glimmer of the boy who once chased waves and laughter with equal fervor. "Fishing and festivals, huh? Sounds like old times."

"It can be," I insisted, my heart swelling with the possibility of putting our broken family back together. "Old times with a new beginning."

"Maybe."

As we walked back up the hill, thoughts whirled in my head—possibilities of reconciling with the past and embracing whatever future lay ahead.

"Thanks for coming," I said. "For what it's worth, I think Calypso Key has missed having you around."

"Let's just hope I can live up to its expectations." His

eyes caught mine, a flash of uncertainty in their depths. "And I'll try not to add to your list of complications."

"Or maybe," I teased, bumping his side playfully, "you'll be the solution we didn't know we needed."

# Chapter Nine

## Aiden

"OH, COME ON, DAMMIT!" My hands, oil-smeared and deft, worked with a surgeon's precision on the boat engine before me. It wasn't human flesh that yielded beneath my touch, but the familiarity of repair—a rekindling of something broken—held its own kind of satisfaction. Late afternoon was trending to early evening, but the warm air caressed my bare back. My shirt hung from the mast nearby.

The marina around me was a comforting background—a chorus of seagulls arguing over scraps, the lapping of water against docks, and the distant hum of voices. With one final twist, I secured a stubborn bolt and wiped my brow, probably leaving a faint streak of grease above my temple. Rising to my feet, I let out a breath, feeling the ache in my back from a solid hour bent over this labor of love.

"All right," I murmured, stepping behind the wooden console with a mixture of hope and trepidation. "Moment of truth."

I turned the key, a silent prayer lifting from my

thoughts. The engine coughed, a spluttering protest before it settled into a steady purr. A grin split my face—there it was, the reliable thrum that spoke of open waters and the freedom only found in waves and wind.

"Didn't think I'd lost my touch, did you?" I asked the sailboat, patting the side of the console affectionately. To anyone else, she might have appeared as a weathered collection of wood and paint. But to me, she was a testament to resilience, a beauty worn by time and tide.

"Okay, let's see if you still remember how to dance."

I eased the boat out of the marina. As I glided past the breakwater, the endless expanse of ocean opened before me, and I felt the familiar thrill of freedom. The ripples parted around us, and when I cut the motor, the scene became nearly silent. Hurrying to the mast, a smile lit my face. The breeze caught the sail as I unfurled it, and for an instant, the world was nothing but the snap of canvas and the taste of salt on my lips.

*Perfect timing.*

Warm hues spilled over the western horizon. The sun was taking its final bow over Dove Key, casting a palette of pinks and oranges across the clouds. I tightened the mainsheet, catching the wind at a better angle, and the boat responded with a gentle increase in speed.

The ocean's vastness welcomed me, and I found comfort in the rhythmic creak of the mast and the whisper of the hull slicing through the water. Setting a southeasterly course, I allowed the beauty of the scene to wash over me. Moments like these reminded me why I'd returned to this small town, to the simplicity and honest truth of nature. I sat down on the padded seat behind the wheel and opened my reusable water bottle to down a long drink. Then the sound of my phone ringing jarred the silence. I picked it up mid-drink and froze. *Mom* flashed across my home screen.

I had some personal rules, and always answering her calls was one now that we were on speaking terms again. I swiped to answer. "Hi, Mom. How's it going?"

"We're fine. It's so good to hear your voice again." Her voice on the other end of the line was soft and filled with longing. "I've missed you so much. How are you getting along?"

I smiled as I glanced out at the ocean, its waves shimmering in the golden light. "I'm doing all right. Settling in well, and I'm even winning over a lot of Dr. Nelson's old patients. I'm happy here."

"I'm glad to hear that, and I understand why you left Michigan." There was a momentary pause, as if she was considering her next words carefully. "I'm sorry I drove you away. I never should have pushed you and Ainsley together. Neither should Maggie. I'm even sorrier it took me so long to realize that."

Maggie Booth was Mom's best friend and Ainsley's mother. After we'd moved to where our family had roots in Michigan, the two women became convinced that Ainsley and I would make the perfect pair. They were wrong. Unfortunately, she and I spent years together before realizing we were doomed as a couple. Years I regretted with every fiber of my being. I rubbed my eyes, trying to ward off the unpleasant memories.

"It's all in the past now, Mom," I assured her gently, my fingers tracing the intricate patterns etched into the wooden console. "I'm where I'm supposed to be."

"Have you seen Stella?" Her voice was deceptively calm and even.

"Yes, Mom. I've seen her." Skipping any mention of the clinic debacle, I recounted how we ran into each other at the farmer's market and that she'd realized her dream of becoming head chef at Orchid.

"Sounds like you two had a nice reunion."

"It was very... careful. I'm not sure anything will come from it."

"I won't pry. But if you two are meant to be together after all these years, you'll find a way."

A smile raised my lips. "Thanks, Mom. I'd better get going. I'm sailing right now and headed toward Cuba."

That made her laugh. "That won't do! I don't speak Spanish, you know. Good night. I love you."

"Love you too." I ended the call and set my phone on the console as I changed course to head north. Despite my quip about Cuba, I hadn't wandered too far offshore.

I put my parents and our unsettled history out of my mind. I was finally out on my boat, and I meant to enjoy the experience fully. The wind was light and fickle, but I didn't mind as I traveled in a counterclockwise circle around Dove Key. With a canvas of stars winking to life above, the bow of the boat cut a solitary figure ahead. I gripped the wheel, feeling the gentle rock of the vessel beneath me, a rhythmic dance I'd thought would be enough. Tonight, it felt like the ocean itself was taunting me with its vast emptiness, mirroring my hollowness inside.

Though surrounded by beauty, I was completely alone.

Stella's laughter echoed in my memory, as clear as if she were right there beside me. We'd been kids, barefoot and carefree, and our futures open and limitless. But as much as I tried, I couldn't hold onto the past. It slipped through my fingers like grains of regret.

I'd been a stupid kid, too scared to stand up for what mattered. I thought back to those college days, how I'd let my mother's expectations chart my course, too afraid to admit that her dreams weren't mine. My parents had given up their home and careers here in the Keys to give me my dream. They paid for every textbook, every late-night study session, and in return, I'd given them the son they wanted.

All while losing the woman I loved.

And the man I wanted to be.

Stella's young face appeared in my mind, her flashing dark eyes and glossy hair. Her mischievous smile. That smile had been a solace to me over the years. Through the difficult times of medical school and residency. Through stormy relationships and breakups. Especially Ainsley.

I imagined Stella next to me, her hair whipping around in the sea breeze. Despite Mom's assurances after moving to Michigan, my relationship with her hadn't been some teenage infatuation. Even after I cowed to my parents' demands to move on, the years hadn't dimmed my feelings for her. With Ainsley, everything had felt forced, like I was trying to fit a square peg into a round hole.

*Can't compare apples and stars.*

"Dr. Mitchell, taking over old Dr. Nelson's practice," I murmured, mocking myself. "And half of it's because she's here."

It was a truth I'd skirted around. But out here, on the open water, there was nowhere to hide. At the farmer's market, Stella had been beautiful, her hair falling over her shoulders. I took solace from the much more pleasant conversation we'd had. And her bare left hand. Which of course didn't mean she wasn't involved with anyone. But if she were, wouldn't she have shut me down flat? As I rounded the southwest corner of Dove Key, I gazed across the water toward the mysterious dark shape of Calypso Key.

Once again, my course steered me back to Stella.

Turning the bow east once more, I headed toward the marina and lowered the sail. With another silent prayer, I turned the key. The engine started again, and I slowly motored through the narrow cut separating the two islands. My gaze fixed on the wild mangroves of Calypso Key, their gnarled roots holding tight to the earth amidst the changing tides. It felt symbolic, how something could remain so steadfast through the ebb and flow. The two islands rose on either side of me, and soon Calypso Causeway arched overhead, connecting the two as I traveled beneath, unnoticed.

Uncertainty loomed as large as the silhouette of the Big House atop the bluff, just the peak of its roof visible, but hope flickered inside me. A decision of sorts had formed. I couldn't make Stella forgive me, but I could make her understand I wasn't the same boy who left the island nearly fifteen years ago. I just needed to figure out how to explain it to her. I guided the boat into its slip and tied off the lines with steady hands. After one final look, I stepped down into the cabin, my heart beating a rhythm that spoke of new beginnings.

The next day, I sat in my office, dictating my note for the patient I'd just seen. My office was in a corner of the clinic, with windows on two sides that overlooked a side street and the parking lot. Not the most picturesque perhaps, but private. My business phone rang from the front desk, and I picked up. "What's up, Susan?"

"You have a call, Dr. Aiden. It's... Stella Markham."

My heart dropped into my stomach. After my sail, this seemed like fate. Of course she could be calling to tell me to go to hell, too. "Put her through, please."

I took a drink of water to coat my suddenly parched throat as Susan transferred the call. When the line clicked open, I tried to sound cool and casual. "Hi, Stella. What can I do for you?"

My heart started climbing back into my chest as her laugh sounded through the phone. "Well, funny you should put it that way. You actually can do something for me. For the whole family."

I was more than a little surprised when she asked me to work in the medical tent of the Sun and Sand Festival, but excitement thrummed through my veins at the opportunity. "Of course I'll do it. I'll make sure to bring plenty of first-aid supplies and maybe some IV fluids in case someone gets really dehydrated."

"Thank you. Dr. Nelson always helped out, and it's great you'll be continuing the tradition."

"That festival has always been the unofficial start of summer—it's hard to believe we're almost to June already. I'm glad to add to the tradition. Are you going to be there?"

"Of course! Who do you think will be manning the resort barbecue stand?"

I grinned and sat back in my executive chair, hardly able to believe our casual, easy banter. "If you're doing the cooking, I'm definitely in."

"I'll save you a plate. See you next week."

My smile faded. "Stella?"

"Yes?"

I hesitated, gripping the phone as I tried to figure out

what to say. "Thanks for asking me. It means a lot. I'll see you at the festival."

After I hung up the phone, I laced my fingers behind my head and spun my chair in a circle. My smile turned into a soft laugh, and my eyes dropped to the calendar on my desk. Next Saturday couldn't come soon enough.

# Chapter Ten

## Stella

THE SEA & Sun Festival had transformed Calypso Key's grassy meadow into a lively scene full of colors and vibrant laughter. Located between the resort and the Markham residences, the area teemed with locals and tourists alike mingling under a sky so blue it hardly looked real. Flame trees scattered throughout the meadow were in full, bright-orange bloom and added their own color to the event. The early-June air buzzed with the hum of conversation and the sizzle of barbecue grills, most notably mine.

"Stella, you're supposed to be cooking, not daydreaming!" Grace's voice, tinged with amusement, snapped me back to reality.

"Yeah, I know." I grinned, turning several brats to ensure even cooking. "Just soaking in the festivities."

"Save the soaking for later, honey. We've got a line longer than the beach volleyball net out there." With her blonde hair tucked under a Calypso Key Resort baseball hat, Grace nodded toward the distant sandy BBQ area where a lively game was in full swing. Laughter erupted as a particularly robust spike sent the ball flying into the ocean. Three kids dove into the warm water to retrieve it.

"Speaking of which, ten bucks says the Johnson brothers take the cornhole trophy again." I nudged her as I passed over a loaded plate. A dozen wooden cornhole boxes were placed nearby, and the tournament was slowly whittling away the competitors.

"I'm not taking that bet. Those two win every year." Grace winked at a customer as she handed them their order. I laughed, watching as a small child attempted to drag his father toward a booth with a face painter. Next to me, chef Felicia shot Grace a grin of agreement as she stirred a huge stock pot of simmering beans, her own family recipe.

Grace watched me rapidly flip half a dozen burgers. "You might want to save some energy for paddleboarding with me later."

"Only if you promise not to *accidentally* tip me over this time."

"Cross my heart." She gave me an angelic look while crossing her fingers behind her back.

"I see how it is. Traitor."

The Conch Republic's beer garden was bustling nearby, a reggae band harmonizing with the laughter. Luke was serving up cold ones with a flourish that drew an appreciative crowd.

"Looks like business is booming all around." I wiped my sweating brow and took a moment to watch the festival unfold. My heart filled with both pride and belonging.

This was home.

"Sure is." Grace's eyes followed the arc of a Frisbee before it was caught by Orchid prep cook Matt, his dark hair flying. He tossed it to Rea with a laugh as my friend continued, "He's kind of hot. Those blue eyes! Which happens to remind me that the festival is also prime time for people-watching—especially the eligible bachelors of our quaint little town. Like the one in the next booth, maybe?"

A sigh escaped me, almost inaudible against the backdrop of festive noise. But I couldn't stop myself from glancing at Aiden's medical tent, positioned next to our barbecue booth. The proximity was no accident, I was sure. Maia had been in charge of the layout. And though convenience no doubt played a part, I was sure my meddling little sister wanted us close together.

"Stella, go say hi." Grace nudged me, her voice dripping with both encouragement and mischief.

My gaze lingered as I observed Aiden. He looked effortlessly charming in his polo shirt, his clinic logo a stark contrast against the fabric clinging just right to his athletic shoulders. Gray slacks and boat shoes completed the ensemble that screamed casual, yet competent and professional. He was currently handing out free sunscreen packets to a gaggle of women, and I frowned.

"Or you could stand here and burn those patties while fantasizing about Dr. Dreamy," she teased, following my line of sight.

"Shush." I redirected my attention to the grill, flipping the burgers and rearranging shrimp skewers.

"Come on, you've been stealing glances at him all day." Grace's tone softened. "Why not just talk to him?"

"Because—" I started, then stopped. What was I afraid of? Rekindling something I wasn't sure I wanted? Trusting someone who had hurt me so deeply? "Because it's complicated." I could feel the weight of our history in those three words.

"Complicated is just another word for *I'm not done with him yet.*"

"Am too," I countered weakly as I slid a burger onto her waiting bun. But my protest died on my lips as I watched the women at Aiden's tent, their laughter carrying over to us. My stomach squirmed as he helped them, oblivious to his attractiveness.

"Sure." Grace arched an eyebrow. "And they're only after his sunscreen packets."

I rolled my eyes but couldn't ignore the twinge of something—annoyance, irritation?—as the women lingered and chatted with Aiden, who was all politeness and smiles. It was apparent to anyone but him that they were less interested in UV protection and more in the man providing it. Of course that slithering in my gut couldn't be jealousy. That would only make sense if I was interested in him myself. Right?

"Let's focus on the burgers, okay?" I said, a touch sharper than I intended.

"All right, all right." Grace relented, but not without giving me a look that said we weren't finished with this conversation.

The grill sizzled after I collected another batch of burger patties from Felicia. A loud cheer erupted from the cornhole competition, and the two Johnson brothers high-fived each other.

"Stella, you're hard at work in your domain, I see," Evan's voice called out above the din, his tone warm and rich with amusement as he appeared next to me.

I glanced up to find my brother's handsome face split by an easy grin that reached all the way to his eyes—a stark contrast to his tense demeanor at our family lunch. As the general manager of the resort, he was in his element here, overseeing the festivities with a practiced eye.

"Only the best for Sea and Sun." I matched his smile as I plated another perfectly seared brat.

"Looks like business is booming," Evan said, taking in the scene around our booth. "You, Felicia, and Grace are killing it."

"Thanks to your impeccable planning," I replied, and we shared a look. Evan thrived on this—the logistics, the community, the controlled chaos of events like these. "And maybe even Maia's too."

As we chatted about the turnout, my gaze drifted once again to Aiden's medical tent, its proximity a constant pull on my attention. Nona, back to her usual wardrobe of Wrangler jeans and a denim vest, appeared, and the hand holding my spatula paused. Her trademark snowy hair was braided down her back as she ambled up to Aiden with her usual confident step.

*Oh, no!*

"Stella, earth to Stella," Evan teased, following my line of sight. "Worried about what Nona might say to Dr. Mitchell?"

"How could I not be? She's got no filter!"

"Hey." Evan gently placed a hand on my shoulder. "Despite her love of meddling, Nona wouldn't do anything to upset you on purpose."

"Right, like she did with you?" I barked a laugh. Nona had inadvertently begun Evan and Liv's relationship. Though she could be nosy, she wasn't malicious about it.

"You could always go over there and shoo her off."

Nona said something that made Aiden throw his head back and laugh, his blue eyes crinkling at the corners. He was so effortlessly charming, and it irked me that I still found it endearing.

"Look at them. It's like they're old friends," I murmured the words, more to myself than to Evan.

"They kind of are, you know?" Evan squeezed my shoulder sympathetically before making his rounds again, leaving me with my thoughts and the ever-present view of Aiden's tent. For distraction, I inspected the juicy heirloom tomatoes and tried not to worry about Nona.

"Stella?" Grace's voice drew me back, her concern evident. "You okay? You're frowning at those tomatoes like they've personally offended you."

"Yeah, just lost in thought." Shaking off my funk, I turned back to the grill with renewed focus. "Let's keep this food moving."

I threw myself into the work, flipping patties and sliding the finished product onto Grace's waiting plates, letting the rhythm of the task anchor me in the present. The festival was meant to be a celebration, and I was determined not to let old memories spoil it.

The next thing I knew, Nona had ambled up to my booth, her braid shimmering like spun silver. "Stella, dear, whip me a shrimp kebab, would you?" She perched on an unused stool with the ease of someone who had navigated this festival for more years than I'd been alive.

"Coming right up." I flashed her a smile and set to work, grilling the shrimp to pink perfection. "Good turnout for the festival, huh?"

"That's for sure. Lots of people to talk to. Speaking of which..." Nona tilted her head toward Aiden's tent, where he was now tending to an overheated tourist. "Seems like you have a handsome neighbor today."

Her elbow nudged mine lightly, and a playful spark lit

her eyes. I couldn't stop the laugh that tumbled out, even as my gaze betrayed me, stealing another glance at Aiden. He was easing his patient onto a cot, the very image of the dedicated doctor... and undeniably attractive.

"Old flames are old for a reason, Nona," I countered, but my heart wasn't in the jest.

"Perhaps they just need a little stoking to burn bright again." She winked before taking a hearty bite of shrimp.

"Enjoy your meal, firestarter." I did my best to ignore the heat rising to my cheeks.

"I always do when you're cooking." She held up a skewer in a toast, making me grin.

"Shame Hunter couldn't join us today."

"Yes, it is." Despite Nona's disappointment at his absence, her eyes softened at the mention of my brother. "Him and his mysterious job assignments. But he made it to lunch, and that's something."

I nodded, handing her the kebabs, one of grilled shrimp and another loaded with fresh veggies. Hunter had called me a few days ago to report he'd received a new case and would be unavailable for the entire week. Whatever that meant. "Yeah, it was nice having him around, even if just for a bit."

"Hopefully the start of things to come." She took several more bites before rising and sauntering off into the crowd, presumably to butt into someone else's life.

I let out a sigh, watching Nona disappear into the sea of festival-goers. When our mother passed away giving birth to Maia, Nona had stepped into those impossible shoes. She raised us with a firm hand and a fierce love that bound us all together, no matter how far we roamed.

The fair buzzed with upbeat, tropical energy, the kind that seeped into your bones and demanded you laugh and join in the cacophony. I leaned against the wall of our booth, taking in the spectacle—the vibrant streamers fluttering above like captured rainbows, and the unmistakable thud of bean bags hitting wooden boards.

I turned to watch as the cornhole tournament reached its climax, teams huddled in fierce concentration, their supporters' rallying cries rising up from the sidelines. It was impossible not to get swept up in the enthusiasm, the community spirit—it was what made small-town life so sweet.

"All right, folks!" Evan's voice boomed over the speakers. "We're down to the final throw!" The crowd held its breath, and for a moment, all of the festival seemed to pivot on this single point of suspense.

"Ooh, so close!" I murmured as the bag missed its mark by a hair's breadth, the collective sigh of the audience echoing my sentiment. Smiling, I turned back to my next task. My fingers were slick with juice as I sliced through a crimson tomato, and the tangy scent filled my nostrils. My movements were self-assured and confident, having performed this task thousands of times.

Until my sharp knife slipped in a jagged, very wrong motion, which was immediately followed by a deep sting across the outside of my left palm.

"Damn!" I hissed, dropping the knife with a clatter. My hand reflexively clenched, but that only brought a fresh wave of pain and a bright ribbon of blood that dripped onto the wooden cutting board. I turned away and grabbed a stack of paper towels, holding pressure on the wound to ensure I didn't bleed on anything else.

"Stella!" Grace gasped, rushing over with wide eyes. "Your hand!"

I tried to laugh it off. "I can't believe that happened! I

haven't cut myself in years." I lifted the impromptu bandage for a peek, but blood welled immediately.

"Let me see." Her tone dismissed any argument I felt like raising.

Reluctantly, I uncurled my fingers and lifted the wad of paper towels to show her the cut, wincing at both the pain and the concern etched on her face.

"Stella, that looks bad. You need to—"

"I'll be fine," I interrupted, stubborn pride flaring up. But I knew she was right. The steady flow of blood was a clear sign that I wouldn't be able to handle this with just a Band-Aid.

"The bleeding isn't stopping." Grace's voice was laced with a seriousness that contrasted sharply with the merriment around the booth.

"Maybe I should just wrap it with gauze," I said, trying for nonchalance as I fumbled with fresh paper towels one-handed.

"Wrap it? With what, hopes and dreams?" But Grace's jest couldn't mask her worry. "I think you need stitches, hon. Felicia can handle things here."

I glanced over at the chef, who nodded firmly from behind the barbecue. "Go, Stella. I've got this."

Hesitating only a moment longer, I gave in to the inevitable. The pain was starting to make itself fully known, a sharp reminder of reality biting through the adrenaline. I pressed the now thoroughly red paper towels harder against my wound "Okay. I'll go see Aiden."

"Good. Hurry!" Grace gave my back a supportive pat before ushering me away from our booth.

My legs carried me toward the medical tent with more resolve than I felt. Each step beat a rhythm with my pulse, throbbing in time with the flow of blood. As I neared the tent, I caught sight of Aiden, smiling as he spoke to an ample, rather red-faced woman. He waved as she and a younger version of her walked away. He was the picture of professionalism, in his element as much I had been in mine. Until I'd made a rookie mistake.

"Excuse me!" I called out as I reached the entrance, doing my best to keep my voice steady. My other hand was still clamped down on the cloth, the red stain spreading ominously.

# Chapter Eleven

## Aiden

A FOND SMILE remained on my face as Mrs. Reynolds slowly walked away, supported on one side by her daughter. Heat exhaustion had crept up on her during the hot afternoon, but at least she'd come to see me before it became serious. Now she was on her way home to spend the rest of the day in air-conditioned comfort.

"Excuse me?"

I knew that voice. The years might have passed, but some things remain forever. At the tension in it, I snapped my head around, heart hitching when I saw Stella. She stood at the tent entrance, clutching a wad of paper towels to her left hand—a blotch of crimson blooming through the white. And steadily growing.

"Maria. Kit," I said crisply, already moving.

Maria nodded, understanding flashing in her eyes. She grabbed the supply cart just as I reached Stella's side. "What happened?"

"Cut myself with my knife," she replied, trying to

mask her distress with nonchalance, but the tightness in her jaw betrayed the pain she felt. "I haven't done that in years!"

"Let me see." My fingers brushed against hers as I gently pried the makeshift bandage away. The sight of the deep gash brought a clinical clarity to my thoughts. "We need to clean this up and get a good look at it."

"Can't you just slap a Band-Aid on it? I've got—"

"Stella, this is serious." My tone left no room for argument as I led her to the back of my tent, where two makeshift examination tables were set up. Maria had laid out the necessary supplies, her efficiency a silent blessing.

"Sit," I instructed, helping Stella onto the edge of the table Mrs. Reynolds hadn't used. We hadn't had a chance to clean it yet.

Her face was pale, a stark contrast to the vibrant red of her wound. "Thanks, Aiden."

"Of course."

I removed the paper towels to expose a fairly impressive laceration nearly two inches long on the outside of her palm. As I cleaned the cut meticulously, Stella hissed through her teeth. I met her eyes briefly, offering a silent apology before continuing.

"Looks like you'll need a few stitches," I told her, trying to keep my voice light. "You're in good hands, though."

"You've done this before, right?" Stella managed a smile, though her eyes couldn't hide the discomfort.

"Flattery will get you everywhere," I joked, hoping to ease the tension as I opened the suture kit Maria had laid out and prepared the needle. "Don't worry, I've stitched up plenty of people. And one pot-bellied pig too."

She laughed, and it had the effect I was going for. Her shoulders dropped and her hand relaxed slightly in mine. I reached for a syringe and a vial of one-percent lidocaine, preparing to numb her hand.

"Hold on a second," she said as I glanced up at her. "I can't have my hand numb. I need to go back to work."

"Stella, this is going to hurt without the local anesthetic."

She frowned, her brows drawing together. "It's just a few stitches. I'll be fine. Your pig-stitching experience has filled me with confidence in your abilities."

I didn't smile back this time. "You sure?"

"Yes. Just go quickly."

"Let me know if it's too much."

As I took her hand and placed it on my impromptu operating table, I allowed myself a fleeting moment to revel in the softness of her skin beneath my fingertips, the delicate lines of her hand that I once knew by heart. But one moment was all.

As I placed the first stitch, Stella pressed her lips tightly together. She had always been strong, never one to show vulnerability. Throughout the day, I'd stolen glances at her booth several times. I couldn't help noticing how the years had both changed and preserved her—the same dark glossy hair that caught the sunlight, the same fierce independence etched into the curve of her jaw. The sight of her was a bittersweet pang, a reminder of what could have been and what we had lost along the way. What *I* had lost.

And yet here she was right next to me. "Doing okay?"

She nodded, a small but reassuring gesture, and I continued. "How are the new orchids doing?"

"Oh! They're adjusting beautifully."

My distraction worked. I figured if anything would take her mind off her discomfort, it would be her favorite flowers. She went on to discuss the merits of each.

"What are they called again?"

She gave me both the common and Latin names, and I hummed appreciatively, though not committing the names to memory. That wasn't the point. Her hand relaxed a little in mine. The stitches had to hurt, but she was holding up to the discomfort well. I placed four stitches quickly and efficiently, then looked up. "There. All done."

"I have to compliment you on your bedside manner." Stella's voice was laced with a combination of pain and humor that made the corners of my mouth twitch upward.

I still held her hand in mine, reluctant to let go, and gave her a smile. "Thank you. I aim to please."

Our eyes met, and something unspoken passed between us—a current as tangible as the sea breeze that wafted through the canvas tent. We lingered there, in that long look, the world around us fading to a distant murmur.

Then I returned to the soft, yet incredibly tough hand I held. "Just take it easy with that hand for a while."

"Take it easy?" Stella's voice was laced with a mix of irony and resignation. "There's no way Felicia can handle all that cooking by herself. Bandage me up so I can go back to work, Dr. Mitchell."

"As you wish."

Our eyes held again as we both smiled at the *Princess Bride* reference. I set about wrapping her hand in gauze, ensuring the bandage was snug but not constricting. If she could handle getting stitches without lidocaine, I figured she was safe to go back to the grill for a couple of hours. As I worked, her fingers brushed against mine, sending a jolt of electricity up my arm. The contact was accidental, or so I told myself, yet it lingered like a promise.

"There, all done," I announced, securing the end of the

bandage. "You should be able to get back to work without too much trouble."

Stella flexed her fingers experimentally, a shadow of concern crossing her features before she nodded. "Yeah. Thank you. I should head back—they'll need me at the booth."

"Maybe stay away from knives for the rest of the afternoon."

She tipped me a wide smile, and I didn't want her to leave, not yet. Her presence made me feel alive, vibrant even.

"Stella," I blurted, the words tumbling out before I could rein them in. "You still know a lot about boats, right?"

Her laughter was light and genuine, if somewhat tinged with surprise as it filled the space between us. "Of course. Look around! I grew up here." She gestured vaguely toward the canal where the three boats bobbed gently.

The sound of her laughter was a balm to old wounds that suddenly ached furiously. I wanted more—more time, more laughter. And most of all, more Stella.

"I remember very well."

Her gaze remained on the fiberglass charter boats. "I helped my dad all the time on those boats. I loved it."

"I'm glad to hear that. Could you—would you—help me with something boat-related?" The question hung awkwardly in the air, my heart thrumming in anticipation of her response.

"Maybe," she said, her expression curious. "What do you need?"

"I bought a sailboat. She's operable but a little rough around the edges. I could really use a hand with the wood-work." I felt suddenly vulnerable under her steady gaze, reminiscent of when I'd asked her out the first time in tenth grade. "I'm not just a landlubbing doctor, you know."

"Is that so?" Her eyebrow arched playfully, and it struck me with almost physical force how much I had missed this easy banter with her.

"I've always loved sailing. When I moved back here, it made sense to take it up again." I grinned, hoping the gesture would mask the flutter of nerves in my stomach. "When is your next evening off from Orchid?"

She opened her mouth but hesitated, and I thought for sure a refusal was coming. Stella was anything but stupid. She knew I was asking her out. Then her eyes softened. "Tuesday."

I resisted the urge to pump my fist. "I'm done at the clinic by five. How's that sound?"

"That works." A hint of surprise colored her tone, making me wonder if she was as affected by this rekindling connection as I was.

"Five p.m. at Dove Key marina, then?" I asked, my pulse racing at the thought of seeing her again.

"Yes." She slipped off the cot and stood, offering me a smile that reached deep into her eyes—maybe a smile that held a whisper of things to come.

As she walked away, I was left with a sense of hope. Perhaps this small town held more for me than just a medical practice. Maybe it held possibility—the possibility of righting the biggest wrong of my life.

# Chapter Twelve

### Stella

AS I WALKED BACK to my booth, the sting of the needle lingered. With every flex of my fingers, I could feel the pull of the stitches on my outer palm—a dull, throbbing pain that echoed Aiden's precise handiwork. Yet, it was more than physical discomfort distracting me. Aiden had surprised me. Not so much how quickly and effortlessly he'd stitched my hand—I'd always known he'd be a great doctor. It was more the unexpected tenderness he'd shown. The way he'd kept me talking and distracted while he worked.

His quiet confidence was not just in his profession but in the way he approached life, and it had a calming effect on me. I might be a woman who thrived on self-reliance, but I wasn't immune to a comforting touch. Especially when a disarmingly handsome, tender, and competent man gave it. I frowned, unsure whether that was a good thing.

"Stella, you're back! Let me see." Grace reached for my bandaged hand with concern etching her features. Then her face smoothed after a close examination. "Very professional-looking. You all fixed up?"

The disposable gloves felt foreign as I slipped them over both hands, the latex sticking awkwardly to the gauze. "A few stitches. Nothing I can't manage. Besides, we've got hungry mouths to feed."

"Uh-uh, no knife work for you," Grace insisted, her tone brooking no argument as she steered me toward the grill. "Felicia, you're on chopping duty!"

From behind the counter, Felicia gave a hearty laugh and selected her knife like a seasoned warrior preparing for battle. "Got it."

"All right, all right." Conceding, I turned my attention to the flames before me. Cooking was so second nature, I lost myself in the rhythm of flipping burgers and charring corn on the cob, the sear of meat merging with the salty sea breeze.

"Smells incredible, Chef!" A guest who'd been a regular at Orchid leaned over the barrier with an appreciative sniff.

"Thanks," I replied, pride filling me despite the day's misadventures. "Try the blackened hamburgers—seasoning, not burned!"

"Bring it on." He beamed, accepting the plate Grace handed over with a flourish.

I passed the next order to a waiting guest with care. "Here you go—Stella's signature shrimp skewers. Watch out, they're hot."

My movements were slower, more deliberate, but the quality remained unaltered. Today's hurdle hadn't dampened my spirit, nor my determination to shine, even if it was just at a small-town beach festival. And my confidence had soared since settling into my new role. I still had moments when the spotlight of being on center stage brought forth butterflies, but I reminded myself that I wasn't just a seasoned chef. I was a Markham, working at Calypso Key Resort's own restaurant.

If this wasn't fate, I didn't know what was.

Amidst the sizzle and crackle of the grill, my gaze wandered across the festival grounds and the cornhole platforms now being collected. It landed on the medical booth where Aiden, with his dark-blond hair falling over his forehead, was gently placing an adhesive bandage on a young boy's arm.

He must have sensed my observation because he glanced up, locking eyes with me. We both stilled, frozen in a moment that seemed to stretch beyond the mere seconds it occupied. His gaze didn't waver, and those deep blue eyes pierced mine. Warmth spread through me, not from the grill's heat but from the unexpected connection we'd forged over a simple injury. After a small smile, he bent back to his patient, and I returned to the grill.

"Another round of shrimp, please," Grace called out.

"Coming right up," I answered automatically, turning over several skewers while my mind continued to dance with thoughts of Aiden.

As the afternoon waned, the festival's energy mellowed, and the crowds began to disperse. Guests returned to their cottages, and locals to their homes.

"So." Grace bumped my elbow with a gentle nudge as I plated a blackened fish taco. "Is your hand holding up?"

"Yes. Surprisingly well." After handing the taco to a waiting customer, I sighed at a break in the action, the hungry celebrants now sated. "It's sore, but I can work fine. Aiden was... thorough."

"And?" she prodded, her eyes sparking with curiosity.

"He asked me out."

Her hand, poised to stack some paper plates, froze mid-air. "Really?" Excitement lit up her features.

"Sort of. Maybe." Hedging, I rubbed my face with the back of one glove-covered hand. "It's not really a date. He just invited me over to look at his sailboat. Maybe help with sanding the deck."

"Stella." Grace laughed, finally straightening the plates into a neat vertical tower. "That's a date, girl. You're going to be alone, on his boat, working on it together? That's the kind of thing people write songs about. Just sayin'."

The corners of my mouth threatened to curl into a smile, but I held my ground. "We'll see." I turned back to the grill, but inside, my heart fluttered at the possibility.

Grace leaned in, her voice lowered. "Give him a chance, Stel. I know he hurt you, but Aiden's not the same kid who left all those years ago. People change."

I glanced over at the medical booth, where Aiden was examining a crying child's face. The intensity in his focus was visible even from here. I remembered that same concentration directed at me earlier, his hands steady as they sutured my skin. And the softness of his voice as he tried to distract me.

"Maybe." I placed a patty on the grill, telling myself it was the heat from the grill warming my face. "I'm thinking about it."

"Thinking about it?" Grace echoed with a playful huff. "Stella Markham, you're going on a date. Admit it."

"Fine," I said, the word escaping me like steam from a pressure valve. "It's a... tentative date."

She grinned, triumphant. "That's more like it."

As I handed out the last couple of dishes to the dwindling line of festival-goers, I couldn't deny that the idea of seeing Aiden outside the context of an emergency had a certain allure. I was curious about who he'd become. The glimpses I'd had so far hinted at a man I wanted to know better.

———

THE CLINK of plates and quiet chaos filled Orchid's kitchen, creating a sound that always energized me. It was Monday evening, and the dinner rush was like a well-rehearsed dance—steady but not overwhelming. I moved between the various stations, ensuring every entree and appetizer was being lovingly tended to before settling at the stove. Rea's laughter echoed as she seared a steak. Luis, our experienced sous chef, orchestrated the stoves with a conductor's precision, his good mood infectious.

"Table seven's chicken cordon bleu needs another minute," I called out to him, checking the chicken's sear.

"Got it, Chef!" he responded without missing a beat.

I was about to turn back when the shrill ring of the wall phone cut through the buzz of activity. All calls to the kitchen came from the hostess station. Luis wiped his hands on his apron and answered it. "Kitchen. What's up, Suze?" A pause, then a glance in my direction. "It's for you, Stella."

Curiosity piqued, I took the phone from him as he moved to take over my chicken dish. "This is Stella."

"Hey, it's Aiden."

Just hearing his name sent an odd tingle down my body. "Hi. Is everything okay?" I was relieved to find my voice more composed than I felt.

"Yeah, everything's good. I don't have your number, so calling you at work seemed the most obvious choice. I just wanted to check in about your hand. Make sure you're doing all right."

I couldn't resist a smile at his concern. The cut on my palm flared slightly beneath my glove—as if reminding me of the incident. "It's less painful every day. I've been keeping it clean and dry, just like you ordered. Thanks for checking in—that's very thoughtful of you." The disposable gloves crinkled as I flexed my bandaged hand. The kitchen's clamor faded into the background.

"Of course," he replied. "Take care of it, okay? Infections are no joke."

"Will do, Dr. Mitchell," I teased lightly, though I warmed at his protective tone.

"I'll take a look at it tomorrow when you come by." Aiden paused, the moment drawing out. "We're still on for tomorrow, right?"

"We are," I replied, my smile widening with the suspicion that this was the real reason he'd called. "I'll be there."

"I'll meet you at the marina entry gate, so you don't need to worry about finding the boat."

"Oh, I figured it would be the one half-sunk in the harbor."

He laughed. "I promise. She floats just fine. See you at five?"

My hand gripped the phone tighter at the sound of his laugh. At the warmth and relaxed tone within it. I'd missed that, and only now did I realize it. "Five it is."

"See you then, Stella. And... take care," Aiden added, almost hesitantly.

After the line went dead, I replaced the receiver and turned back to the controlled chaos of Orchid's kitchen. The scent of seared scallops and citrus zest filled the air, grounding me once again in the here and now.

With a renewed focus, I approached the pass, surveying the dishes lined up like an edible art gallery. Each one was a testament to our team's skill, an explosion of flavors waiting to delight our guests. As I checked the seasoning on a velvety lobster bisque, my mind momentarily wandered to the marina's salty breeze and the gentle sway of sailboats.

I wiped the rim of a bowl, ensuring the plating was perfect. But as much as I tried to concentrate on the present, thoughts of Aiden lingered. A question burned brighter than any prospective romance. I wanted explanations—needed them. But that was going to be a tricky conversation, fraught with emotion. I'd wait for the right moment, under a canvas of sky over the marina.

That's when I'd ask Aiden Mitchell why he left me behind.

# Chapter Thirteen

## Aiden

LEANING against the weathered marina gate, my hands were fidgety, a stark contrast to the languid sway of the boats moored in their slips. It was almost five and my pulse thrummed in an anxious rhythm. Beside me, the water shimmered like spilled mercury in the golden light, and every ripple felt like it echoed in my chest.

When I turned back to the parking lot, my lungs froze. Stella walked toward me, her strides confident, her glossy dark hair catching sunbeams that slipped through the palm fronds. Dressed in a simple lavender shirt and denim shorts, she was the epitome of understated elegance. My heart skipped, lodged somewhere in my throat as she approached.

"Hey there," Stella greeted with a casualness that belied the electricity sparking through the air.

"G-good evening." At least my mouth only stumbled a little when I greeted her. "Glad you could make it."

We started down the dock, our footsteps making rhythmic thuds on the seasoned planks. Boat by boat, we passed the small community of fishermen and sea lovers, each vessel tethered to its own little piece of the marina's world. Though it was a near-empty world as the day wound down.

"Here she is," I announced, coming to a halt beside my beauty.

"She's really nice." Her experienced eye skipped over the boat and the admittedly roughhewn deck.

"Thanks." Warmth and pride bloomed in my chest. "I want her to feel like new, you know? She's a classic Gulfstar 37, and I'm refinishing the teak decking." As we stepped aboard, I pointed out the sanded wood beneath our feet. "It's taking forever, but I enjoy the work. She's got great character, and I'm trying to preserve that."

"Character's important." Stella traced her fingers along the curved railing I'd sanded down to perfection.

"Each plank has its story. Like us, I guess." I smiled, but now that she was here, my insides were a tangled mess of hope and history. I gestured toward the stern where the setting sun painted everything with hues of tangerine and rose. "And see here? I reinforced the rudder mount. No shortcuts, all craftsmanship."

*Oh my God. I'm babbling!*

"Looks solid." She leaned slightly over the edge to peer at the structure. Her proximity sent a fresh wave of awareness coursing through me, the subtle scent of her roaring through my senses.

"Doesn't she deserve a name?" Stella asked, peering at the blank space where the name should be.

"Well, that's a work in progress." I rubbed the back of my neck with a sheepish grin. "I have a few ideas, but nothing concrete yet. It'll come to me." Nothing seemed to encapsulate all the dreams I had for this boat.

"Fair enough. She looks seaworthy, that's for sure."

"Seaworthy and ready for adventure. Just like her new crew member," I said with a teasing lilt, waiting to see if she'd respond in kind or be pissed at me.

"New crew member?" Stella's eyes sparkled, and my stomach unclenched. "I just got done working two jobs. I had to give notice at Blue Nirvana in Key West in addition to starting at Orchid. So I'll stick with chef for now."

"Chef, then. The part you were made to play." Part of me yearned to see her on this boat beside me, wind in her hair, the way I often pictured in those quiet moments alone with my thoughts.

"Still, you've got to give her a name," Stella pressed, a playful challenge in her voice as she leaned against the stern wall. "You're not superstitious about it? Renaming a boat?"

"Superstitions be damned." I laughed, shaking my head. "The stern was so weathered when I got her, any name that was there is long gone. I picked her up at an auction in Key West right after I arrived." I stroked the freshly sanded railing, feeling the smooth wood under my hand. "Besides, I like to think she's getting a fresh start with me."

"Fresh starts." Stella's words held weight—a shared understanding that resonated deep within me.

"Exactly," I replied, and our gazes locked for a long moment. She was so beautiful, with a hint of something... maybe vulnerability, hiding in her gaze.

Breaking the trance, my eyes dropped to her bandaged hand. "Let's have a look at that." We sat on the padded bench near the stern. Gently taking her hand in mine, I unwrapped the gauze and examined the healing cut, the black stitches neat and even.

"Looks like it's healing well." I unconsciously traced the lines of her palm with my thumb before I caught myself.

"You should come by the clinic on Friday, and I'll take the stitches out."

"Thanks. I'll do that," she said softly, her hand warm in mine.

After rewrapping the gauze, I lingered a moment longer than necessary, reacquainting myself with the feel of her skin. I released her hand with reluctance, and the absence left a cold void. To cover my discomfort, I pushed to my feet and picked up a hand sander.

Stella rose to stand by me. "What do you need help with?" Her voice was eager, and she was already rolling up her sleeves.

"The two current tasks are varnishing and sanding the deck up here," I said as if presenting the two tasks like choices on a menu. With her cut being on her left hand, neither should present much difficulty for her. "Take your pick."

"Varnishing," she decided with a decisive nod and twirled her hair into a messy bun with a casual, efficient grace I found extremely sexy. It would be so easy to undo that knot of hair and rush my hands through her tresses.

"Here you go." I handed her a paintbrush. As she took it from me, her fingers grazed mine, sending a jolt of electricity up my arm. Stirrings and emotions were definitely waking up in me, and I wasn't sure yet if that was good or bad. Masking the sensation with a smile, I moved to continue my work on a rough patch I had been tackling earlier.

We fell into a rhythm, the sound of my sanding block scraping against the boat's deck pairing with the gentle swish of Stella's brush. The sharp tang of varnish filled my nostrils, mingling with the salty breeze. Waves lapped against the hull in a soothing cadence, underscoring the quiet that settled between us, a comfortable silence punctuated by our shared task.

I stole glances at Stella as we worked, studying the way her brow furrowed in concentration, or how a loose strand of hair would occasionally dance across her face before she'd blow it away with a huff. Being here with her, doing something so simple, made me feel like I was finding pieces of myself I hadn't even realized were missing.

"Looks good, if I do say so myself," she said after a while, standing back to admire our handiwork. She wiped a bead of sweat from her forehead with the back of her hand, leaving a faint streak of varnish.

"You're a natural." I gave her a lazy smile and returned to my sanding, deciding we were on solid enough footing to fish for some updates on her life. "Blue Nirvana," I said between long strokes. "That's always been one of the hottest restaurants around. Did you like working there?"

Stella set down her brush and stretched, rolling her shoulders back. I took a deep breath as her shirt stretched over the full curve of her breasts. "It was the best apprenticeship I could've asked for. Taught me more about cooking than any class ever did." Her eyes caught the last flicker of light, and I saw a glimmer there that hadn't been present earlier.

"Life lessons in Key West, huh?" I laughed, imagining a younger, carefree Stella navigating through throngs of tourists and sea-salted adventures.

"Something like that. And what about you? Medical school must have been interesting."

I paused, the memory surfacing like a buoyant thought. "Well, there was this one time during my OB rotation..."

The story slipped out effortlessly, an anecdote involving a fellow student prank and a doll that had Stella laughing, her head thrown back and the sound mingling with the waves. As our laughter subsided, the evening settled around us. The moon rose, casting a silver path across the water, guiding us into the night.

"I'm starving," Stella said, staring at the stairs leading into the cabin. "Do you have a working galley on this thing?"

"Yeah, but I don't have much in the way of gourmet food on board. The marina market doesn't exactly scream haute cuisine."

She shrugged, the marina's lights playing off her sly smile. "I can make a meal out of anything. Trust me."

I grinned back. "If anyone can, it's you. But you might be stuck with macaroni and cheese along with a can of pork and beans."

"Challenge accepted."

I shook my head, amused by her confidence, and we made our way to the small store nestled at the edge of the marina. The shelves were half-stocked, the produce less than perfect. But Stella moved through the aisles with purpose, selecting ingredients with a magician's flair.

"Are you sure about this?" I eyed the eclectic assortment in our basket as we headed toward the front of the store. "We could pick up something from Conch Republic."

"Positive," she replied, not missing a beat. "I've got everything I need."

At the checkout, I slid my card before she could protest. "In that case, dinner's on me."

The galley below deck was tight but serviceable. With deft hands and a concentration that drew me in, she maneuvered around the small stove like it was her own gourmet setup at Orchid. The sizzle of vegetables hitting the pan mixed with the tangy scent of a lone orange she'd found and savory herbs, creating an aroma that was downright seductive.

"Can I help with anything?" I leaned against the bulkhead that separated the galley from the bedroom, captivated by her ease in this culinary dance. Even as a teenager, her love for cooking had been evident. But what I saw now was a seasoned professional, at home in her element.

"Sure. You want to set the table?" she replied without looking up, her focus never wavering from the task at hand.

"I can do that. We'll eat upstairs." After tossing a blanket down on a section of varnished deck, I laid out the plates and cutlery. The wood gleamed under the soft glow of lights lining the dock.

Dinner was a simple affair but nothing short of spectacular. We sat opposite each other, sharing stories between bites of the delectable meal she conjured from the market's humble offerings. A late fisherman had brought in a snook that had made Stella light up, and she found a bag of salad greens that were still in date. The rest was a mix of crackers, scraggly vegetables, and herbs that somehow melded into perfection. Her laughter was warm, spilling over us in waves, and I found myself drawn into the comfort of her presence. How naturally she fit into this setting. With me.

"Did you learn to cook like this from the resort chefs?"

"Partly." She tucked a loose strand of hair behind her ear. "But mostly afterward. First culinary school, and then Blue Nirvana."

"You were always meant to be a chef. This proves it even more."

After dinner, we cleared the plates and settled back with the rest of the bottle of wine we'd opened. Also her choice—a rich, surprisingly good blend considering the dusty bottle came from the market. The ruby-colored wine complemented the lingering flavors of our meal. As the stars above us glinted, we reclined on the blanket, the bottle passing smoothly between us as we refilled our glasses. Every brush of her fingers against mine sent a current through my body, and I fought to keep my longing in check. Her hands were both strong and feminine—an incredibly sexy combination that only made me want to discover the rest of her even more.

Rediscover her.

"Beautiful night, isn't it?" Stella's gaze followed the path of a shooting star, exposing the length of her supple neck.

"Stunning," I replied softly.

My eyes lifted to study her profile, the way her lips curved ever so slightly, the gentle rise and fall of her chest with each breath. She turned to stare at me, her eyes dark pools of desire, and I didn't drop my gaze. As her full lips parted slightly, I leaned closer, helpless to resist her magnetic pull. Her breath caught audibly as I reached out, my fingertips softly grazing her flushed cheek. Desire roared through me, pent-up longing that had been building for over a decade.

I closed the distance between us, my lips hovering a hairsbreadth from hers. Her soft, warm breaths danced tantalizingly over my mouth. When our lips finally met, our kiss was a joining of past regrets and present desire. Her hand came to rest against my chest, fingers splaying over my pounding heart as she stroked in long, sweeping motions. And the control I'd been fighting so hard to maintain crumbled. With a deep groan, I finally reached up and pulled out her hairband, sending that glossy dark mane tumbling over her shoulders.

"Yes, Stella."

My words came out deep and gruff, hoarse with

passion. I slanted my mouth to capture her lips more fully. Our mouths melded together seamlessly, hungrily. Her plump lips were impossibly soft yet insistent against mine, and I coaxed them open. She breathed a soft moan as our tongues met, tasting, exploring, stoking the flames higher. The electrifying heat was overwhelming, she was far more intoxicating than the wine we'd shared.

We kissed under the starlit sky, lost in the moment, and in each other, until there was only the avalanche of sensations. It was a remembrance of deep, pure intimacy from another lifetime, and a discovery of something entirely new. *This* was what I'd been missing. What I'd let go of and spent years regretting with every fiber of my being.

Then, with a gentle sigh, Stella's lips stilled, remaining against mine as she pressed a single word against them. "Why?"

I knew what she was asking, and my heart plunged. She had every right to ask that question. The inevitable one. And looking back with the benefit of experience, my answer seemed so childish, so... ordinary.

So unworthy of the love we'd thought would last forever.

I pulled back to look her in the eye. "Because my parents were hell-bent on me being with the daughter of their friends. And I was too young and too scared to stand up to them. They moved back to Michigan for the sole reason of me attending college there, then medical school. I owed them everything." The admission came out more vulnerable than I intended, but this was not the time for pride. I sat back and took another sip of wine. "I was afraid. Afraid of their expectations, of failing them. But in the end, I failed you."

Her gaze held mine, unwavering and intense.

I rubbed a hand through my hair, trying to ground myself. "Mom and her best friend started pushing Ainsley and me together right away. At first, I was resistant. Of course I was. But Mom kept pointing out that a relationship between you and me couldn't work. Our lives were going in such different directions. I read every one of your texts, your emails. But I was such a mess I couldn't respond. And eventually, you stopped sending them."

Stella shifted her position on the blanket but didn't interrupt me. So I continued. "Ainsley and I began dating when I started college. We were in the same dorm." I took a deep breath, not sure how she'd take this part. "We got married our senior year. I felt like I was on a train, but it was moving too fast to get off. Then I was consumed by medical school. During my second year, she told me she wanted to have a baby. I was flabbergasted—we could barely make ends meet, and she wanted to add another mouth? Things only grew more acrimonious as I continued through med school, then residency. We got divorced as soon as I started my internal medicine residency. The strife our marriage created caused a rift between me and my parents, my mother especially. I went two years without speaking to them. It's only been in the past year or so that we've made up."

I dared a glance at Stella, and her eyes held something I wasn't expecting—compassion. "That's not a happy story. I'm sorry you had to go through that."

"You're not the one who needs to apologize. I'm sorry for being a coward." The words spilled from my mouth in a rush now. "I just felt like I was... trapped. Trapped by obligation to my parents who sacrificed so much. And obligation to Ainsley too, once we were together. That period after we moved seems so stupid now, and it caused so much pain. All because I didn't have the balls to stand up for myself. You didn't deserve that. Ending our relationship how I did is the biggest regret of my life."

She took a deep breath, the seriousness etching deeper lines around her eyes. "It's the biggest regret of mine too, Aiden." Her voice was steady, but I could hear the tremor of old wounds beneath it. "I thought we were on the same page, were looking toward the same future. But all I got back was silence. You nearly destroyed me."

Guilt twisted in my gut. Carefully, I reached out and took her hand, my thumb tracing the lines of her bandage. "I know I did. And I want to earn your forgiveness. Can we move forward?"

Stella stared at our entwined hands, her expression unreadable. "I'm not sure. I don't have time for a serious relationship. My career comes first. It always has, and now I've finally got what I've spent years working for. Orchid. And you don't exactly have a casual job either."

I nodded, understanding the gravity of her words, but desperate to make a chink in that armor of hers. "No, but that doesn't have to stop us."

"I can see that you're not the same boy who left. But that doesn't mean I'm ready to forgive and forget, Aiden."

"I understand. Whatever you're willing to give, I'll take. I want... No, I *need* to make it up to you." I cupped her cheek, and she didn't pull back. "I need you to understand this. Whatever we do together, it will be on your terms. I owe you that. But I want you to know, I'm not giving up on us. Not this time. I *will* win you back, Stella."

# Chapter Fourteen

## Stella

ORCHID WAS BUSTLING with the dinner crowd, plates clinking and glasses chiming in a way that was like a beautiful melody to me. I stood at the pass, my mood buoyant. Last night's date had wrapped me in a rather unexpected cocoon of bliss that not even the busy evening rush could penetrate.

"Stella, table five loved your dorado catch of the day," chirped Lucy, our ever-energetic server, as she whizzed past me with two empty plates.

"Thanks! Glad to hear it." My lips curved into a smile. I'd completely revamped the menu, putting my own signature stamp on it, and my feet wanted to dance at how well it was going over with diners.

I continued to check orders, my hands moving unconsciously, even as my mind wandered. The gentle rock of Aiden's boat, the salt in the air mixing with his scent, and the moonlight, all taking me back to that kiss—it was all etched in my memory.

The way he'd looked at me, with that intensity that seemed to see right through to the center of me, made my stomach do somersaults. Aiden Mitchell was no longer the determined boy who had left Dove Key in his wake. He was now a man, steady and sure, his blue eyes reflecting the depth of the ocean he so loved.

I was still processing his story. He'd hurt me deeply, and part of me didn't want to find sympathy for him. But somehow, I had. And now I had a name to go with the missing years. Ainsley. And instead of feeling outrage and betrayal, compassion had filled me for their shattered relationship. Then a sense of relief that she was firmly in his rear-view mirror. As Aiden had recited the tale, regret had been written all over him, along with the deep desire to make up for his mistakes. He was here and wanted to be with me. Now.

The fluttering in my abdomen gave way to a familiar tug of war within me. Our complicated history wasn't the only issue in our way. My career was my current love, and Orchid was the ambitious venture that consumed all my attention. Could I really afford to lose focus now? Yet, the idea of Aiden wanting to win me back, to prove we were worth a second shot, made my smile return.

Because, despite the heartache and the catharsis, that kiss was what I kept returning to. I wanted more of that.

"Chef, table seven sent this back." This time when Lucy returned, her tone was apologetic. She placed a dish in front of me. "They said the risotto is... overdone." Her pause let me know the diner had said more than that.

"Overdone?" My jaw dropped, and my feet didn't feel like dancing anymore. I had made the dish myself. I glanced down at the creamy swirl of shrimp risotto, the pink crustaceans peeking through like hidden treasures. Tasting a spoonful, I let the flavors settle on my tongue. It was cooked to perfection, just the right bite to the rice, the richness of the stock marrying beautifully with the seafood.

"Lucy, this is exactly how it's supposed to be." My frustration simmered beneath my calm exterior.

Lucy rolled her eyes. "I know. This guest has been complaining about everything since she got here. She ate at Dorado this afternoon and I heard all about it. The coffee was too hot, the toast on her sandwich too crispy—"

I shook my head decisively. "Doesn't matter. The last thing I want is her unhappy and making a scene. Tell the woman I'm sorry to hear the risotto wasn't acceptable. I can make her another one, but risotto isn't Minute Rice. It'll take a little while."

But Lucy was already shaking her head. "She said she doesn't want a replacement."

I schooled my face into a mask of professional regret. "Offer her a dessert on the house, then. Maybe the lemon panna cotta? That's Rea's specialty and everyone loves it."

"You got it." Lucy nodded, already pivoting on her heel to smooth things over.

As she scurried away, I stared at the offending dish. Doubt crept in, wrapping its gnarled fingers around my confidence. *Was* it perfect, though? Orchid was the culinary heart of the Lower Keys. Every dish that left my kitchen carried my reputation with it. And my dreams.

"Chef, you okay?" asked Luis, concern furrowing his brow.

"Fine," I lied, plastering a smile on my face. "I think I'll step out for some fresh air for a few minutes, though."

He nodded, looking unconvinced, and returned to his station. I drew a deep breath, the familiar scents of thyme and garlic grounding me. I couldn't let self-doubt sabotage me. Not when I had fought tooth and nail to get here. Orchid was my vision brought to life, and I'd be damned if I let one persnickety guest shake my resolve.

Stepping out the back door, the bracing air was a welcome respite. The breeze tousled my hair as I walked toward the covered outdoor area where guests often enjoyed their meals al fresco.

But my reprieve was short-lived when I saw several empty hangers dangling from wrought iron posts along the path. Empty hangers where handmade lanterns should have been. I stopped cold, gaping at the edge of the path. The lanterns weren't just decorations. They were antiques that had hung for decades, part of the Calypso Key legacy.

Like the orchids that had gone missing.

And the hedge trimmers might not be ornamental, but they hadn't grown fins and swum away either.

"Ben Coleridge," I muttered under my breath. It had to be. All the thefts had taken place outdoors, where he worked. And God knew he'd never accomplished anything productive or upstanding in his whole sorry life. My phone vibrated in the pocket of my chef's jacket. Pulling it out, I saw Hunter's name flashing on the screen. A smile tugged at my lips despite my frustration. "Hey, you."

"How's my big sister doing?"

The smile dropped off my face. I glared at the ground, dirt scattered on the side of the path. "It's been a pretty stressful shift. And it's only half over."

"You sound pissed. What's up?"

"You have great timing. I just noticed several missing lanterns outside Orchid. You know, the antique ones?" I paced, kicking at an innocent pebble. "And of course, there's the whole Aiden situation."

"Wait. Back up. Missing lanterns and Aiden? That's

one hell of a cocktail. I take it things have heated up between you and the good doctor."

I'd always been able to discuss my problems with Hunter. Though not a big talker about his own difficulties, he was a great listener. I eased out a long sigh. "Yeah. He kissed me. And I... well, I guess I kissed him back. But I'm not sure if I should dive into whatever this is. Not now, with everything at stake career-wise."

"Stella, you're the most stubbornly independent woman I know. People do manage to juggle both careers and boyfriends rather regularly."

"Whoa. Boyfriend is a strong term. And how would you know? When was the last time you dated anyone?"

He didn't rise to the bait or the subject change. "No comment. Focus on what matters, sis. I doubt Aiden's the same guy who took off years ago. And you're not the same girl."

I bit my lip, considering. "Enough about my love life. Let's get back to the theft. Ben Coleridge works on the landscaping crew that's doing the grounds update. It's an awful big coincidence that he shows up and shit starts turning up missing, isn't it?"

"Ben, huh?" The protective edge returned to his voice. "Don't go playing detective, Stella. And for God's sake, don't confront him. Do you even have proof he's involved?"

"Well, no. But he's such a snarly shit." I'd come across him on my run the other day as he dug a trench. He'd barely stopped to acknowledge me, his eyes going hard as I gave him a cool nod.

Hunter's sigh came through the phone. "Being an asshole isn't a crime, or else I'd be in jail. This isn't exactly your territory, you know. I can come down, poke around a little."

We both knew Hunter's suggestion was more than just a casual visit to see family and sightsee. With his background in military Special Forces and current private security work, he'd know exactly what to look for.

"That might not be a bad idea." I rolled my shoulders, the weight of both issues bearing down on me. The conversation left me with a mix of relief and worry—not just about the thefts, but about the possibility of letting Aiden back into my heart. "We'll talk about it some more. I need to head back to the kitchen."

"Anytime. Stay safe, okay?"

"Always do."

I hung up, my resolve hardening. Ben Coleridge was the worst apple in a bad bunch. Who knew, maybe he had a grudge against me. The thefts hadn't started until I took over as head chef. As for Aiden... well, that was a storm I'd navigate when the skies inevitably opened up.

THE FOLLOWING AFTERNOON, I shaded my eyes with my hand as I wandered down the path toward the restaurant. *Shark Bait* was entering the canal after the morning dive trip, and Maia tossed a line to Gabe, where he tied it around a cleat on the dock. The sight brought on a pang of longing inside me. Like my other siblings, I'd grown up on the water and been certified to dive as a teen. It was practically the family pastime, but I hadn't been diving in far too long.

Though if Hunter came around more, that might change. Evan accepted that he couldn't dive anymore and didn't resent any of us who did. But I was under no delusions that his easygoing attitude would extend to Hunter, who had caused the diving accident that left Evan paralyzed. They'd only been nineteen and eighteen that day they dove the shipwreck the *Benson*, and things had gone horribly wrong. Evan's body had mended over the years, but only over the past few months had he been willing to speak with his little brother. And though Hunter also carried deep scars from that day, they were on the inside. Hunter had planned on a fun adventure that day, not a trauma that would derail both their lives.

But I didn't have time for diving right now anyway. I turned my gaze away and skirted the lobby on my way to Orchid to start my shift. My mind should have been on my prep work, but it was cluttered with the thefts—those missing lanterns had tipped me over the edge. Ahead, the landscaping crew was busy planting a new palm tree, standing tall and expectant, its fronds still bound. And there he was, in the midst of it all.

Ben—his name alone was enough to raise the hackles on my neck.

Gabe had mentioned to me that he and Ben had recently had a conversation. Apparently, it hadn't been an overly friendly one. But since neither of them ended up in jail this time, it had to be considered an improvement. Ben and Gabe had gotten in a bar fight when Gabe first moved back, and both had spent the night in the local lockup. I shook my head. Coleridges and Markhams were like bleach and ammonia—a very bad combination.

Hunter's advice to stay out of the theft situation filtered through my mind, then I disregarded it. I'd never depended on a man to fight my battles, and I wasn't about to start now.

"Ben!" I called out, striding toward him with purpose sharpening my every step.

He turned, his green shirt sticking to his back with sweat, hands covered in dirt. His normally light-brown hair was darker where sweat matted it to his head. Seeing me, his broad shoulders tightened, as did his jaw. I couldn't deny he was a handsome guy. Too bad it was wasted on such an asshole.

"Stella." The neutrality of his tone and light-blue eyes failed to mask the tension already coiling between us.

"So last night, I noticed that three of our antique lanterns were missing." My voice was tight with accusation. "You wouldn't happen to know anything about that, would you?"

"Huh?" His brows knotted together as he leaned on his shovel. "Why would I know anything about that?"

He was tall and I had to stare up at him, which only pissed me off more. "Because things have been missing for weeks. Ever since you started working on the grounds. Coincidence?"

"Yeah, Stella. Coincidence."

I stepped closer. "I don't believe you."

Ben let the shovel drop to the ground and braced both hands on his hips. "Oh, I get it. You think because I'm a Coleridge, I'm automatically a thief?"

"Not just that. How many times have you been picked up for drunk and disorderly again?" I crossed my arms as my question hung heavy in the air, unspoken history coloring every syllable.

"Not for a while. Not since *your brother* picked a fight with me. I'm working this job to get a clean slate. Not to be hassled because of old news." His voice rose, and the muscles in his neck tensed, cords standing out.

"Then who is it, Ben? Because someone's stealing things around here, and I can't just ignore it!"

"Look, I get it. You're pissed off. But slinging mud at me without proof is low."

"Low?" I echoed, incredulity lacing my retort. "I've known you practically my entire life, and I know what you're capable of. What's low is thinking you can walk onto this Key and not be held accountable."

"Accountable for what?" His hands spread in a gesture of innocence—or perhaps defiance. "I've done nothing wrong, Stella. And I sure as hell don't need your family breathing down my neck."

"I think maybe you do," I snapped.

"Whatever."

With that, he turned back to the fledgling palm tree, leaving me to grapple with a storm of emotions. Frustration surged through me, and my head pounded with my racing pulse. Hunter's words echoed in my head, urging caution, but he wasn't here. Ben Coleridge might deny any wrong-doing, but I wasn't ready to let this go.

Gritting my teeth, I stalked off, then veered toward another landscaper who was filling in dirt around a newly planted croton. "Excuse me," I called out to a wiry man and doing my best to be polite. His nametag read Marcus. He halted, wiping sweat from his brow with the back of his hand.

"Ms. Markham." His greeting was cautious but polite.

"Have you seen anything strange around here? We've had some things go missing." Though he must have over-heard my tense conversation with Ben, I kept my tone even, not wanting to seem too accusatory.

Marcus shook his head, his eyes reflecting sincerity, or what I hoped was sincerity. "No, ma'am. We come here, do our work, and leave everything as it is. No touching."

"Are you sure? You've seen nothing?" Frustration seeped into my words, despite my efforts to contain it.

"Believe me, we wouldn't risk our jobs," he said firmly

before returning to his task. His denial did little to assuage my suspicion. Of course the crew would speak up for each other.

I whirled toward Ben, who worked a short distance away. "My family has let you continue working here despite—"

"Despite what? My last name?" His eyes flashed with a mix of challenge. It was clear that Dove Key hadn't offered him the fresh start he'd hoped for. "Maybe I was a fool for thinking it'd be different this time."

"Maybe you were," I shot back. "Having things disappear isn't exactly helping your case, you know."

"Yeah, well, neither is accusing people of things they didn't do," Ben replied without looking at me, his voice laced with a bitterness that made me bristle. "Should have known better than to expect more from a Markham." The way he sneered our family name made my breath catch.

"Take it easy, Ben." The foreman, a stocky man named Walt, approached with a protective stance, like a bear guarding his territory. "Miss Markham." He nodded in my direction. "I can assure you, we don't hire thieves. Ben has done good work for me."

"We've had several items go missing since you guys started working," I pointed out, my voice steady despite the frustration boiling within me. "Someone took them."

"Then look elsewhere because my guys are clean." Walt crossed his arms over his chest, his crewcut almost bristling. Every line of his body spoke of unwavering conviction, challenging me to argue further.

But I knew a brick wall when I saw one. A united brick wall. "Fine. Thank you for your time," I said evenly, while biting back the words that wanted to escape.

Then I spun on my heel. Leaving the gardeners to their

tasks, I could feel the weight of their stares on my back. A mixture of anger and helplessness churned inside me as I walked away. I hadn't expected Ben to just fall to his knees and confess, but I felt better having had my say. Now he was on notice.

I marched to the front of the restaurant, where my eye caught the beautiful Phalaenopsis Aiden had found at the farmer's market. The other sat across the entryway, and both were stunning additions. I took several minutes to calm myself, closing my eyes and listening to the gentle rhythm of the waves against the shore. Finally, I entered the kitchen and nodded to the two prep workers hard at work for tonight's service. Slowly, methodically chopping potatoes, Matt was coming along well. I patted him lightly on the shoulder. "Nice job with those. Your knife skills are really coming along."

Glancing up briefly, he shot me a smile. "Thanks, Chef. I'm getting faster every day."

I grabbed a scoop of ice and pushed through the double doors into the empty dining room. Could Ben be innocent? The timing was too much to ignore, but maybe it was someone else on the crew. I shook my head. What better way to keep a low profile than by convincing everyone you've changed?

Continuing the therapy I'd started outside, I stopped before a beautiful specimen of Oncidium, its delicate pink blossoms ready to dance away. I placed an ice cube in the pot, letting the soothing, familiar motions of tending to my orchids distract me from my troubles.

# Chapter Fifteen

## Aiden

THE WEIGHT of the day crashed down on me as I flopped into my chair in the quiet of my office. The last patient had left, and the clinic grew silent as my staff left. My hands, steady from years of medical training, now betrayed a slight tremor as I rubbed my face, trying to wipe away the exhaustion.

I thought about Mrs. Jonas, the seventy-year-old dynamo who used to organize neighborhood block parties during my childhood. Time hadn't been kind to her. She'd hobbled into my clinic today, a shadow of her former vivacious self and her face lined with pain. But at least this second conversation about her hip had gone better than the first. She finally agreed to see a surgeon in Marathon about a hip replacement.

"You know best, Dr. Aiden," she'd said with a trust that felt like a warm blanket on a cold night.

As I stared at the darkening sky through my window,

my mind wandered. Once upon a time, I might have been the one performing her surgery. But life had had other plans, and here I was, in this small-town clinic instead of a chilly surgical suite. If things had turned out differently... I shook my head, trying to dislodge the what-ifs.

Nearly every day, my interactions with patients made it clear that I wasn't the only one who had changed in the past fifteen-plus years. Unfortunately, most of their changes weren't for the better. Informing them of bad news was a part of the job, but one I'd struggled with more than I thought I would. But dealing with loss was inevitable for a small-town doctor who saw patients through all phases of life. And I was learning to let the victories outshine the more troubling interactions I had with my neighbors.

The clock on the wall ticked, and I needed something—anything—to lift my spirits. Which of course sent my mind racing to Stella. And the feel of her lips under mine. A smile rose on my face to find I was stroking my mouth with one finger. She had taken my confession as well as I could have hoped for, and my soul now felt lighter for the telling. As a grown man with the experience of many years behind me, the stupid boy I'd been seemed inexplicable.

Indefensible.

Yet Stella had listened, and a new beginning had been formed. A week had passed since that night. We'd seen each other several times, going to Key West one evening where Stella showed me all the local haunts, and spent a morning on Big Pine Key. Our nights together had been like rediscovering a lost treasure, though our different schedules made getting together a bit of a juggling act.

Unable to resist, I reached for the phone and dialed Stella's number, once again in my contacts where it should be. "Hi there," I said as soon as she picked up, pleased my voice betrayed none of the heaviness that clung to me like fog. "Just checking in. How's your day going?"

"Good. I'm in my office working on my catch of the day idea for tonight. I'm almost there but haven't figured out the missing ingredient yet."

That made me smile, taking my mind off my day. "I didn't realize so much thought went into fish specials."

"Oh, yes. More than any other dish, the catch of the day is the chef's signature, especially at a destination restaurant like Orchid. And since the catch changes every day, the recipe needs to also. Citrus for a light flaky fish, a hearty sauce for a meaty dorado—stuff like that."

I could listen to her voice for hours. Now I needed to get that passion aimed at me and not her kitchen. *Give it time. I need to be patient here...* "I had no idea. Guess that's why you wear the chef's coat."

"Especially for me, trying to make a name for myself at Orchid. The daily catch is what I'm trying to make our signature dish. It's what keeps me on the right course." She laughed. "Sort of like a compass for you. But enough about culinary dreams. How was your day?"

And my smile fell as I told her in general terms about the conversation with my patient. "Thanks for listening. It helps."

"Of course. And if I'm being honest, pouring over my recipe is serving as a distraction for me. My day hasn't been so stellar either." Stella's voice floated through the line, now tinged with annoyance. "Someone stole our antique lanterns from Orchid. The ones outside near the patio."

"Damn." I straightened in my chair, concern swamping my own troubles. I couldn't remember exactly what they looked like, but that wasn't the point. "Isn't this the second thing that's gone missing? You were at the market replacing missing orchids."

"Actually, it's the third theft. We lost some lawn edgers not long ago."

"Shit. It sounds like you guys might have a problem."

"Yeah, and Ben Coleridge is always lurking somewhere," she replied. I could picture her rolling her eyes, a gesture so quintessentially Stella it made my lips curve upward despite everything. Obviously, the Markham-Coleridge feud hadn't dimmed over the years.

"We kind of got into it today," she continued. "I asked him if he knew anything about the thefts, and of course he was all innocence."

"You confronted him? Stella! Maybe I should swing by and give you a gentlemanly escort home from work…" I trailed off, hoping she didn't think I was overstepping.

"Thanks." The soft warmth in her tone told me she appreciated my concern as much as her words did. "I'll be fine. I think Ben got the message loud and clear today. Just another day in paradise, right?"

"I don't know about that," I said. "Calypso Key has always been so safe. Maybe it's time to look into more security around the resort."

"Actually, I talked to Hunter about it today."

Last night, we'd cautiously caught up with each other, and she'd given me updates on her siblings. Including that the tall, weedy boy I'd once known had grown up to become a mammoth Special Forces Marine. My forehead creased with concern. "Didn't you say he's all the way in South Beach? How does that help?"

"Aw, are you offering to be my Dr. Knight in Shining Armor?" Stella teased, a playful lilt in her voice.

"Hell yes," I said as all traces of levity left me. My heart thudded against my ribcage. "You needed me once, and I let you down. I've regretted it. Every. Single. Day. Since." The words hung between us, heavy and fraught.

There was a pause, a hitch in her breath that told me my confession meant something. "It means a lot to hear you say that," she finally murmured. "But I don't have a long walk after work. That's one of the perks I negotiated." Her laugh came down the line, making me smile despite my concern.

"Then at least text me when you get home?"

"I'll do that. I need to get going. We'll get together soon, okay?"

"Okay," I replied, giving in before reluctantly ending the call. As soon as I did, a deep desire to see her coursed through me. Her voice coming through the phone, no matter how seductive, paled in comparison with the real thing.

And hell if I'd just sit by this time.

I hardly tasted the sandwich I wolfed down for dinner, my mind already halfway to Calypso Key. After scraping my plate into the trash, I grabbed my keys and headed out into the warm evening.

The drive was short, the roads nearly empty as I drove over the two-lane Calypso Causeway that separated the two islands. When I parked in the main resort lot near the lobby, my stomach tightened as I exited my car. Taking a quick glance at the softly lit grounds, I blew a low whistle. Stella had mentioned a recent remodeling, and what I saw before me bore little resemblance to the resort I'd known as a teen. Gabe was serious about his renovations. I hardly heard the low voices of guests enjoying the evening as I strode toward the pale pink structure hugging the edge of the island. The area around the back door was deserted, and as I approached, the anticipation within me built to a crescendo.

Stella slipped out the back door, her silhouette graceful and familiar, and stopped before a potted orchid.

"Stella," I called softly.

She whirled, eyes wide and surprise lighting up her face. "Aiden? What are you doing here?"

"I wanted some company, and only you will do," I admitted, offering her a hand. "You sneak out for a break?"

She nodded. "I insist everyone take theirs, no matter how nuts the night is. I figured I'd better practice what I preach. And it gives the crew confidence that I believe in them to handle things without me for a while."

I pointed toward the path with my head. "Walk with me?"

Her smile brightened the night as she slipped her hand into mine. Together, we strolled toward the beach, the landscaping lights casting long shadows on the sand. Caution tape surrounded a long trench where the landscapers had dug up the ground, reminding me of the theft. That was the last thing I wanted to think about, so I raised my eyes upward. The moon had begun its ascent, a crescent of silver in the dark sky.

"Isn't this a bit out of your way?" Stella asked, her voice teasing but her eyes searching mine.

"I decided a text wasn't enough." I squeezed her hand gently.

Our slow walk led us down the beach, then to the paved path toward Orchid. The sound of the waves had been a soothing backdrop to our meandering conversation, but now, as we approached the end of our interlude, tension threaded through the air. I could sense Stella's reluctance to return, mirroring my own.

"I'm glad you came by." Stella's voice was soft, her gaze fixed on the cement beneath our feet.

"So am I."

At the same time, we halted at the edge of the path a short distance from Orchid. She faced me, and the world seemed to still around us. The manicured trees arched overhead and provided a measure of privacy, though I couldn't see anything but the woman before me.

Her dark, liquid eyes caught mine, holding me captive. Her normally tan face was bathed in pale moonlight, her sharp cheekbones softer. We were silent as words became unnecessary, superfluous. Without thinking about it, I leaned down, my lips meeting hers. The kiss started out tentative, an expression of two people who weren't quite sure where the boundary between them lay.

I was sick of being restrained.

As I tilted my head, I clutched a handful of her hair, pulling her closer. Stella responded with equal passion, her hands finding their way to my shoulders and yanking me closer. Every nerve ending in my body ignited in a wildfire sparked by her touch. When she pulled back, her breath came in quick gasps that matched my own. Our eyes met in a mixture of desire and uncertainty. Questions danced unspoken in the air.

What does this mean? Where do we go from here?

"I have to get back to work," she whispered, regret lacing her tone. "I've already been longer than I should."

"Of course," I managed, feeling the loss of her warmth instantly. My lips felt cold. Wrapping an arm around her waist, we walked to the kitchen door where we'd started. "I'd still like that text tonight."

That made her smile like I'd hoped as she promised she would. Reluctantly, I released her and watched her slip back into the building, her silhouette briefly framed in the doorway before vanishing. I stared at the closed door after she disappeared. My heart pounded a fierce rhythm, urging me to stay, to not let this night end. Slowly, I turned around and walked to my car, only to stand beside it, keys jangling in hand. Unable to drive away.

Instead, I returned to Orchid. I found a carved wooden bench nearby, under a palm tree swaying gently in the night breeze. Easing out a sigh, I stretched my legs and crossed my feet at the ankles. I settled in to wait.

Hours passed, but I didn't mind. The sounds of the warm, welcoming night lulled me into a reflective state. Thoughts of Stella danced through my mind, replaying the feel of her kiss, her laughter carried by the wind, and the way she fit so perfectly against me. And distracted me from thinking about my eight o'clock patients tomorrow morning.

Just after midnight, she emerged from Orchid once again. This time her face was etched with the fatigue and relief of a shift now complete. Rising from my bench, I approached her silently as a small smile stretched my lips.

When she saw me, surprise flickered across her face. But it was quickly replaced by a radiant smile that outshone the moon above. "You waited? I guess texts really aren't enough for you."

"Couldn't let the night end without making sure you got home safely. I recall someone saying something about me being a doctor in shining armor."

I offered her my arm, and she looped hers through with a laugh. "This is very sweet. Thank you." Her words teased, though her eyes shone with something softer, warmer.

"You're welcome."

"No early patients tomorrow?" Stella asked, a hint of concern edging her question.

I shrugged, dismissing the thought. "I'm used to working on little sleep—I did it all through residency. And right now, I'm much more interested in tonight."

As we climbed the gentle hill toward the Big House, Stella's arm with mine, I felt the pull of something undeniable between us. The garden next to the grand old structure spread out like a green sea, its edges defined by the vibrant red and yellow hues of bougainvillea hedges. The blooms stood as silent sentinels, creating an intimate alcove that seemed to invite stolen moments. As it had all those years ago. Our first awkward, fumbling sexual encounter had been right here. But tonight, instead of filling me with regret, the sight brought a powerful wave of nostalgia. Not to mention renewed desire.

I stopped to take it all in. "It looks exactly the same. All these years later."

"But we're not, are we?"

I lifted her hand to my lips, brushing a kiss over the soft skin. "No, I think we've both learned a thing or two since then."

"Gabe and April got married here a few months ago," Stella said as her gaze swept over the serene expanse. "No need to change a setting that's so perfect."

My focus shifted from the garden to her profile illuminated by the soft glow of the moon. The way she bit her lower lip, a hint of anticipation in the curve of her mouth, stirred something deep within me. The grass beneath our feet smelled like summer, and as we ventured nearer to the edge of the garden, the sounds from the nearby sea became muted whispers. We stopped, surrounded by the fragrance of flowers.

Without another word, I closed the gap between us, pressing my lips to hers in a kiss that spoke volumes of years lost and longing reignited. As our mouths moved together, tenderness quickly gave way to passion, to an explosion of desire that had simmered below the surface for far too long. We became a clash of teeth and tongues, each searching. The sensation of her was familiar and yet completely new, all at the same time.

I pulled back slightly, breathless, my hands framing her face. "This." I managed to say between pants. "This is what I've thought about for years. Being with you."

"Then don't stop," Stella whispered back, her fingers tracing the line of my jaw before pulling me into another deep, consuming kiss. "I think we can do a much better job this time."

My arousal was a fierce, rhythmic current that threatened to sweep me under. With every touch, every sigh that escaped her lips, my desire grew. Her hands slipped under my shirt, and her fingertips grazed my skin. Everywhere she touched lit on fire.

"God, Stella," I groaned, pressing her closer against me. "I've missed you so much."

"You make me feel alive." As she spoke, the heat of her breath sent more pulsing waves rocketing through me. Her hand skipped down my abdomen, stopping to palm me. I twitched, gritting my jaw at the intensity of sensations flying through me. I pressed hard into her hand and raked my mouth over hers.

"I don't want to stop. Not now. Tell me you're prepared," she said between gasps, her voice a sultry whisper that was almost lost in the breeze around us.

My heart hammered against my ribs as I nodded. "Yeah, I've got a condom in my wallet. I always keep one."

Her lips curved into a smile, full and swollen from my kisses, a silent message of intent that sent blood pounding through my body. With a swift motion, she tugged at my hand, pulling us both down onto the soft, fragrant grass that seemed to welcome us into its embrace.

"I'm very glad to hear that," she purred, her eyes alight with desire. "Because I plan on making this night unforgettable."

# Chapter Sixteen

### Stella

THE SWEET SCENT of bougainvillea hung thick in the air, mingling with a fragrance that was pure Aiden. My fingers tightened in his hair as his mouth moved down my neck, each kiss igniting a blaze that raced over my skin. Over a decade of pent-up longing and desire surged through me as we tangled in the grass.

*What will this mean for us in the long run?*

I shoved the thought away. Right now, all I cared about was the feel of his hands sliding under my top, the rasp of his stubble against my collarbone.

"I've dreamed about this," Aiden murmured, his voice rough. "About touching you again. I've missed you so much, Stel."

Heat flooded my veins at his words. I arched into him, craving more, and he groaned. His hands slid higher to cup my breasts under my bra, his thumbs teasing the tight peaks. I gasped, desire swirling hot and fast inside me. The garden was shadowed and silent, but that didn't stop the thrill of anticipation at possibly being caught. Everything felt more intense, more desperate.

As if we were making up for all the lost time we'd been apart.

Aiden lifted his head, eyes dark and half-lidded. "Tell me you want this as much as I do."

"More," I said, my voice catching. "I want you, Aiden. I never stopped wanting you."

A smile curved his lips. "Good. Because I'm not letting you go again."

His mouth claimed mine in a kiss that obliterated thought, that spoke of possession and promise. And as his hands continued their intimate exploration, I gave myself up to the pleasure. Expectant... Anticipating... because this time we weren't fumbling novices. Aiden broke the kiss, nudging my chin up to trail hot, open-mouthed kisses down my throat. I shuddered, desire pooling low in my belly as he tore off my shirt and bra.

"Tell me what you want." His breath was deliciously warm against my skin. "Anything, Stella. It's yours."

I sucked in a sharp breath as his fingers found my breast again, pinching lightly. "You. I want you inside me."

He groaned, the sound vibrating against my neck. "Not yet. I want to taste you first."

My cheeks heated at his words, but the throb between my legs intensified. "Here?" I asked, glancing around the shadowed garden. "What if someone sees us?"

"The risk makes it hotter." Aiden nipped at my collarbone, then soothed the sting with his tongue. "But if you're not comfortable..."

I shook my head, desire overruling caution. A low laugh tumbled out of my mouth that made him shudder. "I don't want comfort. I want you. All of you."

Another smile, this one wolfish. "Your wish is my... desire."

Aiden kissed his way down my body, fingers deftly unbuttoning my shorts. He started by tracing the edges with his fingers before slowly sliding both shorts and panties down my legs. He took his time, savoring each inch of exposed skin he revealed. Once they were discarded, he gently nudged my knees apart, opening me to his gaze.

His eyes held mine as he lowered himself to my thighs. His warm breath fanned over the sensitive skin there, causing shivers to ripple through me. Then, ever so slowly, his mouth descended. The first press of his lips was soft and teasing against the inside of my thigh, making me squirm.

His mouth, warm and teasing, continued its tantalizing journey upward. Each kiss left a trail of fire on my skin that seemed to echo long after his mouth moved on. He stopped just shy of where I yearned for him most, a playful smirk pulling at his lips.

With a shift in position, he retraced the delicious path down my thigh before embarking on the same slow expedition up the other one. His mouth and tongue worked together, and the tension within me spiraled, every nerve ending screaming for his touch where I craved it most.

Shivers rippled through me as I waited breathlessly for him to reach that pinnacle, each second feeling like an eternity. My heart pounded in rhythm with the rising tide of desire pooling within me.

And then finally, after what felt like an eternity of exquisite torture, he gave me what I wanted. The first stroke of his tongue had me gasping out loud, fingers threading into his hair as pleasure surged through me.

"You're so ready," he said, voice rough with desire. "You taste like heaven, Stella."

I could only moan in response, lost in the slick glide of his mouth. He knew exactly how to unravel me and drive me wild. As if we'd never been apart. The coil of heat in my belly tightened with each flick of his tongue. I rocked against his mouth, chasing the bliss hovering just out of reach.

"Please," I gasped, fingers tightening in his hair. "Aiden, I need..."

He pressed his tongue harder, faster, and I shattered with a cry.

I lay trembling in the aftermath as he kissed his way back up my body.

"You're even more beautiful than I remembered."

I smiled up at him, brushing my fingers over the sharp angle of his jaw. Time had carved faint lines around his eyes and mouth, but he was still the boy I'd fallen for at seventeen—kind-hearted, playful, passionate. "You're so different... yet the same."

Without warning, I pushed both hands against his chest, rolling him onto his back. Lifting his shirt, he ripped it off. Unable to resist, I raked my hands down his chest, his abdomen, and shot him a smoldering stare at the hiss that issued from his lips. Then, straddling him, I unbuttoned and unzipped his shorts. "It's my turn now."

His eyes darkened with need as I slowly pulled his length free from his shorts. It was hard and throbbing, a testament to his desire for me. I wrapped my fingers around his shaft, stroking gently, savoring the feel of him in my hand. Shimmying farther down, I ran my tongue along the length. Aiden groaned, his hips bucking slightly. I smiled around him, loving the power I held in this moment. Then I lowered my mouth onto him, taking him in deep.

His hands threaded through my hair, holding me close

as I sucked and licked, exploring every inch of him. In response, he grew harder still. His groans filled the air, mingling with the sweet scent of bougainvillea and the heat of our passion. I could feel him getting ready to climax, a certain tension building within him. With a deep breath, I pulled away, moving up his body until our lips met in a kiss.

Pushing both hands against my shoulders, he rolled me over as he stretched out over me. He kissed me, deep and claiming, and the hard length of him pressed against my hip. I reached down to stroke him, enjoying his indrawn breath.

"Inside me," I said, urgency lacing my tone. "Now, Aiden."

He didn't need to be told twice. In moments, he grabbed his shorts and wallet, then rolled on a condom.

He plunged into me with a forceful thrust, causing a sharp gasp to escape my lips. My legs instinctively wrapped around his waist, pulling him closer as we moved in sync. We moaned in unison, a perfect harmony of pleasure and completion. He filled me so perfectly. I clutched at his back, nails scoring lightly down his skin as he began to move.

"You feel so good," he groaned, bracing his hands on either side of my head. "So right, like you were made for me."

"I was," I said, lifting my hips to meet his increasingly rapid thrusts.

His body was rock-hard against mine, pulsing with every thrust. As we moved harder and faster, his gaze never left mine, the intensity in his eyes reflecting the depth of his desire.

Until Aiden's lips crushed against mine with a fierce hunger, his tongue plunging deep into my mouth. My body trembled beneath his relentless pace, each thrust sending shockwaves coursing through me. I clawed at his back, arching up to meet him.

With every breathless moan, we reached new heights. He ravished my mouth in a searing kiss, muffling my cries as I shattered again around him. A few more strokes and he followed, burying his face against my neck with a hoarse shout.

For long moments, we lay there in a tangle of limbs, hearts pounding in time. I stroked his back as he caught his breath, a bone-deep contentment settling through me.

Aiden lifted his head, staring down at me as he brushed a lock of hair from my face. "I don't want this night to end. When I'm with you, it's like the rest of the world fades away."

"I know what you mean." I traced the lines of his face, rough with stubble. "It feels like we're the only two people left, and nothing else matters but right now."

"Because it's true."

I brushed a kiss over his jaw. "Now we have a second chance. Let's not waste it."

"Never." He kissed me softly, sweetly—a promise and an apology all at once. "I'm here to stay this time."

"Good." I smiled up at him, filled with giddy joy.

The moon hung like a silver sickle in the black sky, its light painting us in ethereal hues as we lay entwined in the fragrant grass. And reminding me of how late it was. The air had cooled, and a gentle breeze whispered over our skin, raising goose bumps in its wake.

"Stay," I murmured. I wasn't just feeling the need for warmth—I needed him. "Spend the night with me."

Relaxing, Aiden pulled me closer. His lips brushed my forehead in silent assent, and something within me unfurled —a hope I hadn't realized I'd been holding onto so tightly.

"I'd love to," he murmured back, his breath warm against my skin. "I'm not ready to end this night."

We stood up, brushing off blades of grass that clung to our clothes. After quickly redressing, we made our way through the veil of darkness that shrouded the path to the Big House. Each step felt like a secret dance, our shadows melding together, and a ripple of excitement surged through me.

The old wooden door creaked softly as we slipped inside and closed it gently behind us. My heart raced, not from fear of being caught, but from the thrill of sharing the forbidden with him once more. We couldn't help but exchange amused glances, feeling like teenagers sneaking past curfew. Our ascent up the staircase was a careful ballet, avoiding the familiar creaky steps that would betray our presence. Aiden laughed quietly, a sound that was free and uninhibited.

"Quiet," I whispered, grinning as I led him through the dimly lit hallway to my bedroom door. "For God's sake, don't wake Nona!"

After entering, my door clicked shut behind us, sealing us away from the world, from the past, and from all the complex threads of life that waited beyond. Our silly mirth died as we stared at each other. Here, it was just Stella and Aiden—no expectations, no judgments. Just two hearts seeking solace in the quiet storm. His gaze became hot and intense, igniting a spark that hadn't truly died down.

My bedroom, steeped in moonlight, cast a serene glow over the soft contours of my sanctuary. A display of my favorite orchids stood near the balcony door to catch the light. The gentle splash of waves against the bluff whispered through an open window, a steady rhythm that mirrored the beating of my heart. Aiden's presence, both reassuring and exhilarating, sent anticipation rolling through me as we stood mere breaths apart.

"Stella." His voice was a low rumble that resonated within the walls of my chest. His hands reached for the hem of my shirt, fingertips grazing my skin with deliberate tenderness. I lifted my arms, allowing him to peel the fabric away.

"I still can't believe you're here. You're so hot," I breathed the words, tracing the planes of his athletic form before making quick work of his shirt. It fell to the floor, joining mine in a pool. Our breaths hitched in unison, a sign of that magnetic pull between us.

We navigated the remaining barriers of our clothing with an impatient pace, each layer discarded. Naked and unguarded, we climbed into my bed. Lying side by side, our bodies became a landscape of rediscovery.

"God, I've missed this," Aiden murmured, his blue eyes reflecting the moon. Each touch was a discovery, a home-coming that whispered promises of shelter in each other's arms.

"Me too." My fingers tangled in the dark blond strands at the nape of his neck, pulling him closer until our lips met.

Aiden's mouth journeyed from my lips to the hollow of my throat, eliciting moans that danced once again on the edge of restraint. He breathed against my skin. "I want to remember every inch of you, memorize how you feel, how you taste..."

"Then don't stop," I arched into his touch as we fell together once more.

# Chapter Seventeen

## Aiden

THE OLD HOUSE creaked around us, the only sound in Stella's bedroom as we lay with our limbs entwined like vines. The moonlight spilled over her bare shoulders, highlighting the drying sweat on her skin. I inhaled the faint hints of her floral shampoo along with a muskier scent underneath, then grinned at the ceiling.

"I can't believe we're back in your bedroom again," I whispered as I pulled her closer, her back nestling perfectly against my chest. The beat of her heart was steady against my hand, a rhythmic assurance that this wasn't just another dream from which I'd wake, alone and yearning.

Stella let out a soft laugh, tilting her head to grant me access to the side of her neck where I planted a gentle kiss. "It's similar in some ways, different in others." She turned onto her back and met my gaze. Her eyes, reflecting the night sky outside, were deep pools I drowned in all over again.

"I definitely don't remember sex being *that* good." A low

laugh tumbled out as I ran my fingers through her hair, marveling at the silkiness. Every touch, every shared breath, felt like stroking the edges of a favorite book—familiar, comfortable, yet somehow more heartfelt with age.

"Of course it's different," she said, her languid stroking of my chest making me twitch. "We're not bumbling teenagers anymore. We've got more... experience."

"I'm not complaining."

"Though I admit my experiences paled compared to this." She laughed quietly, a light and carefree sound I wanted more of.

"Mine too. Because we're special together." I kissed her forehead gently before capturing her lips with mine.

"Speaking of experiences..." Stella shifted the topic as she rolled onto her side to face me, her eyes searching mine as if trying to read an unwritten chapter of my life. "Do you enjoy being a doctor?"

"Every day," I replied without hesitation. Medicine was more than a career. It was an integral part of me. "Even the difficult ones like today. It's what I've wanted since I was a kid."

"Why didn't you become a surgeon?" Stella had no way of knowing her innocent question probed at one of my deepest scars. "It was all you talked about when we were together before."

"I found out dreams and reality are sometimes very different things. Being a surgeon..." I trailed off as memories flashed through my mind. Inhaling, I continued, trying to put years of strife into context. "It requires a certain kind of courage. A willingness to hold lives in your hands in a very direct way, and the risks that come with that."

"Isn't that what you do every day anyway?" She tilted her head, her gaze full of curiosity and concern.

"Family practice is different." Searching for the right words, I flexed my hands, which had balled into fists. "It's about the long game, getting to really know the people I'm helping and guiding them through life's ups and downs." My voice was steady, but inside I was grappling with the complexities of choices made and paths not taken.

"What aren't you saying?"

I met her gaze, and a line formed between her brows. She knew me too well.

"There was an incident during my surgical rotation."

She propped herself up on one elbow, her eyes searching mine. "What kind of incident?"

"A patient who didn't make it." My voice faltered, the room suddenly feeling smaller, as if the walls were witnesses to my confession. "It was supposed to be a routine, simple gallbladder procedure, but nothing is ever really routine in surgery."

Her hand found mine, her grip both delicate and firm. "What happened, Aiden?"

"Complications. He had a massive heart attack on the table." I swallowed hard, the memory of that day still so vivid. "Everything spiraled. I felt like I was outside my own body, watching this disaster unfold, and there was nothing I could do to stop it."

"That must have been terrifying," she whispered, her thumb brushing across my knuckles.

"It was paralyzing. I froze, my mind completely blank, and the attending surgeon had to take over. I just stood there, gaping." I closed my eyes, inhaling deeply. "But there was nothing he could do. After that day, I questioned every-thing—my skills, my decisions, my path. I wondered if I was cut out to be a doctor at all."

"Yet here you are," she said softly, pulling herself closer. "You didn't let that stop you."

"No." I opened my eyes to meet hers, wanting her to see the truth in them. "But it changed me. This was also when my marriage was falling apart. It was... a very dark time. Every decision I'd made had led me to that point. Leaving Florida, leaving you, getting together with Ainsley even though I knew it was a mistake, medical school... I kept telling myself that when I was a surgeon, it would all be worth it." I pressed the heel of my hand against my eye, then gave Stella a faint smile when she kissed my shoulder.

"I'd let myself become so single-minded on one goal that I couldn't comprehend any others. Losing that patient made me realize that my blind ambition had truly made me blind." I swallowed, fighting off the utter despondency of that time. Of feeling like my life was over. "My parents couldn't understand it when I said I didn't want to be a surgeon anymore. They thought I was overreacting to the whole thing, especially my dad. He'd always wanted me to become a surgeon—he practically worshipped a distant relative who was a neurosurgeon. When added to the stress caused by my marriage to Ainsley—a marriage they'd wanted so much—I couldn't take any more of it. Of them. I cut off communication with them. Didn't speak to them for several years."

"I'm so sorry, Aiden. But you're on better terms now?"

I smiled, feeling a little lighter. "Yeah. About a year ago, we got together again and hashed everything out. They'd finally realized how much damage they'd done. And they believed me when I told them moving back here might actually help our relationship. I email them pretty often and my mom and I talk on the phone regularly."

"I'm glad to hear that. I can see how losing a patient

would be devastating. But... Don't you have to face that in family practice too?" Her words were the verbal equivalent of walking on eggshells, and it made me smile. I kissed her temple to let her know I didn't mind the question.

"Definitely, and I have to admit that that part of my practice is taking some getting used to. But operating is a very different situation. This is hard to explain, but losing that patient made me realize there were other paths open to me. Ones that were every bit as valid as surgery. All I had to do was open my eyes."

She laid her head back down. With her hair fanning out around her, she looked like a mermaid. "I think you're very brave. To face that and keep going. You're exactly where you're supposed to be."

"I hope so." The lingering doubt crept in, weaving through the contentment like a shadow in the moonlight.

"Of course you are," she said, her voice steady. But there was something unsaid hanging between us, a recognition of the fragility of our rekindled connection.

"Being a doctor," I continued, "it's more than a job for me—it's a part of who I am." The confession felt intimate, even after the physical closeness we'd just shared. "When I first got into med school, I thought being a doctor would be like solving complex puzzles day in and day out."

"But it isn't?"

"No." I exhaled, tracing the curve of her shoulder as I spoke. "It's about the people behind those puzzles." The realization had dawned slowly since taking over Dr. Nelson's clinic, washing over me like the tide—steady, persistent, undeniable.

"I did a lot of soul-searching after the surgical debacle and my divorce, and I finally decided to stick it out. Internal medicine was my next rotation. And I saw the real impact I could have from getting to know my patients, their stories, their families." A smile tugged at my lips as I recounted the way a patient had insisted on baking me a pie after I'd helped manage her diabetes.

"Building relationships, not just solving problems over a few hours," Stella said.

"Exactly. That's the surprise—the joy in those small moments. They've... fulfilled me in a way I never anticipated when I first set sail on this path. As a surgeon, your interaction with patients is often fleeting." My chest swelled with pride, not for accolades or accomplishments, but for the genuine connections I'd woven into the fabric of Dove Key.

The room was silent save for our breathing and the distant sound of waves crashing against the bluff. I held Stella close, her heartbeat a rhythm that had become essential to my own. I traced the line of her collarbone with my fingertip. "So tell me about Orchid. About being a chef there."

She settled down on her side again, her hair spilling over her shoulder. "It's been a whirlwind. Being a chef is part passion, part madness. I'm always chasing flavors, textures—the perfect balance."

"Sounds exhilarating." I loved watching the way her eyes lit up when she spoke about her craft. It reminded me of how I felt when I figured out exactly what was bothering a patient.

"It is," she agreed, "but it's also long hours and endless pressure. There's this dance in the kitchen, fast-paced and precise. Every service is a performance."

"And I'm sure you handle it with grace."

"It's what I was born to do. I really believe that." Stella sat up, drawing the sheet around her as if it were a protective barrier. Her expression grew solemn, her eyes searching mine. "Aiden, I need to be honest with you. I care about you. And reconnecting has been like finding something I thought I'd lost. But I can't make any promises about where this is going between us." Her voice was firm, resolute.

I nodded slowly, my heart sinking a fraction. "I understand. We're both starting over, in a sense."

"Exactly. And Orchid—it's not just a job for me either. It's my shot at proving myself. Here, where everyone knows your story before you've lived it." She glanced out the window, where the silhouettes of trees swayed. "I belong here, in Calypso Key. And I'm going to make it as head chef. That has to be my focus."

I brushed the hair off her forehead, smiling. "Your ambition is one of the things I love—respect—about you." I corrected myself quickly, though the truth of my feelings threatened to spill over. "I'm sure we can work out any scheduling conflicts that might come up."

She gave me a soft smile. "Thank you for understanding."

I set the alarm on my watch, trying not to wince at the hour and how soon morning would come. We settled together, and letting out a long, contented sigh, she relaxed immediately. But as I held Stella close once more, a ripple of disquiet butted into my contentment. I stared at the ceiling, the shadows now moving with the fickle breeze—nothing was ever truly still. I wanted her, and I wanted to dive into the depths of her world again. Except a part of me wondered if the surface was all she'd allow me to explore. And that could be a problem.

Was she truly wanting to focus on her career? Or was that an excuse to guard her heart from me?

As my body relaxed, I held onto the warmth of her

body, the gentle sound of her even breaths. I was falling fast and hard for her without a lifeline in sight. I understood that she needed time to fully trust me again, and I was willing to take whatever she could give. But a nagging thought made my eyes pop open again.

Would that be enough?

# Chapter Eighteen

## Stella

AS GOLDEN LIGHT poured through my window, I stretched luxuriously. Over the past two weeks, Aiden and I had spent as much time together as our dissimilar schedules would allow. He mentioned implementing evening hours at his clinic one day a week to give him an extra morning off, and I'd been incredibly touched.

He just shrugged in that self-effacing way he had. "It's good for patients too. Lots of people struggle to make daytime appointments. I'll look into it some more." Then he closed the distance between us, his mouth so close to mine I could feel his breath. "If changing up clinic hours gives us more time together, I'm not complaining."

Grinning, I turned on my side and stared at the empty spot next to me. He'd left before dawn. Now it was after 8:00 a.m., and still languid from his embrace, I stretched beneath the cool sheets, reliving the way he had explored me, assured and incredibly in tune with what I wanted. What made me bite my lip to keep from screaming. My skin still tingled from where his lips had wandered. I sighed into the new day, reluctant to leave the bed, but the thought of coffee finally lured me downstairs.

I received a distraction as soon as I walked into the kitchen, where Dad was eating breakfast. I'd barely smiled a greeting at him when a smoke gray cat with vivid green eyes padded up to me and rubbed against my legs. "Pilar! You're back from the whorehouse. Well done."

I laughed and scooped up our cat as Dad looked up from his plate, frowning. "I would hardly call the Hemingway House a brothel."

Still grinning, I stroked her head as she purred in my arms. "Did you just get back with her?"

He nodded. "Yes, yesterday evening. I got confirmation the deed had been accomplished multiple times and I could collect her again. Hopefully, we'll have more Hemingway kittens in two to three months."

One of our Markham ancestors had been friends with the great writer and been gifted one of his famous six-toed felines. We'd kept up the bloodline ever since, breeding our cats with those located at the Key West estate to keep bloodlines fresh. And now hopefully Pilar would carry on the tradition. I gently deposited her on the wooden floor, and she padded out of the room.

"Oh, how exciting! I love kittens." I fetched a mug from the cabinet, throwing a smile at chef Martin, who was already preparing my oatmeal and fresh fruit. I filled my cup and took a seat adjacent to Dad. "I'm surprised you're still here. No fishing charter to lead this morning?"

"No, I scheduled myself a day off." He shrugged, putting his fork down and giving me his full attention. "I'll head down to the fishing shed and tie some flies soon."

He looked years younger since he'd started leading our

fishing charters, releasing the mantle of resort leadership to my brother. "Gabe had a great idea with the fishing charters. Though I hardly get to see you anymore."

"I'm always around anytime you need me." His eyes gleamed with the same adventurous spirit that mirrored my own.

"I know you are. You always have been."

"The reservation book at Orchid has really filled up," he said with a smile. "Coinciding with when you took over as chef."

I tried to look demure and sipped my coffee. "The staff is great."

He grinned at me. "I think we both know it's more than that." A gust of wind blew in through the open kitchen window and I slammed my hand down on a napkin to keep it from flying away. "Good thing that storm went south. Well, good for us anyway. Hopefully, we have a calm storm season this year."

At the same time, we both rapped our knuckles on the wooden table. I laughed, though hurricane season was no joking matter, and we were in July now. "Thefts and hurricanes would just be too much to deal with. Let's keep our fingers crossed for a nice, calm summer."

Dad nodded and sipped his coffee. "You'll get no argument from me."

The sky outside was a stunning crystal blue and a light breeze wafted through the trees. "Looks like excellent fishing weather out there."

He nodded. "The last week has been as good as it gets. The people on my charters positively gush about your daily catch specials."

I reached out and squeezed his forearm, grateful for these

rare mornings when the world seemed to pause just for us. He and I had come up with an idea a while back, and it occurred to me that now was a perfect opportunity to discuss it. "Do you think you'd be able to catch enough every morning for us to serve at Orchid? I love the idea of the family connection to my signature dish, and I'm sure guests will too."

Dad nodded. "That shouldn't be too difficult. And if for some reason I come up short, you can always get more from one of our suppliers. Orchid has always been known for its connection to the sea, and you've taken that to a whole new level."

"I love working with the challenge the daily catch presents. Every day is different and a new chance to shine. It's the perfect dish to make my reputation with."

"And you certainly have, sweetie. Your mother would be so proud of you."

"Thanks. I'd like to think so." I smiled softly, the distant memory of her laughter like a warm blanket around my shoulders. "I miss her."

"Me too, kiddo. Me too."

We sat in companionable silence for a while, the only sound being the sharp squawks of seabirds outside and the occasional clink of silverware. No matter how busy life got or how far apart we were, these shared silences always brought us back together.

"If you don't mind me butting into your business," Dad said, breaking the silence as he took a sip of his coffee, "How are things between you and Aiden?" He'd had breakfast here a couple of times, but so far we hadn't managed to arrange our schedules for a family dinner.

*Soon.*

I couldn't help but smile at the thought of Aiden—his

blue eyes that seemed to see right through me, his laugh that reverberated in my own chest.

"Things are going well." I smiled as Martin set my breakfast in front of me, but I wasn't about to discuss my sex life with my dad. "We're both more mature now and have a little more perspective on life."

"Is it serious?" His brow arched, curiosity etched in the creases of his weathered face.

I stirred my oatmeal, considering how to answer. "It's... messy and tangled."

"Messy and tangled can be good. Keeps life interesting."

"Maybe." I sighed, my thoughts swirling. "We're both trying to establish careers here. I don't want to get involved seriously, and Aiden needs to focus on his medical practice. I'm lasered in on my goal, always reaching, while Aiden is trying to mix pleasure with his business. He even lives on a sailboat he's restoring. In some ways, we aren't alike at all."

Though I enjoyed the nights I spent on his boat, the cabin was cramped and stuffy. We'd spent a night on deck, snuggled under blankets and under a starlit sky, which had been absolute heaven. But Aiden's living situation seemed... tenuous, not in character with a man wanting to set down permanent roots in Dove Key.

"Your mother and I were night and day, Stella. She was all fire and passion, and I was content to let the world come to me. We ran a busy resort together and had five children along the way." He reached across the table, covering my hand with his. "Work and love can coexist, you know."

"I just don't want to get sidetracked from what I'm trying to accomplish at Orchid." My career was my identity. And Aiden, with his cautious nature and intense focus on his medical practice, seemed like another world away.

"Listen," he continued, "just remember that taking risks

is part of living. Your mother never hesitated to dive into life headfirst. I see her spirit in you every day."

"Thanks, Dad," I said, warmth spreading through my chest. His belief in me was a buoy I could always count on.

"I spoke to Hunter yesterday." Dad's voice was casual, but his eyes held a hint of concern. "He's worried about the thefts at Orchid and is thinking about coming down to look into it himself."

I nodded, swirling the last of my coffee in the cup. "Yeah, we talked about it too."

There had recently been another theft, this one a glass sculpture that had stood near the entrance to Orchid. Right next to the path where the landscapers were adding a flower bed. I scowled at my oatmeal.

My father eased out a sigh. "As much as I want to see him again, I don't like the thought that petty theft is what is inspiring his visit. I hate the idea that we might need a security presence here."

"Me too, but it's kind of the way of the world now. If Hunter comes down for a visit, maybe we should do something... fun." The idea came to me like a sudden breeze. "A pool party? Get everyone together. It could be another chance for him to reconnect with Evan too."

"That could work." The corners of his eyes crinkled with his smile. "As long as Evan doesn't push them both into the pool this time."

"I think he's still pretty appalled about that. This could be an opportunity to put that episode behind them for good, and maybe even the accident too." Excitement rippled within me.

"Don't get your hopes up too high," Dad said quietly. "There's a lot of water under that bridge. But you're right—

it's a great idea. Nothing brings family together like food, sun, and a pool."

"Maybe Hunter can put the pieces together regarding Ben and the thefts."

Dad folded his arms, his eyebrows knitting together. "I'm looking into security cameras. But you need to be careful—I heard about your altercation with Ben. Don't go confronting anyone about this again."

I sighed, knowing he was right. "I just hate sitting back and doing nothing."

"I know, and I love that fire in you. But if anything else goes missing..." He paused, meeting my gaze with a mix of sternness and affection. "It's time to call the police. Agreed?"

"Okay, Dad." I conceded the point, not completely convinced but willing to drop it for now.

"We'll see what Hunter has to say. Now I'm off to tie some flies. And make sure my big rods are in good condition so I can catch enough to feed an entire restaurant." He pushed to his feet, planting a kiss on my forehead before heading out to his fishing shed.

I took a fresh cup of coffee outside, the flagstone patio still cool beneath my bare feet. The pool's surface rippled gently as it reflected the clear blue sky. Wanting a distraction from family drama and petty thefts, I dialed Aiden's number. Even though I wasn't sure where I wanted our relationship to go, I missed him already. Missed the warmth and sexiness in the tone of voice he used with me.

"Hey there, gorgeous." His deep voice was a balm, instantly soothing me. "What's up?"

"It's a gorgeous morning, and I had an irresistible urge to hear your voice."

"Mmm. I like the sound of that." A smile raised my lips

as he laughed. "I have an irresistible urge for more than just your voice, and I've been running over an idea in my head. When was the last time you went diving?"

"I've been thinking about that! I can't even remember."

"Well, I happen to have two sets of gear on my boat. How about you join me for a sail and dive?" There was a hint of something more in his voice, an invitation I couldn't resist.

"That sounds like the perfect date," I replied without hesitation. "How about Sunday? I have that night off."

"And I have the day off. Don't you love it when a plan comes together?"

We both laughed and my toes curled at the rich sound of his. "Can't wait."

I felt like a stupid, giddy teenager, and I didn't care. After we ended the call, the corners of my lips still curled upward. Except the idea of diving left me with a rather large problem. Jumping to my feet, I headed down the hill toward the resort.

The dive shop always smelled of neoprene, a pungent scent that reminded me of happy times as a child. Maia was elbow-deep in a crate of new masks when I walked in, her long hair loose over her shoulders and back—every bit the siren of the sea.

"Hey, mermaid." I leaned against the glass counter laden with colorful brochures of underwater adventures.

"Landlubber," she shot back without looking up. "What brings you to my watery kingdom?"

"I need a favor." I shifted from one foot to the other. "A refresher course in scuba. It's been a while."

"Oh! You're going diving?" Maia quirked an eyebrow, finally giving me her full attention.

"Maybe. Well, yeah." Staring at the brochures, I tried to avoid her knowing gaze.

"Spill it, Stella. Is this about Aiden?"

I sighed, sitting on a stool. "We're going diving on Sunday."

"Keeping things casual, huh?" Her voice was laced with mischief as she began sorting through the masks.

"Yes," I confirmed, trying my best to sound nonchalant. "Just casual."

Maia let out a peal of laughter that bounced off the tanks and wetsuits lining the walls. "Yeah, so were Gabe and April. Who are now married, I might add."

I rolled my eyes but couldn't suppress a smile. "Well, Aiden and I are not them."

"Sure, sis." She winked at me and stood, walking behind the glass counter. "I'll get you sorted, don't worry."

She ran a finger down her computer terminal, studying the schedule. "Okay, how about Friday morning? I can have Nona watch Skye for a few hours, and you don't need to start work until the afternoon."

"That's perfect. Thanks, Maia. You're a lifesaver."

"Anytime." She paused, her eyes still dancing. "If you're happy, I'm happy. Besides, I don't want you dying on me."

"Jeez, way to increase my confidence!" Despite my words, a rush of affection for my sister washed over me. "And who knows? Maybe a little adventure is just what I need."

She waggled her brows. "Or maybe, it's what you both need."

# Chapter Nineteen

## Aiden

DOVE Key Marina slid slowly past as I motored out at an easy idle. Once past the breakwater, I turned the key, and the rhythmic purr of the engine gave way to more natural sounds—a chorus of lapping waves and the soft flutter of the sail I unfurled. The late morning sun cast an iridescent gleam on the water, like a thousand diamonds scattered across a blue velvet floor.

"Feels good, doesn't it?" I said to Stella, who stood beside me with the kind of easy grace that comes from years of being in tune with the sea. The breeze tugged playfully at her hair, making her look like the wild, carefree creature she was out here.

"Better than good. It's magical."

On impulse, I wrapped my arm around her and pulled her toward me. I kissed her soundly, tasting and exploring those incredible lips. We'd settled into a happy routine, as routine as we were able to, anyway. When we weren't together, I missed her with an ache that felt almost physical, a phantom pain from a part that wasn't there. Her mouth drove me to extremes, and this kiss was no different. A slight vibration in my hand holding the wheel made me end the kiss with a reluctant groan. The boat, still unnamed, was yearning for direction, like a living thing waiting for a command. I slightly adjusted course as Stella laughed beside me.

"Oh, this is wonderful!" She inhaled the bracing air. "We're firing on all cylinders, aren't we?"

"That would be an understatement. Want to take the wheel?" I gestured toward the helm with an inviting tilt of my head.

"Really? All our boats are motorboats." Stella turned to me, her eyebrows arched in playful skepticism. "I'm not experienced with sails."

"You'll be fine." I stepped aside to make room for her. "Just keep her steady into the wind. You want to maintain our heading at about forty-five degrees off the bowline. Watch the luff of the sail—if it starts to flap, ease up on the wheel just a bit."

"Got it, Captain." She shot me a mock salute before confidently taking the wheel. Immediately, she altered course slightly and the thrum running through the sail vanished.

"See? You're a natural. Just feel the response of the rudder. Let it guide you."

Stella nodded, focused, her hands firm on the wooden wheel as the boat obeyed her every subtle command. The clinking of the rigging was as familiar to me as my own heartbeat as I nudged her side. "See? I could fall overboard and drown, and you'd have no trouble finding your way back to the marina."

She burst into laughter, though her concentration never

wavered from the task at hand. "Don't even say that! But I guess skills transfer over. Kind of like riding a bike, I guess."

"Except with more water and less likelihood of scraped knees."

"True, but there's something about the ocean. It's unpredictable, thrilling…" Her voice trailed off as she absorbed the enormity of the open waters around us.

"Thrilling, yes," I mused, leaning against the wooden console. "But today, she's being kind to us. A perfect day for sailing and diving."

I watched Stella work, admiring the way she blended with the elements, becoming part of the boat, the water, the sky. It was a dance of sorts. The sail billowed above us, full and taut, harnessing the power of the wind. Around us, the world was boundless, a horizon that promised adventure and whispered tales of the deep. Moments like these made all the complexities of life on land dissolve into insignificance, leaving only the simplicity and purity of the sea.

It was easy to let my mind wander back. Back to those carefree high school days, before we knew what pain and heartache were. They were fond memories. "Hey, remember that time in high school when we borrowed Coach Thompson's kayak and ended up tipping into the ocean?" Grinning, I sidled up next to her.

Stella's eyes lit up with the memory as a large swell lifted the boat and lowered it, making her wobble. "Borrowed is a generous term for what we did. And by *tipped*, I take it you mean you showing off and capsizing us?"

"Me? Never!"

Tucking a windblown lock of hair behind her ear, she gave me a side-eye. "I have more faith in your seamanship now. Why don't you take over? The swell is bigger out here."

I nodded and took the wheel from her hands. "And for the record, you were the one who dared me to do the Eskimo roll."

Stella shook her head in mock disapproval. "Only because I thought there was no way you'd actually try it." Standing next to me, she bumped me with her shoulder, a familiar gesture that warmed me more than the sun overhead.

"Never underestimate what I'd do on a dare, especially when it comes from you." I guided the boat with ease, my muscle memory aligning perfectly with the vessel's response. The wind became a willing accomplice, carrying us forward like a whispered secret between old friends.

"Look at us now, huh?" Stella mused as she slipped her arm around my waist and rested her head against my shoulder. "From capsizing kayaks to sailing into the great unknown together."

"Life has a way of coming full circle." I glanced at her, catching a glimmer of something in her expression—a mixture of nostalgia and anticipation. And maybe something stronger lurking in her eyes.

Or was that just wishful thinking on my part?

I wrapped an arm around her shoulders, pulling her close. It felt right, like she'd always belonged there. We snuggled together comfortably, watching the horizon stretch out before us, the sea a canvas on which our day would unfold.

As we settled into silence, my mind tried to turn to those days after I'd left Florida, times I had no desire to relive. The contrast was so dramatic between how I'd felt about life then and what I was experiencing now. Even in Michigan, I'd always felt this was home. It took more than a decade, but at last I'd made it happen. I wondered if Stella's thoughts were similar.

Then she turned and answered my unasked question, her expression sobering. "So how did you end up back in Dove Key?"

I took a deep breath. "After medical school, I joined a large internal medicine practice in Lansing. It was difficult, especially with family expectations."

"Your parents?" Her voice was soft, understanding.

"Yeah." I looked away, focusing on the horizon. "My mom had a hard time dealing with my divorce from Ainsley, and Dad... he had his heart set on me becoming a surgeon." The words felt heavy, like anchors dragging behind me. "When I chose internal medicine, they tried to be supportive, but I could tell they were disappointed."

"God, that's harsh!" Stella's brow furrowed, and her eyes flashed. "They should've been proud of you—internal medicine isn't exactly a walk in the park. You realized your dream of becoming a doctor. Who cares what specialty you decided to go into?"

"Thanks." I offered her a half-smile that probably didn't reach my eyes. "It was pretty rough between me and them for a while. I'm glad we reconnected and cleared the air. Especially my dad—he's not the most emotional guy. And when he finally apologized and said he was proud of me, it meant a lot. But I really wanted a change—location, mindset, everything. I needed a reset. So when I heard about Dr. Nelson retiring, I jumped at the opportunity."

"I'm glad you did," she said, her words as soft as the breeze.

"So am I."

Leaning in, I caressed her lips with mine. As I returned my eyes forward, the conversation I'd had with my mother yesterday ran through my head. More gentle probing about how things were going with Stella, and I was pleased with how happy Mom sounded about us being together again. I even talked to my dad for several minutes about the upcoming football season. This move had been more than a rekindling between the woman I'd let get away and myself. It was also a bridge to repair my relationship with my parents.

The boat rocked gently beneath us, and I steadied myself with a hand on the wheel as our shoulders bumped. "I hated being estranged from them. Now, despite the distance, we get along better. Maybe it's the miles between us that make the heart grow fonder, or just time doing its thing."

"Distance has a way of putting things into perspective."

"Exactly." I glanced at her, then back at the sea, gathering the courage to say what had been weighing on me since she stepped aboard. "Us getting back together has meant a lot to me. I've missed you more than I let on."

Her smile was a sunrise, slow and beautiful as it banished shadows. "I've missed you too."

A weight lifted off my shoulders, one I hadn't fully acknowledged carrying. The past couldn't be rewritten. But under the vast dome overhead, with Stella by my side, maybe the future could be something different. Something better.

"Hey," Stella said, nudging me playfully. "No more of that brooding sailor look, okay? We're on the water, and it's a perfect day. Embrace the adventure, Captain."

"Affirmative, Admiral Markham." I laughed, the last of the seriousness ebbing away. Our laughter mingled with the sound of the waves. And just like that, we were back to where we started—just Aiden and Stella, two souls adrift, and yet finding their way back to each other.

Stella reached out to stroke the back of my hand. "It means a lot to me. Your being so open about everything. It's not easy, I know."

I glanced at her, catching the sincerity in her eyes. That other thing flickered through them again, but this time I couldn't deny what it was. Hesitation. My heart hitched as I sensed the conflict within her. But I just smiled, because that's what you do when you want to believe everything's fine. I might be doing everything I could to convince her this time would be different, but I hadn't finished the job yet.

I reached out to smooth her hair. "We can't get past what happened without reliving it, at least to some extent. You deserve the truth. You deserve so much more."

* * *

As we neared a small, nameless key, I pointed out the vibrant reef below the clear, warm water. "This is it."

Stella leaned over the side, peering into the depths. "It's so clear," she exclaimed, her face awash with wonder. Then, with a playful glint in her eye, she turned to me. "You keep two sets of gear on board, huh? Isn't that perhaps a little presumptuous?"

"Ah." I laughed, running a hand through my hair. "Both belong to Luke. He's completely obsessed with diving. I keep them on board in exchange for being able to use them when needed." I didn't add that since he brought the gear on board, part of me had been hoping she'd share it with me one day.

"Convenient," she teased. "I'll have to thank Luke the next time I see him."

"Don't. He'd just want to join the dive with us." I joined in her laughter, grateful for the ease between us.

This site had a mooring ball, and I tied us off, double-checking the clasps to make sure the boat wouldn't go anywhere. I caught her gaze, the same sparkle from years ago still alive within them. My pulse quickened, not from the adventure ahead but simply because I was with her. "You okay with the sway?" I asked, watching her for any sign of discomfort.

"I don't get seasick." She grinned, steadying herself with a hand on the bench. "It's like dancing with the ocean."

We set about gearing up, the neoprene wetsuits a second skin. As we slid into our scuba kits, anticipation rose within me. This was more than a dive. Scuba had been one of our favorite activities during high school. Submerging under the water would be a step toward something lost, a bridge across years of silence.

I helped her walk to the makeshift removable platform Luke and I had built, then handed Stella her set of fins. "Remember how to put these on without tipping over?" I teased, recalling the first time we'd tried snorkeling together.

"Watch and learn, sailor." Her reply was playful, but determination was clear in her eyes as she slipped them over her neoprene booties. "Maia gave me a refresher a couple of days ago, so you better look out. I'm ready to show you how this is done!"

Laughing, I checked her tank a final time, ensuring everything was secure. "Yeah, yeah. I'm not quite as lucky as you, with half your family being dive professionals."

"Not half. Just two—and both women, I might add."

"You won't get any argument from me about the capa-bilities of women, believe me. I see that every day. Luke might not be a dive pro, but we've gone diving several times since I've moved back. I'd forgotten how much fun this is, though you are much hotter than him."

"Oh? You noticed I'm not a guy, huh?"

"Pretty sure I've demonstrated that knowledge multiple times now." I waggled my eyebrows at her. She responded by pushing me in the chest, and I staggered a little before getting my footing again.

We did a final buddy check, ensuring everything was secure and operational. Both of us perched on the edge, the crystal waters beckoning below. My heart raced with the adrenaline of embarking on a new journey with the one person who had always made my spirit soar. Our eyes met as smiles widened our mouths.

"Are you ready to jump?" I asked.

# Chapter Twenty

## Stella

I DRIFTED DOWN through the clear blue water, my lungs finding a rhythm with the hiss and bubble of my regulator. The ocean cradled me, vast and yet soothing, as Aiden descended by my side. I caught glimpses of him through my peripheral vision—his dark-blond hair waving gently, his trim form floating through the sea with athletic grace.

He pointed toward a school of tiny fish. Nearing at impossible speed, they stopped and swooped around us in a silvery dance. Their movements were synchronized, enchanting in their fluidity as they swirled and darted. I could only nod, mesmerized by the simple magic of this underwater ballet.

Reaching sixty feet, we glided along a wall of solid coral painted with vivacious streaks of color—soft and hard corals of crimson, emerald, and azure. Colorful butterfly fish flitted about, their delicate fins brushing past corals like the strokes of an artist's brush. Several lobsters, armored in shades of scarlet and burgundy, played hide-and-seek within the crevices of the reef. I stopped to watch one, its long antennae reaching toward me and twitching.

After moving on, a twinge of unease rippled through me at the realization that we were alone, without the guidance of an experienced dive leader like Maia or April. But Aiden and I were both certified divers and qualified to dive in a buddy team.

There was no current to fight, and I craned my head up, spotting the shadow of the boat moored overhead. Relaxing, I kicked on, letting myself enjoy the immersive experience. Aiden's movements were confident yet gentle, his presence reassuring. As he gestured toward a particularly intricate formation, I followed, my fins propelling me closer. It was an overhang of coral, festooned with swaying fans and dotted with the tiny, brilliant sparks of luminous fish peeking out from their coral homes. I locked eyes with Aiden, and his eyes glinted through the mask.

Being submerged in this alien yet familiar world brought a serenity unmatched by any other experience. The loudest sound was our exhaling bubbles, a soothing rhythm that accompanied our quiet tour. Above us, life was all honking cars and ringing cell phones, but down here, there was just the hush of the ocean.

As we continued to explore, Aiden and I rediscovered each other in a place where words were not only impossible, they were unnecessary. Every gesture, every shared look, spoke volumes. When he inspected the edge of a massive brain coral, beckoning me to admire the complex patterns, a smile tugged at my lips. My heart swelled with a warmth that had nothing to do with the tropical waters.

We communicated in hand signals and shared laughter captured behind our regulators. Easing through the dappled light that filtered down from above, Aiden and I glided side by side. As we rose toward the sun-dappled surface thirty feet above, our fins acted as silent engines, driving us through an elaborate canal that wound beneath the ocean's skin. This winding channel felt like the keyhole to a world unseen by most. The surge of water, like a playful sprite, teased at our bodies with its gentle tug.

The channel was a living tapestry of soft and hard corals. Lacy sea fans swayed seductively, delicate dancers in a ballet choreographed by nature herself. The stoic hard corals were interspersed between them. Their calcified structures stood firm against the push and pull of waves, creating permanent, solid homes for aquatic life.

Schools of fish darted around us in synchronized motion. A yellow-tailed damselfish flitted about, its body an impossibly vivid cobalt with iridescent turquoise sequins. One snap of its bright yellow tail sent the shy fish scurrying into the reef.

I'd forgotten what this felt like, the intimate connection of diving. It was more than just admiration for the sea's beauty or fascination with its complexity. I felt woven into this underwater fabric—not as an outsider intruding upon nature but as an integral thread adding depth to its design.

Then I spotted it. And rejoiced.

First just a dark brown shape nearly eight feet long. But the closer we got, the more recognizable it became. A nurse shark, its broad, flattened body motionless but for the rhythmic flutter of gills, lay on the sand under an over-hanging shelf.

The creature's deep brown color was perfectly designed to blend with the coral. Its small, barbel-fringed mouth gaped, drawing water over gills that heaved with a hypnotic cadence. The shark's eyes held an ancient, unblinking calm that rooted us to the spot.

I could feel Aiden's gaze on me and turned to find my excitement mirrored in the wide-eyed wonder behind his mask. My heart pounded not from fear but from the thrill of sharing this moment. Aiden extended his hand, palm open and inviting. Our fingers met, and his thumb brushed against mine as a silent language of emotion flowed between us. I squeezed Aiden's hand tighter, my smile reaching him through the softening of my eyes.

Suspended in the water's embrace, we lingered a moment longer before exchanging a look that said it was time to move on. Reluctantly, we released our hands and began to ascend, the nurse shark fading into the shadows below as we returned to the world of sun and air. At fifteen feet, we leveled off to complete our three-minute safety stop. And our hands found each other once again.

The sensation of breaking the surface was like waking from a dream. Climbing back on Aiden's boat, sunlight played on my skin, chasing away the chill as I peeled off my mask and fins.

"God, that was incredible," I breathed, my voice sounding foreign after the long silence underwater.

Aiden's smile matched mine, his eyes still holding echoes of our dive. "I'd never be able to tell you don't dive every day."

"Thanks. That just reminded me how much I love the ocean." I reached out to brush his arm. "*You* reminded me of that."

"I'm glad we got to experience it together."

As we stood on the deck, Aiden twisted the knobs of the fresh-water shower, and crystal droplets cascaded over us, warmed from being in the sun. It felt like a baptism, washing the salt from our skin and hair, sealing the experience within us.

With the water spilling over his strong shoulders, Aiden laughed. "The butterfly fish were cool—that one with the stripes kept following you."

"Maybe it liked me." I shrugged, unable to suppress a laugh.

"Or it sensed your kindred spirit." Aiden paused, turning serious for a moment. "You have a way of drawing things—and people—in, Stella. Underwater or not."

His compliment warmed me more than the sun overhead. I allowed myself to bask in the glow of his admiration before shaking off the sentiment like droplets from my skin. "What about that nurse shark? That was the best part of the dive."

"It was." He reached for a towel and offered it to me. As I wrapped it around myself, I caught his gaze lingering on me for a heartbeat longer than necessary. "It didn't even care that we were there."

"Like it knew we meant no harm." I broke down my gear, then settled onto the cushioned bench at the stern of Aiden's boat. I watched as he secured our equipment with focused attention to detail. The sun was past its zenith now and cast its warmth like a net, including on Aiden's bronzed skin. His movements were fluid, methodical, and I found myself hypnotized by the play of his muscles.

"Enjoying the show?" he asked with a grin.

"Nature has a way of putting on quite the display," I replied with a wink. My heart beat a little faster as he approached.

He sat beside me, close enough that our knees brushed. The contact sent a ripple through me, amplified by the intensity in his eyes. Aiden reached for my hand, his fingers entwining with mine. The action was gentle but deliberate, sparking a connection that vibrated through my body.

"Today reminded me how much I've missed... this. Just being together."

I looked down at our joined hands, feeling the strength in his. "Me too. I loved every minute. Because I was with you."

Cupping the back of his head with my hand, I pulled him to me. Our mouths met in a salty kiss as the warmth of shared experience gave way to a completely different kind of heat. His lips were soft yet demanding, moving against mine with a fire that reignited old flames and sparked new desires. With a quick tug, he untied my bikini top and slid his hand around to cup my breast.

"Mmm," I said softly, nipping his earlobe. "Why do I get the feeling you've got something else in mind now?"

With a deep laugh that made my core clench, he grabbed my wrist and moved it to his board shorts, and the rapidly growing bulge there. "Whatever gave you that idea?"

After a quick squeeze, I lifted my hand to run it through his wet hair, closing it and pulling him tighter as my lips moved back to his. This time our kiss was a storm of passion, threatening to break over us both.

"Did you know," Aiden murmured against my lips, breaking away only enough to speak, "there's a comfy bed just down those stairs?"

A smile tugged at the corners of my mouth. "I remember. So let's go."

My bikini top slid completely off as I stood and reached out my hand. Aiden's eyes went on a slow, leisurely journey from my feet upward. They paused for a long moment on my breasts before he stood, his eyes pinning me. His fingers interlocked with mine as he guided me toward the cabin.

# Chapter Twenty-One

## Aiden

A WEEK LATER, the warm breeze tousled Stella's hair as we walked hand in hand along the pedestrian path running parallel to Seven Mile Bridge. Though less than ten miles away from our little islands, it felt half a world away. The endless stretch of turquoise water below competed with the sky above, both captivating shades of blue. I couldn't help but think the water won, reflecting Stella's vibrant energy back at us.

An osprey soared overhead, its sharp gaze surveying the waters before it chose to alight on the railing a few feet away. Its talons gripped the metal with easy authority, and Stella squeezed my hand, pulling me to a stop to admire the large raptor.

"Look at him," she said, her voice laced with awe. "He's magnificent."

The mottled brown and white bird surveyed us without fear. "I wonder how close he'd let us get?"

She smirked. "Do you really want to find out whether he'd attack or fly away?"

"Good point. Let's keep going." I bumped my shoulder with hers as we stepped around the bird. It watched us pass but didn't move otherwise.

As we continued our stroll, I found myself just enjoying the moment. The salty air filled my lungs, and it felt like inhaling a piece of home. A piece of us. "I'm so glad I moved back. I've missed this so much. The warmth, the water, the fresh air." I glanced down at her and winked. "You..."

Her fingers tightened around mine, and she turned to give me that mischievous, heart-stopping grin. "I'm pretty happy about it too."

As we walked, a splash in the water below caught our attention. We wandered over and rested our arms on the metal railing. A fishing boat bobbed on the waves, and a man on deck was engaged in an epic battle with a fish that leaped and danced on the water's surface. One particularly majestic leap revealed it as a tarpon—its silver scales flashed brilliantly under the sun.

"Look at him go!" Stella exclaimed, pointing as the fish thrashed wildly, trying to shake free from the line.

"Kind of like us," I said. "Always wrestling with something or other."

"Except we usually came up for air at some point." She laughed, then grew contemplative. "You know, growing up on Calypso Key and being able to dive or fish whenever I wanted... I didn't realize then how precious that freedom was. How lucky I was."

"Sometimes we don't see the value of what's right in front of us until it changes," I mused, watching the man finally reel in the tarpon.

Stella leaned against the railing, her hair blowing gently

in the breeze. "There was this wild sense of adventure that came with every dive, every catch. And Dad made sure each of us got the experiences we craved. It felt limitless."

Limitless was a fitting word for Stella too. She had an untamed spirit that matched the ocean's depths. As if to prove my point, she stood on her tiptoes and bent over the railing, peeking straight down.

"Hey, what do you think about jumping off this bridge right now?" She wagged her eyebrows at me.

I stared at her for a moment, incredulous, before bursting into laughter at the solid hundred-foot drop into the ocean. The idea was ludicrous but so quintessentially Stella. "Only if you plan to sprout wings or start practicing your mermaid skills. And you go first."

"Mermaid skills, huh? You haven't seen anything yet, Mitchell." Her laughter mingled with mine, a sweet sound that filled the space between us.

The laughter hadn't quite died down as we strolled farther along Seven Mile Bridge, hand in hand. I couldn't help but feel that every smile and giggle between us was stitching the past and present together, weaving a portrait of what could be.

"Life doesn't get much better than this," I said, my voice carrying a note of contentment that had been absent for too long. "Simple pleasures—walking beside someone who means the world to you."

Stella's gaze met mine as our steps slowed, then stopped. She stood on her tiptoes, and her lips found mine in a kiss that felt like coming home. A kiss that spoke of second chances and unspoken promises.

"Agreed," she murmured against my lips, then broke the kiss to flash me a smile brighter than the sun glinting off the water.

And as I watched the light dancing on her dark hair, my heart skipped a beat. Stella's vibrant laughter, her fearless approach to life—it all hit me straight in the chest like a physical blow. I was falling in love with her all over again, each laugh and smile deepening the emotions stirring within me. The realization was as exhilarating as it was terrifying. How had I let her slip away once before?

After finishing our walk, we got in my truck and headed north on Highway One to Marathon's quiet charm. The lunch spot we stumbled upon was the epitome of small-town allure, a tiny hole in the wall that promised more than its unassuming exterior suggested. *The Salty Crab* was etched onto a weathered wooden sign that swung gently above the door, the paint chipped but the name clear.

Inside, the air was thick with the aroma of spices and grilling seafood, and the buzz of conversation filled the cozy space. Nautical decor—nets, buoys, and old photos of local fishermen—adorned the walls, while a chalkboard menu boasted the catch of the day in colored scrawl.

"Look at this place," Stella said, her eyes scanning the intimate restaurant as we took our seats at a corner booth. "It's got character."

"Character and some amazing scents," I added, taking in a whiff of garlic and sweet herbs that wafted from the kitchen. I pointed at the chalkboard. "Look. Catch of the day. Must be a good place."

Stella perused the menu with the eye of a seasoned chef, her fingers tapping rhythmically. When our meals arrived, she assessed her plate with a glint in her eye, giving the blackened snapper an approving nod before sampling a bite.

"Wow," she exclaimed after a moment, her taste buds

clearly delighted. "I should hire whoever's back there to bring a little of this magic to Orchid."

"Is that so?" I laughed, watching her savor each forkful. "I'll still take your Cajun seafood pasta over this."

"Flattery will get you everywhere, Dr. Mitchell." Her grin was as delectable as the food we were enjoying, and I got caught up in the simple pleasure of our banter.

But her use of my title reminded me of something. I arched a brow. "Being here in Marathon reminds me... have you made your appointment with your new gynecologist yet?"

She wrinkled her nose in that adorable way. "Yes, though you are rather familiar with my lady bits now. I don't see what the problem is."

Smiling, I refused to rise to her bait. "The problem is that it's a conflict of interest. A doctor needs to maintain impartiality as much as possible to make the best treatment decisions. And, darling"—my voice turned to a low drawl—"I'm anything but impartial where you're concerned."

"Glad to hear it. And you're off the hook, though I couldn't get an appointment for a while yet. No more horrifying meetings in your exam room."

Laughing, I covered her hand with mine. "I still feel awful about that."

"It wasn't the best way to see each other after nearly two decades, was it?"

"No, but it led us here. So at least some good came from it."

Lunch stretched on, punctuated by laughter and the clink of silverware. As Stella talked animatedly about flavor profiles and cooking techniques, I realized that these moments—the easy conversations, the shared smiles over a meal—were what I'd been missing in my life. Why I was back.

I watched her across the table, the sunlight filtering through the window and casting a golden glow on her skin, and I wondered how long I could keep my heart's truth silent. Would she ever be ready to hear just how deeply I'd fallen for her? I pushed the thought aside, determined to savor the present, uncertain as the future might be.

The clatter of dishes and the hum of conversation filled the little diner, a quaint sanctuary from the bustling heat outside. I leaned back in the booth, feeling the stickiness of the vinyl against my skin, and watched as Stella took another bite of her key lime pie, her eyes closing in what I could only describe as pure culinary bliss.

"It's kind of nice not to work all the time, huh?" I teased, taking a swig of my ice-cold beer.

Stella's eyelids fluttered open, and she set her fork down with a gentle clink. "You know," she began, dabbing her mouth with a napkin, "I've been so wrapped up in the restaurant lately that I forgot how good it feels to just... breathe."

"Sounds like you needed this break more than you realized." I leaned forward, resting my elbows on the table, intrigued by the softness that had overtaken her usually fiery demeanor.

She nodded, a strand of hair falling across her face. "I need to remember that there's still room for fun and adventure," she said, tucking the errant lock behind her ear. "Especially now." Her gaze held mine, and the corner of her mouth lifted in a smile.

"Then here's to rediscovering each other." I raised my bottle. "And to remembering that the best parts of life aren't on any menu."

"Cheers to that," Stella agreed, her glass chiming against mine.

"How are you feeling about the pool party next weekend?" I'd been pleased she wanted me to attend such a big family event. She might not be quite as into this relationship as I was, but inviting me was a step in the right direction.

"A little nervous, of course. The last time those two were around the pool, it didn't go so well. But I'll keep trying. Both of them need to move past what happened, but I think they're too stuck to reach out on their own."

"And here you are, ready to step in and help. They're lucky to have you."

She smiled and blushed a delicate shade of pink but didn't reply to the compliment. Once again, that deep, clenching wave of emotion swept through me. A trio of pelicans swooped by outside, inches above the water's surface. I picked at the label on my beer as I tried to sort out the tight warmth in my chest.

"Hey, you've gone quiet on me." Stella nudged me gently, her voice pulling me back. "What's on your mind?"

"Nothing," I lied, forcing a smile. The truth was, my heart was so full it felt like it could burst through my chest. The words *I love you* perched on the tip of my tongue. But I swallowed them down, along with another mouthful of beer.

She raised an eyebrow, clearly not buying it, but she let it go. Maybe it was the way I looked at her just then, the intensity and vulnerability making her uncomfortable. She picked up her beer and took a swallow, her throat moving in a way that made me want to kiss it. To kiss everything. I wanted to savor this simplicity, this easiness between us. It was a rare treasure—one I knew all too well could be fleeting.

The pelicans rose in a graceful arc and then one slammed into the ocean, coming up with a wriggling pouch under its bill a moment later. Stella's eyes widened and her mouth stretched into a broad smile. Her delighted look nearly did me in right then and there.

But just as I opened my mouth to spill my heart out, I thought twice. Of the times I'd glimpsed that flicker of hesitation in her eyes. It was enough to give me pause. Because despite spending the perfect day together, she wasn't ready to hear my declaration. And even as I forced a smile on my own face, I had to wonder.

Would she ever want to hear those words? And would she ever return them?

# Chapter Twenty-Two

## Stella

THE LOW HUM of conversation and splashing underscored a warm, gentle afternoon as I sat at a patio table. Across from me, April pushed her lower lip out, her eyes faintly tinged with disappointment. "Well, at least *you're* here."

"Aiden's sorry he couldn't make it." I handed her a glass of iced tea, beads of condensation trickling down its side. "An emergency came up at the clinic."

Just as I was getting ready to come downstairs, he'd called, apologizing that he wouldn't be able to make it. I'd felt a pang of regret, though a tiny part of me I didn't want to acknowledge had been relieved. Introducing him to my entire family was a big step, and one I wasn't entirely on board with. My focus needed to be solely on my family today, not worrying about how Aiden blended into the mix.

April exchanged her frown for her trademark smile. "It's okay. I understand. The life of a doctor is never dull, huh?"

"Emergencies come with the territory." I smiled, but yet again, my eyes wandered to the pair standing on the other side of the pool. The pair we were all pointedly trying not to watch. Hunter and Evan both had pleasant expressions on their faces as they stood talking, and neither looked like they were about to push the other into the water. The four of us sitting together had been craning our necks subtly, curiosity piqued by the brothers' interaction. Liv perched on the edge of her seat as she tried not to inspect Evan's every move.

"Looks like Hunter and Evan are getting along." Gabe's voice was even, but I knew him well enough to hear the hope in it.

"No signs of fireworks, anyway," I said.

Across the pool, Evan nodded and something unspoken passed between the two men before he turned and padded our way. His muscular chest was bare and he wore swim trunks, fully embracing the theme. His limp hardly noticeable today, and his eyes were fixed on Liv. But as he neared, I stood from my seat and wrapped my arms around him.

He returned my hug, laughing. "What's that for?"

At his laugh, the tension I'd been carrying dissolved. I'd been so nervous about this get-together at the scene of the crime, so to speak, that I'd completed a six-mile run earlier at the fastest pace I could maintain. But nothing could blunt the edge of my nerves like the smile on Evan's face. He'd been through so much. I tightened my hold on him. "For being both an amazing man and an amazing brother. Thank you for trying to mend things with Hunter. I can't tell you how much it means to me."

As he sat, Liv looked down and brushed a tear from her cheek. Smiling, Evan placed a hand on her thigh and squeezed. "I can't promise we're going to be close again, but I think we can tolerate each other." His gaze drifted back to

Hunter, whose towering form was headed toward the other cluster of family. He wore a button-down shirt and shorts, all black as usual, and moved with incredible grace for such a large man. Evan shook his head. "I still can't believe that guy is Hunter. He told me he's had most of those tattoos for years."

Gabe was staring at Evan, his face giving nothing away. But I had to wonder if his thoughts were similar to mine. Namely, that for the first time in over a decade, maybe Evan was seeing Hunter as a human being instead of the ghost who haunted him.

Progress...

The so-called party itself had been a carefully orchestrated affair, designed to be as unassuming as possible—a far cry from Gabe and April's wedding reception, which had ended in disaster because of Evan and Hunter. Mostly Evan. The water shimmered with the reflection of the sun, and Hailey laughed as she tossed a beach ball our way. Gabe moved instantly, intercepting it with his foot and then launching it back to his daughter with a grin. Gabe and April both wore swimsuits but were enjoying a reprieve from the water. Catching the ball, Hailey giggled, and the musical sound floated across the area. I'd stayed out of the water today, instead wearing a pretty sundress and wore my hair in a ponytail.

Evan grasped Liv's hand and lifted it. "Come on, sweetness. I'll buy you a beer."

"How can I refuse an offer like that?" With a laugh, she rose, and they slipped their arms around each other as they ambled toward the long white cooler that sat next to the house.

As Hunter crossed the flagstone patio, he caught my gaze, and the corner of his mouth lifted in the barest of smiles. I smiled back, my entire chest filling with warmth at the scene around me. He paused to talk with Dad, Nona, Maia, and Wyatt. Wyatt bounced baby Skye in his arms as she stared at the shimmering pool fixedly. As Hunter and Maia embraced, her face lit up in a wide smile, the kind that only come from rekindling a lost connection. I'd seen the expression on my own face once or twice lately. A resort staff member weaved through the clusters of loungers and tables, collecting empty plates and crumpled napkins from the delicious lunch I'd had nothing to do with for once.

"Stella, you're quiet today," April noted.

"Am I?" I responded absentmindedly, my eyes still on Hunter. "Just taking it all in, I guess."

"Is it weird, seeing him here again after so long?" she prodded gently.

"Yeah. Weird and a little tense." I fiddled with the rim of my glass. "I've visited him plenty in South Beach, but it's important to have him back. This is his home too."

Gabe reached over to rub between April's shoulders, and she leaned into his touch as a long look passed between them. It made me smile. "Well," he said, turning back to me. "It's definitely more interesting when the Markham brothers are together. Hopefully in a good way this time."

"We couldn't ask for more than how today has gone," April added.

"Yeah. I wonder what they talked about." I watched as Hunter smiled slightly at something Wyatt said, his broad shoulders relaxing slightly. He'd become so solemn, guarded. Hopefully reconnecting with Evan would start the healing for Hunter, who needed it just as much as Evan did. He was just better at hiding his emotions.

I allowed myself to imagine what it might be like to have Hunter around more often—to share in these simple pleasures without the weight of the past looming over us. As the laughter from the pool area mingled with the distant sound of waves, Hunter slipped away from the group and headed toward the path leading down the bluff. His gait had that familiar purposeful stride, a man on a mission. I excused myself from the table, leaving Gabe and April to their newly wedded bliss.

"Hey," I called out softly as I caught up to him.

Hunter turned, raising both brows.

"Looks like things are going pretty well today, huh?" I gestured back toward the party.

"It's been all right." His gaze scanned the pool deck. "No bloodshed anyway."

"I saw you and Evan talking earlier. How did that go?"

"Yeah, it was... still awkward, but we had a civil conversation." He rubbed the back of his neck and swept his gaze down the hill to the south. "I want to walk around the property, get some impressions about the thefts before I head home."

"Already leaving?" Disappointment laced through my words before I could rein it in.

"Got to. I start a new assignment early tomorrow."

My phone buzzed in my pocket, pulling my attention away for a moment. Aiden's name lit up the screen.

Aiden: Almost done. Is the party over?

Stella: Just about. Sorry you missed it.

As I typed back, a spark of an idea ignited. Looking up at Hunter, I said, "Why don't you do your snooping while I help clean up here? We can meet up with Aiden at Sweet

Dreams for dessert afterward. You can leave for home from there."

He considered it for a brief moment, then nodded. "Sure. It'll give me a chance to grill your boyfriend."

I stuck my tongue out at him. "Don't be an ass. I hate the word boyfriend. We're both in our mid-thirties, for God's sake. See you in a bit."

He gave me a wave. As he walked away, I watched him go. His tall, athletic frame moved down the hill, and he was ever watchful as he assessed the scene before him. There was something reassuring about having him back, even if just for a fleeting moment. With a satisfied sigh at an important mission accomplished, I turned to help clean up the party.

# Chapter Twenty-Three

## Stella

"AS A TRAINED PROFESSIONAL, I declare this mango cake divine." I tried to hold back a moan, but I might not have been successful given the side-eye Aiden shot me. At Sweet Dreams, the outdoor tables lining the sidewalk were prime real estate for indulging in culinary and sensory delights. The perfectly tropical weather we'd had for the pool party continued as I found myself next to Aiden, with Hunter across from us. Inside, Liv's employees did an admirable job holding down the fort without her.

We sat under the covered canopy of pink and white. Ornamental streetlamps added to the charm, their antique design reminiscent of a time when life moved slower, more deliberately. Next to us, hanging flower baskets spilled over with vibrant colors, swaying gently in the breeze.

My eyes lingered on Bookshop in Paradise across the street, owned and run by Ben Coleridge's younger sister, Brenna. Frowning, I sipped my iced coffee, not wanting to ruin my last minutes with Hunter by thinking about our family adversaries.

And despite his warning about grilling Aiden, Hunter hadn't loomed over him during their first meeting in over fifteen years. At first, Aiden had gaped at the man my little brother had become. I hadn't been able to hide a grin at his reaction, even though I'd warned him that my brother had filled out quite a bit. Hunter had started out polite, though somewhat cool, and he eyed Aiden levelly. As our little get-together progressed, he relaxed.

I was pleased, and a little proud too. As much as Hunter had changed over the years, I still knew my brother. And he wasn't finding anything to complain about where Aiden was concerned.

I turned to my... man? I was *not* going to use the word boyfriend. Partner? No, too committed. And when I beheld his neat, professional appearance after dashing here straight from his clinic, warmth filled my chest. Of course Hunter couldn't find fault with him. Hunter wasn't the only one who had changed since leaving our little islands.

"Try this." Aiden's fork was poised with a generous bite of carrot cake, the cream cheese frosting perfectly finished. He held it out to me, his eyes dancing.

I obliged, savoring the spicy sweetness of the cake on my tongue, the crunch of walnuts adding depth to every mouthful. "Mmm, that's incredible." I glanced at my mango cake, trying to decide which was better, and decided on a draw.

"Liv knows her stuff," he said with a grin, turning to ask Hunter something.

But Hunter wasn't paying any attention.

Across the street, Brenna Coleridge unlocked the door to her literary sanctuary. She paused, adjusting a sign by the entrance, her tall, willowy silhouette framed against the soft light within. Her sheet of long, light-brown hair hung down, and I had to admit she was attractive, even if she was a Coleridge. Hunter's gaze fixated on her and his whole body froze. He became utterly still, watching her every move as she opened the door and disappeared inside.

"Careful, Hunter," I teased, bumping him with my elbow and bringing him back to the land of baked goods and friendly banter. "What's that look all about? She's a Coleridge, remember? I hope you're not thinking about sleeping with the enemy."

Hunter's lips fell into a frown. "Enemy is a strong word, Stella. We haven't spoken in years." His voice was carefully even and guarded, but his eyes darted across the street again.

"Weren't you two in the same grade through school?" Aiden asked him. "Maybe Stella and I weren't the only teen lovers..."

"It was nothing like that," Hunter shot back, his eyes glinting with that familiar hint of defiance. "We were only friends. But we were close... once." Then, in typical Hunter fashion, he took a large bite of his carrot cake slice, staring at his dessert like it could induce a subject change.

"Hey, you okay?" I asked.

He exhaled, long and slow as his eyes took a slow pan around Main Street. "Yeah, it's just that this place stirs up so many memories. I left here under awful circumstances, and I can't just turn back the clock." After another quick glance toward the bookshop, he cut another bite of cake. He seemed a million miles away, lost in a sea of memories that were apparently anything but sunshine and sandcastles.

I caught Aiden's glance and gave him a subtle head shake. Hunter had dark moments, parts of his past he kept locked away like forbidden treasure. It wasn't the right time to dredge up whatever history lay buried between Hunter and Brenna Coleridge. Not after he'd already dug through the painful past he shared with Evan. Today, both had appeared on the other side, unscathed.

Instead, I shifted the conversation back to something more enticing for him. "Did you uncover anything during your little resort tour?"

Hunter's eyes cleared, a spark of interest reigniting within them as he leaned forward. "Right, the thefts. When I looked around, Ben was there with a couple of other land-scapers. They were all working on the other side of the resort today." He snorted. "I'm pretty sure Ben didn't even recognize me."

"I hardly did either," Aiden said softly. "And not just because of the tattoos."

Intricate designs covered Hunter's upper chest visible in the V of his shirt, and points of more ink reached from his massive upper arms toward his elbows. He'd kept his shirt on during the party, forgoing any swimming. And now that I thought about it, I couldn't remember the last time I'd seen him without a shirt.

Hunter just rolled a shoulder uncomfortably. "I've been gone a long time. A lot has changed. Getting back to the thefts, all the items stolen have been outside. So it could be one of the landscaping crew, but it could also be damn near anyone."

"Anything we can do to help?" Aiden offered, and I smiled at his support.

"Keep your eyes open," Hunter said, staring at me. "If you notice anything that seems off, let me know. Or if anything else goes missing."

"Of course," I said.

Aiden leaned back in his chair, the soft light catching

the thoughtful furrow in his brow. "Do you suspect someone is stealing for financial gain, or are we talking about someone with a grudge?"

"It could be either," I chimed in. "We've got staff who've been here for years, no blips on their records. Then there's lots of new hires. And of course, the obvious. Ben."

"But you've said none of the resort employees raise any red flags," Aiden said as he put his fork down on his empty plate.

I shook my head. "Nothing glaring."

"There often isn't," Hunter replied, folding his arms across his chest. "And the items that have been stolen aren't expensive, big-ticket items, so I doubt we're dealing with a pro. But it's still pretty concerning."

Aiden reached across the table to cover my hand with his. His touch sent a ripple of warmth up my arm. "I really don't like the idea of you confronting anyone else about this."

"I'm not a fainting maiden, dammit," I muttered but couldn't help soaking in the comfort of his concern. All the while, I was aware of Hunter's silent observation. Their eyes met briefly, and I caught the micro-exchange—a nod so subtle I almost missed it.

"I agree one hundred percent," Hunter added, acknowledging Aiden's comment. There was respect there, and I got a sense that Aiden had passed a silent test.

I knew two brick walls when confronted with them. "All right. I'll back off Ben. But I'm going to keep an eye on things." I turned to my brother. "Do you have a plan if anything else turns up missing?"

"I'm hoping nothing else will," Hunter said, rubbing a hand over his short, neat beard. "Since the last theft, I've been thinking about baiting a trap of some sort."

"Like what?" I asked.

"I'm not sure yet. I need to think about it some more."

"I'm glad to have your help in this, Hunter. And to have you back." My words hung between us, charged with an unspoken acknowledgment of the bond that still tethered us.

"Of course. It's what I do." Hunter offered me a brief smile before pushing back his chair. "I should get going. I got in my boss's face, and he gave me a shitty assignment as a result. I start at oh-four-hundred tomorrow. Asshole."

"Yuck," I said. "I could never do that. I won't have been asleep long."

I stood so we could embrace. Goodbye for now. Then he was gone, his tall frame disappearing into the growing shadows.

Aiden tossed his napkin on his plate. "You look very happy about how today went. I'm sorry I missed it."

I smiled and reached for his hand, interlacing our fingers. "I was almost afraid to breathe at times. It wasn't like old times, but they're really making progress." I looked at the canopy above our heads. "Thank God Evan met Liv. She's made such a huge difference for him."

He lifted my hand to brush a kiss over the back of it. "Kind of like the difference you've made for me. We've still got several hours of daylight left. Want to head back to the boat?"

I laughed, imagining life aboard Aiden's cherished vessel. "Your boat is nice, but how can you live in such a confined space all the time?"

"Cramped?" Aiden grinned and leaned close. "I never even notice when you're around."

"Smooth talker." Warmth bloomed in my chest at his words.

"Of course," he added with a mock-serious tone. "I have to tread carefully. If I step out of line, your hulking brother might rip me apart."

I laughed, knowing full well the fierce protectiveness my brother wielded like a shield. And I still glimpsed the man he kept deep within, the sweet, shy one. The one I'd been afraid was gone forever when he'd gotten out of the Marines. "Hunter is a man of contradictions. But it sounds like he's got bigger fish to fry right now."

"Good." Aiden glanced briefly in the direction Hunter had gone. Then he turned to me with a smile that warmed me even further. "Come on. There's a can of varnish with your name on it. Let's go, missy."

As we strolled down the sidewalk, the salty breeze tugged at my hair. Aiden's presence was comforting and sexier than hell, yet a part of me held back. Despite our easy banter and the undeniable chemistry, I wasn't ready to dive in headfirst.

Inside me, the battle raged—a longing to give in to the feelings swirling within me, warring with a stubborn streak that urged caution. My heart was a compass spinning wildly. I needed time, time that Aiden seemed willing to give. For now, I'd enjoy the gentle sway of the boat beneath my feet, his laughter mingling with mine under a pale blue sky.

But commitment? That was something else entirely.

# Chapter Twenty-Four

## Aiden

THE EXAM ROOM was soothing yet professional with its clinical whites and blues. After washing my hands, I leaned against the counter and my gaze fell upon eighteen-year-old Kayla, whose eyes were heavy with the impending weight of unexpected motherhood. Beside her, a woman stood with a deeply lined brow and hands that couldn't seem to find stillness—her mother, Gloria.

"Kayla, how are you feeling? You doing okay?" I asked, trying to navigate the tension that seemed to thicken the air between them.

Kayla's eyes darted toward her mother before settling back on me. "I... I'm not sure yet," she mumbled, her voice barely above a whisper. "My head's still spinning."

"Gloria, maybe it'd be best if Kayla and I chat alone for a moment," I suggested gently, fully aware of the controlling undertow in the older woman's stance.

"Doctor Mitchell, we've already decided she's going to give the... child away," Gloria replied defensively, barely able to acknowledge the idea of her grandchild. Her arms were crossed as if to ward off any challenge to her maternal authority. "I've already contacted two agencies."

Kayla's eyes dropped to the floor and my heart twisted.

"I understand this is difficult." I locked eyes with Gloria in earnest. "But Kayla's eighteen. She's legally able to make her own decisions regarding her care and the baby she's carrying. Plus, from what I've seen, she's plenty smart enough too."

The room fell silent, save for the distant hum of the air conditioner. Kayla fiddled with the hem of her shirt, a sign of her nervousness that I'd come to recognize over the past few appointments. Gloria's posture softened slightly, and I seized the moment, pressing on with the delicacy the situation demanded.

"Kayla has options," I continued. "And the best thing we can do for her is ensure she—" I narrowed my focus and Kayla met my gaze. "That *you* know all of them and feel supported no matter what you choose."

It felt like navigating a minefield, each word carefully placed to avoid detonation. Gloria took a deep breath, finally nodding. "I just want her to be safe... and happy." She sighed, the storm in her eyes giving way to a flicker of vulnerability.

"Then we're all in agreement," I said, flashing a smile. It was a small victory, but those were the ones that kept me anchored in this profession. The room exhaled, and so did I. "Maria has a list of resources for you to explore. Take some time to make this decision. Both you and the baby's father, if he's in the picture." From the tight anger flashing across Gloria's eyes and the hope in Kayla's, I had a feeling he would be the next battleground. But today was a win I intended to savor.

As I left the exam room, I gave Maria a surreptitious thumbs-up. She gathered up the stack of brochures with a relieved smile and headed toward the young mother's exam room. The situation with Kayla was one of our biggest worries at the clinic. But as I headed toward my next patient, I had a sense that things were finally going her way.

THE SUNSET WAS a swathe of crimson on the horizon by the time I made my way to the marina. The air was thick with the scent of brine as I stepped into the cabin of my boat.

With careful strokes, I applied light gray paint to the galley kitchen cabinets. The color was muted and calm, like the Dove Key shore on a still morning. The boat was coming along, the deck now fully refinished, and the cabin interior was shaping up too.

My gaze drifted to the bed tucked into the bow, and an involuntary sigh escaped me. It had been three days since Stella and I had last tangled together in those sheets, three days of echoing silence from her end. I told her I'd take what she could give, but the truth was, I wanted more. Hell, I craved it like a ship lost at sea craves the sight of land.

"Stop thinking about her," I muttered and focused on the brush in my hand. But my mind wouldn't obey.

Stella had slipped through the cracks in my carefully constructed life more than I had anticipated. I knew I couldn't rush her, couldn't push for more than she was ready to offer. But that didn't stop the yearning. Didn't stop me from falling in love with her. Again.

I set the paintbrush down and surveyed my work, then turned my attention to the list of potential boat names scrawled on a piece of paper. The name had to be just right, something that captured the essence of my journey from the overcautious boy who almost let fear steal his dreams to the man who was trying to chart a new course.

"*Sea's Embrace?* No... *Odyssey's End?*" I read aloud, trying each one. They felt foreign on my tongue, placeholders. "*Driftwood Heart?*" I paused, my lips curling into a half-smile. But no, these were all too serious. I wanted a touch of whimsy in the name.

The slap of flip-flops on the deck above announced Luke's arrival. Grabbing a six-pack out of the fridge, I trotted up the stairs to join him.

"There you are," he said, dropping into one of two canvas camping chairs I'd set up. "You won't believe the day I've had."

"Try me." I tore off a can and handed it to him. With the day's fading heat, the chill of the aluminum was welcome against my skin.

"The bar was slammed, and this one lady..." He trailed off, shaking his head as he cracked open the brew. "Man, she was relentless. I felt like a goddamn piece of meat. Had to pry her off me like she was superglued."

I laughed, popping open my own can. "You getting tired of the single life?"

"Hardly. I'm not against relationships, though I know better than to get near a harpy like that." Luke took a long pull from the can. "So, Captain Ahab, found a name for your white whale yet?"

"Still searching," I admitted, lifting my can for a drink. The beer was crisp, washing away the lingering taste of frustration.

"All right, let's hear the shortlist." Luke leaned forward, elbows propped on the armrests, his gaze expectant.

"*Odyssey's End, Driftwood Heart,*" I rattled off the names I'd been considering earlier, only to be met with a grimace from Luke.

"Too poetic, too... sad," he decided, waving a dismissive hand. "This is a new beginning, right? Needs something with punch."

"Yeah, I know." A smile tugged at the edge of my lips despite myself. "I want something catchy."

"Okay, so what about... *Phoenix Feather?*" Luke raised an eyebrow in challenge.

"Good God, that sounds like a hipster tattoo parlor," I shot back, unable to suppress a laugh.

"Fine, fine, hotshot. How about... *Horizon Chaser?*" He leaned back, a proud grin lighting up his features.

"Better but still not quite right." I shook my head, though I appreciated his efforts.

"Damn, you're picky. I thought that one was pretty good." Luke feigned being hurt, clutching his chest dramatically.

My eyes wandered over the boat's gleaming deck. "Got to be. Naming a boat is a big deal, you know."

Luke nodded solemnly before breaking into a wide grin. "Well, let's keep brainstorming until we find the perfect fit or until we run out of beer. Whichever comes first."

"Here's hoping it's the name," I replied, raising my can in a mock toast.

"*Sea's Whisper?*" Luke said with a half-hearted shrug as he opened another beer.

"Too... girly." I scowled, staring at the canopy of stars beginning to wink into existence above.

"*Everlasting Tide?*" He slid a wooden crate over to rest his feet on.

"Sounds like laundry detergent," I grumbled. My mind

again drifted to the bed below us, and the memory of Stella and I in it three nights ago. The scent of her skin still haunted the threads, and I couldn't bring myself to wash them.

"Hey, you just went miles away, man. What's up?" Luke's voice pulled me back to the dim light around us.

I sighed, raking a hand through my hair. "Stella. It's been three days, Luke. Three days without a word."

He watched me, his expression softening. "You want more than she's willing to give?" He took a swig, eyes thoughtful.

"Yeah, I do."

"Wanting is one thing." Luke's words were slow and deliberate. "But pushing for it? That's another. You might just push her away if you're not careful."

"Yeah, I know."

"Give her time," he said gently. "Let things happen naturally. Like the perfect name for this boat—it'll appear when it's ready. And so will Stella."

"Easy for you to say." I tried to muster a smile. "You fend off admirers like you're swatting flies at a barbecue."

"True." He laughed, raising his hands in mock surrender. "It's hard work, fighting them off. But I'm not looking for what you are. Not everyone's after the forever horizon."

"*Forever Horizon*," I repeated, mulling over the words.

"Hey, that's not bad!" Luke's eyes grew round, but I shook my head.

"Close, but still not it." I was hesitant to dim his optimism. It was a constant, Luke's ability to brighten a room— or in this case, a boat. I opened a second can and took a long swig.

"Okay, Mr. Picky, how about *Siren's Song*?" Luke grinned, waggling his eyebrows.

"That sounds like a romance novel." I couldn't help but laugh.

"Isn't that your current situation, though?" he teased, and I shot him a mock glare.

"Very funny." I cast my gaze around, looking for inspiration. I caught sight of an old photo tucked behind a toolbox, the edges worn—Dad teaching me to tie knots, a proud smile on his face. Before life became so complex.

"All right, your turn then. What names are swirling around in that head of yours?" Luke crossed one ankle over the other, watching me with the kind of patience only an old friend could muster.

"Nothing's sticking." I ran a hand through my hair, the salt from the sea air leaving it coarse. "Everything I think of just seems off."

"Naming a boat is like capturing a piece of the ocean, Aiden. It's vast, mysterious, all-encompassing." His gaze drifted toward the dock where light from an exterior spotlight danced on the water's surface.

"Thanks, that doesn't put any pressure on at all," I replied dryly.

"Hey, I'm just saying it's got to feel right. Like"—Luke paused, searching for the words—"like coming home."

"Yeah, that about sums it up."

"Or you know, just name it *Boaty McBoatface* and call it a day." Luke laughed, nudging me with his elbow. I joined his laughter, and we clinked our cans together.

As the evening wore on, the list of rejected names grew longer, our brainstorming devolving into absurdity as the beer flowed and the moon climbed higher. But beneath the jokes and jibes, there was an undercurrent of frustration—a longing to find that perfect fit that remained elusive.

"Guess it's not happening tonight," I said finally, tossing my empty can into the trash.

After adding his own, Luke said good night and hopped to the dock with a wave. I watched him fade into the night, unable to shake the feeling that the name for my boat matched the status of my relationship with Stella.

Completely unknown.

And that was frustrating as hell.

# Chapter Twenty-Five

## Stella

I STOOD before my open closet, sifting through a sea of fabric, searching for the perfect dress that whispered romance under the tropical sky. The one I chose was a coral number, its hue rivaling the most vibrant reef fish that darted beneath the waves surrounding Calypso Key.

With careful movements, I slipped into the dress, enjoying how the fabric clung to my body. Tonight, Aiden and I would sit under the August stars at an outdoor play in Key West, and I was amazed he'd been able to procure tickets. My pulse quickened at the thought of him sitting next to me in the dark.

A final glance in the mirror, and I was satisfied. My earrings, a simple pair of silver drops, were the last touch. They were as ready to catch the moonlight as I was to see Aiden again. We hadn't been together in nearly a week, and I had a feeling this special date was his way of gently prodding me to be more available.

And I felt a pang at that. I didn't mean to be distant, but

this summer had been unusually busy at the resort, thanks to a quiet hurricane season. Without thinking, I reached down and knocked on my dresser top. As much as I enjoyed being with him, I refused to apologize for wanting to succeed at Orchid. And I was—my early misgivings and fears had slowly given way to confident assurance. With a sigh, I smoothed my hair as I examined the pains I'd taken to look good tonight. Maybe I did need to make more of an effort.

My phone's sudden ring split the air, jarring against the evening's anticipation. Luis's name flashed across the screen, accompanied by the accompanying photo of him in his black sous-chef uniform, his dark eyes glinting with mischief. I lifted the phone to my ear.

"Stella"—Luis's voice was tense—"you need to come down here. Now."

"What's wrong?" I tried to keep the worry from my voice. I'd taken tonight off partly to let him shine, and he knew how much I needed this break.

"Health inspector," he practically hissed, each syllable laced with urgency. "She's here, going through everything with a fine-tooth comb."

I nearly dropped the phone. "What? Now?"

"I know! I can't believe she came in the evening, after her usual hours." His voice was tinged with panic. Of all nights, it had to be tonight. I could feel the romantic bubble of the evening pop.

"Okay, okay. Keep everything running smoothly and show her whatever she wants. I'll be right there." I ended the call, the phone feeling like a lead weight in my hand.

I stared at my reflection, the woman in the coral dress a stark contrast to the one bracing for battle. My mind raced as adrenaline coursed through me. I swapped heels for flats, practicality taking precedence over style.

I snatched my phone again and called Aiden, already dreading the conversation.

"Hey, beautiful! All set for tonight?" His voice was warm and brimmed with anticipation.

My heart squeezed. "Aiden, I can't believe this is happening, but I'm going to have to cancel tonight. A health inspector showed up out of nowhere at Orchid, and Luis is freaking out. I need to take over."

A pause, then a sigh. "Oh, shit. That's... that's horrible timing."

"I know. I'm so sorry. I was looking forward to tonight." My words rushed out, and not just because I could feel the clock ticking.

"Can I do anything to help?"

I marched down the hall, already mentally preparing. "No, no, it's my kitchen. I need to deal with this."

"Well, if you need me, I'm here, okay? Even if it's just to talk after."

"I know you are. Thank you." I clutched the phone tighter, hating that I had to do this to us.

"Seriously, Stella. Let me help," Aiden pressed.

But my mind was already a whirlwind of checklists and procedures. "We'll talk later, okay?" Without waiting for his response, I hung up, guilt gnashing at me as much as urgency did.

I dashed out the door, leaving behind the promise of a romantic evening. The night air was balmy, but I hardly felt it, my thoughts on the ticking time bomb that was Orchid's kitchen. I rushed down the hill, and before I knew it, I was barging through the back entrance of the kitchen.

Luis stood there, wringing his hands. "Stella! Thank God you're here. The inspector is in the dining room."

I nodded, steeling myself. "Okay, everyone, listen up!" My voice cut through the clamor like a knife through butter. Kitchen staff paused, their expressions fraught with anxiety. "Just do your job like any other day. We do things right, and we're going to prove it."

My team rallied, nodding and murmuring affirmations. I started barking orders, assigning tasks with military precision while simultaneously reviewing every inch of the kitchen. Stainless steel surfaces gleamed under the harsh fluorescent lights, but I checked them anyway, looking for anything amiss. "Check the storage temperatures, rotate the stock, and make sure labels are up to date! Health codes are no joke, folks. Cleanliness, food safety, cross-contamination, we know this. Let's show them how it's done," I called out, moving from the fridges to the prep areas, eyes darting over every detail.

"Sorry about your evening," Luis said with a miserable smile. "Nice dress."

"Thanks. Where is the inspector?"

He pointed through the double doors into the dining area. "She went to the pass right before you got here."

Just then, the doors opened again, and my heart sank as the inspector walked through. I recognized her immediately.

*Oh, shit. Shit!*

The woman examined this side of the pass, her pen scratching against her clipboard as the bright lights reflected off her short brown hair. The sound seemed to echo off the stainless-steel surfaces. Her face was impassive, but I knew her sharp, critical eye firsthand.

"Marjorie," I greeted, a knot forming in my stomach as I

recognized the stickler from my culinary school days. She had struggled as a chef and had taken a dislike to me. Instead, she'd gone to work for the health department, though I hadn't realized Calypso Key was part of her territory.

"Stella," she acknowledged, her voice flat as she raised a hand to adjust her black framed glasses. She looked me up and down, a slight gleam of triumph in her eyes. "I hope you didn't get dressed up on my account. I'm not keeping you from anything, am I?"

"Not at all. I was just finishing." I kept my face professional and bland, though I was already itching to throttle her.

Her gaze panned to take in the large kitchen. "I see you've moved up in the world."

"I'm back where I belong," I replied, forcing a smile while wondering if there was a hint of sarcasm in her voice. Marjorie had been known for her meticulous attention to detail, and I could tell by the way her gaze lingered on the corner of the counter and the undersides of shelves that she was searching for any reason to mark us down.

"Let's hope your cleaning standards have risen along with your ambitions," she said dryly, making a note that felt like a foreshadowing of doom. "I've already found one expired food worker's permit."

My stomach lurched. That was a stupid mistake, but one that was easily correctable. If that was the only infraction she found, I could live with it. We headed to the dishwashing station, where Marjorie got out her thermometer. After letting the hot water faucet warm up, she held the probe under the stream of water. When she read the result, a smug smile rose on her face. "This is below the acceptable range for hot water."

I assured her we'd remedy that immediately, but when she ran a pale finger over the stainless-steel dish sorting counter and came away with a sticky coating on it, the knot of tension in my gut turned to raw acid.

Marjorie slowly turned her head to me and raised a brow. "What kind of kitchen are you running here, Stella?"

THE NEXT DAY, sunlight streamed through the kitchen window of the Big House, casting beams across the wooden table where an inspection report lay before me like an unwelcome guest. My hands shook slightly as I picked it up, reading the grade that might as well have been etched into my skin.

*FAIL*.

"Improper cleaning procedures?" I muttered to myself, my cheeks flushing with indignation. "How can that be possible?"

Evan chose that moment to walk in, his footsteps quiet on the tiled floor. After the inspection, he'd still been up, and I'd taken a moment to fill him in. "From the look on your face, I'm guessing the verdict isn't good."

"Look at this!" I thrust the report toward him. "Marjorie gave us a fail. It's ludicrous."

He sat next to me and took the report, his blue eyes scanning the contents before meeting my gaze. "We all know you run a tight ship, Stella. But we can't ignore this. Especially not when our reputation is on the line."

"Of course we can't," I snapped, more at the situation than at Evan. "She's doing this out of spite." I told him about my history with Marjorie.

Evan's expression softened, but his voice remained firm.

"Maybe. But we also can't dismiss this outright. If there's even a kernel of truth to these claims, we need to address it."

"Deanna just forgot to wipe down that counter. She would have done it within half an hour. Are you doubting how I run my kitchen?" The question hung between us, charged and heavy.

"No," he replied quickly. "But we need to be thorough. You're great at what you do, Stella, but sometimes..." He hesitated, choosing his words carefully. "Sometimes you become very single-minded. You get so focused on the trees that you miss the forest."

"What forest? Evan, I—"

"Look, we'll get to the bottom of this, okay?" He offered a supportive smile, which I returned half-heartedly. "Start by investigating each infraction she found."

My mind was already racing with plans to rectify the situation. I wasn't about to let Marjorie question my competence. My half smile fell as heat rose in my cheeks. "We need to tackle this head-on, Evan. I want to call Marjorie out on some of these minor infractions. A potholder too close to an open flame? Really?"

"Whoa. Hold up." He pressed his hand out like a traffic cop as his voice took on his General Manager tone. "Accusing her won't help. We don't want to make enemies with the health department."

"Enemies?" I echoed, incredulous. "She made herself an enemy the moment she walked through my door with a vendetta."

"Look, I'm not saying you're wrong about the inspector." Evan turned in his chair to face me. "But right now, our focus needs to be on getting everything up to code— whether or not the allegations are true."

"Fine," I muttered, knowing he was right. My pride hurt

more than anything, but Orchid couldn't afford the scandal of a shutdown. Especially with a new head chef. And that made a hollow, twisting feeling roll through me. What if Evan was right, and I couldn't see deficiencies that were right in front of me?

What if this was a sign I wasn't meant to head up Orchid?

My brother was already scrolling through his phone calendar to schedule a meeting. "Let's start by going over procedures again with the staff. We'll document everything, every step of the way."

"Sure," I said, though my hands wanted to do more than just defensive maneuvers. They itched to wring Marjorie's little chicken neck.

My phone vibrated on the table, lighting up with Aiden's name. I glanced at the screen—a missed call and a string of texts asking if I was all right. If there was anything he could do. My chest tightened with guilt. He'd been nothing but supportive, and here I was, burying myself in work. I'd been too worn out to text last night, and after getting the emailed report, now I was too despondent.

"Everything okay?" Evan asked, noting my distraction.

"Everything will be soon," I lied, the words tasting bitter on my tongue as I shoved the phone aside. Aiden would have to wait. For now, Orchid needed the iron-willed chef, not the woman who might just be falling for her ex-boyfriend again. I pushed my chair back and stood. "Let's get to work."

<br>

THE SCENT of fresh orchids clung to my bedroom, a mocking reminder of the date night that never happened.

I'd run home for a quick shower to hopefully wash off some of the surreal haze that had enveloped me during a day of planning with Evan. I put Luis in charge tonight, just so I could focus on our response. But above all, one sentence kept running through my head like a banner at the bottom of a television screen.

How could this have happened?

I dressed in fresh pants and a clean polo shirt. After pulling out my phone, I crossed the room and dropped onto my bed. I'd avoided this call all day, and the weight of the phone felt like an anchor in my palm. Aiden's name still glowed on the missed calls list. With a deep breath that did little to steady my racing heart, I tapped on his number.

"Stella?" His voice was like a warm blanket I desperately wanted to wrap myself in, but I knew better than to linger in its comfort.

"Hey. Look, I'm sorry about not getting back to you." Each word felt like pulling teeth, hard and painful. "The health inspection didn't go well, and I've spent all day cleaning up the fallout."

"Of course. I get it." His tone was supportive yet laced with an unmistakable undercurrent of disappointment. "Why don't I come over and we can talk about it over a bottle of wine?"

His genuine, kind offer was so tempting. But my old, familiar adversary—fear—had dogged me all day, whispering about my doubts and insecurities. I couldn't fit in romance right now. "Thanks, but I don't have time. I need to handle this problem myself."

There was a long pause on the other end. "Okay, if that's what you want." The resignation in his voice came through loud and clear.

I filled the void with action plans and hurried words.

"We're meeting again first thing in the morning. I need to go over procedures, make sure everything's by the book. I'm heading back to Orchid to work some more."

"Stella—"

"Sorry, I have to go." I cut him off, my focus narrowing on the battle ahead. "We'll talk soon, okay?" I didn't give him, or myself, the chance to say more before ending the call.

My reflection in the dresser mirror held a woman whose eyes burned with determination, even as the rest of her world wavered at the edges. The expanse of ocean outside whispered promises of romance and adventure, but within the walls of my restaurant, only challenge and self-doubt awaited me.

"I can do this," I whispered, trying to convince myself. "I have to."

After one last glance at my phone and Aiden's promise of support, I turned away. Shutting the door behind me, I set off to steer this ship off the rocks.

# Chapter Twenty-Six

## Stella

IT HAD BEEN one holy hell of a week, with tension knotted in every corner of Orchid after Marjorie's visit. But now I clutched the new inspection report to my chest like a winning lottery ticket, its clean white edges crinkling under my grip. The kitchen hummed around me, stainless-steel surfaces gleaming in the afternoon sun that peeked through the window. Marjorie had given us one week to rectify all her findings. And now, after days of scrubbing and training and double-checking every inch of this space, we'd emerged triumphant—or rather, spotless.

"Folks, we are officially a top-notch kitchen!" I called, unable to keep the elation from spilling into my voice as I waved the paper at Rea, busy arranging desserts in the display case.

"Back and better than ever," she called back, her smile a mirror to my own relief.

I should have been basking in our success. But instead, a

single nagging thought tugged at the corners of my mind—how had I let this happen?

When I'd delved into the cause of the scare, it turned out to be a simple, silly mistake—an employee's misguided attempt at being thorough in the dishwasher area. Innocent intentions with potentially disastrous consequences. She'd used the wrong kind of cleaner, one not approved for food surfaces, and it had left the germ-attracting residue that Marjorie discovered. The same employee hadn't realized how often she needed to clean the area, another training error. She'd been in tears after her mistakes came to light, and I'd taken her under my wing to make sure she felt valued.

I'd even worked personally with the prep staff, who were there hours before the main dinner shift showed up. I had a soft spot for Matt, who listened closely and took all my suggestions to heart. All were an indispensable part of Orchid's success, and I needed to make sure they understood that.

This afternoon, Marjorie had come back for her reinspection and hadn't been able to find a single infraction. She'd even given me a begrudging compliment on my thorough follow-up.

Now I leaned against the cool metal of the prep table as everyone returned to their tasks. "I should have caught it sooner." Frustration simmered in my chest, a slow burn of disappointment in myself. How could I have missed something so fundamental?

"Hey, you can't see everything," Luis chimed in, his hands never stopping as he chopped a fresh batch of herbs.

I shook my head, a strand of hair escaping my ponytail. "But that's just it, isn't it? I'm supposed to catch these things before they become issues."

"Stella, you trained us well. This was a fluke. Besides, look at this place now." He gestured expansively with his free hand. "You couldn't eat off the floor because it's so damn shiny, you'd slide right off."

A laugh escaped me despite the residual annoyance, and I glanced around the kitchen. He wasn't wrong. The place was practically gleaming, a testament to the hard work and dedication of everyone here.

"Okay, point taken," I conceded, allowing a smile to break through. "Just don't actually eat off the floor, please."

"Well, there goes my break." Luis's eyes twinkled as he winked at me.

The victory was sweet, yet incomplete, overshadowed by the gnawing guilt of having neglected everything—and everyone—else during this fiasco. Including Aiden. I hadn't meant to shut him out. It was just... when crisis mode had hit, my world narrowed to the four walls of Orchid and the challenge at hand.

I slipped out the back door, pulling my phone from the pocket of my chef's coat. Aiden's name sat at the top of my missed calls list—a glaring reminder of conversations deferred and connections missed. My thumb hovered over the call button, and I hesitated. After a week of self-imposed isolation, reaching out felt like taking a risk all over again. But Aiden had always been so understanding. Hopefully, we could pick up right where we left off. My heart thudded a rapid beat against my ribs.

"Hey, it's me," I said as soon as he picked up, my words tumbling out in a rush. "I'm sorry for going dark these past few days. We've been working on the inspection issues all week, and I've been—"

"Busy. I know," he interrupted. His voice was tight and low, a sharp contrast to his usual warmth.

"The good news is we passed our reinspection. Things are settling down, and I promise I'll make it up to you, okay? Maybe I'll make you dinner. Cajun seafood pasta?"

He heaved a long sigh. "Not tonight. I've had a long, rough day. You're not the only one with work issues, you know. I had to tell one of my grade-school teachers she's probably got cancer today."

My good mood evaporated as I recognized the yawning divide opening between us. "Oh, God, Aiden. I'm sorry. Want me to come over after work? Give you a backrub?"

The line crackled with tension, as if even the phone connection sensed the chasm between us. I leaned against the restaurant wall, my fingers tracing circles on the surface in an attempt to ground myself.

"Stella," Aiden finally broke the silence, his voice carrying a tinge of pain that knotted my stomach. "I don't know what else to say. You've been gone for a whole week—no calls, no texts. A whole lot of nothing."

"I'm sorry." I sighed, feeling the weight of my neglect. "It's just been... overwhelming here. The health inspection scare took over everything. I had to make sure Orchid came out clean."

"I get that," he said, and I could picture him running a hand through his hair, a gesture he made when he was frustrated. "But not even a quick message to let me know you were alive? That maybe I actually meant something to you?"

I wilted, closing my eyes momentarily. "I should've found a moment. I didn't mean to ignore you. But don't overreact here—this inspection was a huge deal. That's not fair."

"Fair?" He laughed without humor. "Stella, I was hoping we were past high school drama shit. This is about us. About being there for each other, even when things get messy. You can't just ghost me."

I gasped, my heart nearly stopping in my chest. Did he just use that word? My anger ratcheted up. No, my fury. "I ghosted *you*? Are you kidding me? Because I was dealing with a work emergency for a week? You moved away and completely left me behind! Don't you dare lecture me about ghosting!"

Aiden sighed. "Stella, I get it—your restaurant is your world. But I thought I was part of that world too."

"Of course you are," I snapped, frustration bleeding into my words. "But let's be real, Aiden. We don't know where this is going! You don't even have a home. You live on a sailboat, for God's sake. Ready to float wherever the wind takes you. It's not exactly a foundation for... for anything permanent."

There was a long beat of silence, heavy and charged, before Aiden spoke again. "You think that's what I want? To just drift away? I've poured my heart into my practice here. I've rooted myself in this town. And I thought I was doing the same with you. My God, Stella. We've been together for months! I thought we had the kind of relationship where awful days actually made us want to see the other person. Maybe even lean on them a little."

"I don't know what we're doing, Aiden." My voice still had a hard edge to it.

"I've bent over backward to give you the space you needed. To be the man you needed. What do I need to do to convince you?" Frustration dripped from his voice as his question hung in the air like a sail waiting for the right gust of wind to catch it.

"I don't even know if I can be convinced." My voice wavered, and I cleared my throat quickly. "I'm not looking to be some housewife with two-point-five kids, Aiden. If that's your dream future, then maybe—"

"When have I ever said that?" I could picture his face, his blue eyes widening in shock. "Marriage, kids... none of that has ever been on our radar. I want you. Only you. Are you trying to find excuses because you're scared?"

"Scared?" The accusation stung, more so because it rang true. I was scared—terrified of letting him in, only to be left shattered again.

"Look at what I've built here. Do you honestly think I'm looking for an escape?" His flat, angry voice cut through the static of my fears but did nothing to ease them.

"I don't know what to think," I said, the honesty scraping raw against my heart. "Maybe I am looking for reasons not to believe you've changed. Maybe I'm terrified of taking that risk."

"Aren't I proving that I've changed every damn day? By supporting you, even though you push me away at every turn. Stell, please..."

My heart felt like it was twisting in half. "I'm sorry I ignored you for a week. You're right. I shouldn't have done that. But I'm just not ready for... more."

"Then what do you want?"

"I don't know, Aiden. I really don't."

After ending the call, I leaned against the building's surface as I grappled with tension that refused to dissipate. A tension filled with unspoken fears and unresolved feelings, leaving us both adrift in a sea of doubt.

# Chapter Twenty-Seven

## Aiden

I NURSED the Queen Conch IPA, the froth of beer leaving a temporary mark on my upper lip—a badge of my sullen mood. I wiped it off with a paper napkin as I took in the Conch Republic with a sweep of my gaze. The wooden bar top was polished to a shine, reflecting the soft glow of the lights suspended from the open ceiling and its metal duct-work. The low hum of murmured conversations from the few patrons blended with the tinkling of glasses and the soft clinking of silverware, creating a peaceful backdrop. Too bad I felt anything but peaceful. I bit into my burger, the comfort of juicy meat and melted cheese comforting me for a fleeting moment.

Luke, ever the observer behind the bar, raised an eyebrow as he polished a wine glass. "Bit of a departure from your usual healthy diet fare, isn't it, Doc?"

"Don't give a crap tonight," I grumbled between chews, the saltiness of the fries stinging my tongue with every bite.

"Yeah, I caught that vibe. What's eating you?" He leaned forward, resting his elbows on the bar.

"Stella. Things are still a mess."

I rested my jaw in my palm, scowling. We'd had our blow-up over her inspection nearly two weeks ago. The day before yesterday, I even reached out to talk to her, but she'd let me know loud and clear she was still pissed. I'd complained to Luke numerous times, and since he was a bartender, I figured he wouldn't mind listening to me vent. During our last call, she'd thrown that *ghosting* comment in my face again. "She won't let me get close to her."

"Ah," Luke said, nodding slowly, his face taking on the reflective look of someone who'd seen his fair share of heart-break across the bar top. "And I take it that's not sitting well with you?"

"It's sitting like a lead weight." I pushed the fries around my plate. "I think we're broken up at the moment."

With one brow arched, Luke mixed a gin and tonic. "You don't know?"

"I never know how hard to push her! I've been patient, supportive. But her walls... they're skyscrapers, and I'm starting to wonder if I brought enough dynamite."

"Maybe it's not about blowing them down," Luke suggested, his gaze flickering over to the array of bottles lined up like soldiers ready for battle. "Maybe it's about finding the door."

"Easy for you to say. You're not the one trying to figure out the combination to a lock that keeps changing." I took another swig of my beer, the bitterness mirroring the tang of frustration on my tongue.

"I've known Stella for a long time," he said, shrugging. "She's always been focused on her career. And maybe she's scared of you. You know, of getting hurt again. After all, history does have a penchant for repeating itself."

"Except when people learn from it," I countered.

"True. But learning that takes time. And trust." Luke's voice was soft but carried the weight of truth, much as I hated to admit that.

"Time's one thing I've got, but trust? That's a two-way street. And right now, it feels like I'm stuck at a red light."

"Maybe you need to give her a reason to hit the gas pedal." His eyes sparkled with a mix of mischief and wisdom.

"How am I supposed to do that?" I didn't bother to keep the edge from my voice.

"You, my man, need a grand gesture." Luke leaned on the bar, a knowing smile creasing his face.

"Grand what?" I frowned, racking my brain for any medical condition that sounded similar. I was pretty sure he'd said gesture, not seizure. Though I felt like I was about to have a seizure.

"Gesture, Aiden. Grand gesture." He rolled his eyes as if I'd missed the punchline of a joke. "You know, like in romance movies."

"What in the hell are you talking about? Since when have you been into romance movies?"

Luke grinned and began wiping down the counter with a rag that had seen better days. "My ex-girlfriend was a fanatic for those films. Made me watch tons of them. According to her—and Hollywood, I guess—a grand gesture is some kind of over-the-top act you do to prove your love. It's about going the extra mile, doing something unexpected and meaningful."

"Sounds... exhausting." And unnecessary.

"Maybe," he said, shrugging. "But it doesn't have to be

jumping out of a plane with a banner. It's about showing you understand her—what she cares about, what makes her tick. It's about pushing past your comfort zone."

"Comfort zones are there for a reason," I muttered, but I couldn't shake the image of Stella's hesitancy, the way her eyes darted away when things got too close for comfort.

"Exactly. And sometimes, you need to step out of that comfort zone to show someone they're worth it. You two have a long and not very pretty history, Aiden. And it affected her badly. I've never been best friends with Stella, but I've never seen her in a serious relationship. Maybe she's waiting for you to show her how much you've changed. Now you've gotta ask yourself—Is she worth the risk?"

Hell yes, she was. And I knew it.

I'd caused that hesitancy, that fear in her. I'd left those deep scars, and no one else. "All right." I sighed, capitulating to the whimsical notion. "I'm almost afraid to ask, but what does a grand gesture look like in real life? And don't tell me I have to rent a billboard or hire a skywriter."

He just laughed and went back to wiping out glasses. "Just think about what Stella loves, what's important to her. Make it personal. Tailor it to the woman you know she is."

After thumping my pint down on the bar, a scowl etched itself deeper on my face. I glared at my half-eaten burger, the comfort it once promised now suffocated by exasperation. "Wait a minute, dammit. Why should I be the one doing all this soul-baring? She's the one who went an entire week without contacting me... the one who pushed me away." The words left my mouth more accusatory than I intended, betraying the hurt beneath the anger.

Luke leaned in as if sharing an ancient secret that men have passed down through generations. "Because, Aiden, it's always the guy. Even when the woman screws up too. It's our cross to bear, man." His laughter rang out again, carefree and knowing.

"Cross to bear?" I repeated, incredulous. "What is this, the Middle Ages? Since when did modern love become a chivalry contest?"

"Since always," he shot back with a quick wink, then began rattling off examples like a seasoned professor lecturing on the art of love. "Think Lloyd Dobler in *Say Anything*, standing outside with the boombox over his head. Or that dude who learned Portuguese in *Love Actually*."

"Who the hell is Lloyd Dobler? I don't even know what you're talking about. This is real life." I massaged my temples. My gaze drifted to the array of liquor bottles lined up behind the bar, each reflecting the dim light like gemstones.

"Exactly, man. Life imitates art, or is it the other way around?" Luke shrugged and leaned back against the counter. "Point is, you need to show Stella how well you understand her. That you're willing to take a risk for her. You gotta find your boombox, man."

"Find my boombox. Great." Skepticism laced my tone. The notion was foreign to me, but as much as I wanted to reject the cliché, a sliver of hope threaded through my anger. A hope that maybe there was something to this grand gesture business.

"Look," Luke continued, catching the shift in my demeanor. "You're a smart guy, Aiden. And you know Stella better than anyone. You can figure out your own version of a grand gesture. Something... oceanic, maybe?"

"Oceanic," I repeated, the word rolling off my tongue and into the air, where it hung like a promise. The sea had always been my sanctuary and our shared passion. Could it be the key? Then my scowl returned. "This is impossible. And ridiculous. And unnecessary, I might add."

He leaned close to me. "You are totally full of shit."

"What? That's a bit harsh." I narrowed my eyes at him, but he just wiped out another pint glass with a practiced swirl.

"Never argue with a bartender on matters of the heart, Aiden." His tone was light but not without wisdom. "Especially when it comes to first loves. They stick to you like barnacles. Stella was yours and vice-versa. Lots of baggage there."

I slumped on my stool, the worn leather creaking in sympathy. "Yeah, I know. But Stella... it's like she's anchored in the past, and no matter how much I pull, she won't budge."

Luke leaned forward, resting his elbows on the bar. "And that's exactly why you need to do something big. She's hesitant because you two ended in disaster. You've got to prove that this time, things will be different."

I sighed, the weight of our shared history pressing down on me. How could I convince her that the past wouldn't repeat itself? That I wasn't the same stupid, cowardly kid who had broken her heart? My mind cast about for ideas, each one fizzling out before they could take hold.

"Doesn't have to be like some rom-com airport chase scene," Luke added, a smirk playing on his lips.

"Thank God for that," I grumbled, rolling my eyes. I took a long swig from my glass as I pondered his words. Stella loved the ocean—it whispered to her soul, despite her comment about my boat. We had reconnected while sailing these waters, and while being immersed in the tranquility of the sea. And she was also a chef...

"Meaningful," I muttered, mulling over the possibilities.

"Maybe something tied to her work? Like new knives or something?"

Luke burst out laughing, bending forward at the waist. "Oh yeah. Great gesture. A weapon for her to use on you."

I tilted my head back and forth. "Okay, point taken."

Luke nodded approvingly. "Think about it. You're not just any guy trying to win back a girl. You're Aiden Mitchell, the caring doctor who cures patients and navigates storms. Use that."

"Navigate storms..." I trailed off, picturing Stella's bright eyes reflecting the sunlit waves, the way her laughter melded with the breeze mussing her hair. But nothing came to me. "Thanks, Luke. Guess I need to dive a little deeper."

"Ah, there he is." Luke grinned, proud as if he'd just coached a drowning man to swim. "Go get her, Dr. Love."

"Dr. Love?" After wincing, I couldn't help but laugh, the tension ebbing away over a horrible nickname he'd come up with years ago. "You're never going to let that go, are you?"

"Never." Luke's smile was as broad as the horizon outside the Conch Republic. "Keep thinking," he said, just as one of the line cooks lumbered out from the kitchen, his apron stained with the day's work.

"Hey, Luke." The man's voice was tired as he reached for the fountain sprayer to get himself a soft drink. "Just got the word that our regular fisherman's out sick tomorrow. We're gonna have to wing it for the fresh catch."

"Thanks for the heads-up," Luke replied, shrugging and unbothered by the news. "There's no shortage of fishermen around. We'll manage."

As the cook shuffled back to the heat and clatter of the kitchen, a spark ignited in my chest. I twirled a coaster on the bar top. A grand gesture... something unexpected...

And then, like a flash of lightning across the murky waters of my mind, it came to me. The idea hit with such force that I gasped aloud, startling Luke.

"What?" he asked, peering at me closely.

Laughing, I tossed the coaster aside. The stool scraped against the wood floor as I stood. "I got it!"

"All right! Let's hear it." Luke's eyes widened and he leaned closer.

"Nope. Not saying." I grinned, reveling in the sudden clarity. "But the hardware store closes soon. I gotta run."

"Whatever it is, make sure it counts," Luke called after me as I hurried toward the exit, a sense of purpose propelling my steps.

"I'll do my best," I threw over my shoulder, my grin never fading. Bursting out of the brew pub into the warm evening air, the breeze swept over me, carrying with it a sense of impending hope.

# Chapter Twenty-Eight

## Stella

AFTER TAPPING my code into the keypad, I nudged the door to the Big House open just enough to slip through. The grandfather clock in the hallway struck half-past midnight, its deep chime resonating with my thudding heartbeat. My feet felt like lead as I headed toward the soaring staircase. I'd grown used to the feeling over the past two weeks. Weeks spent alternating between being angry at Aiden and miserable without him.

His call a couple of days ago hadn't gone well. And I hadn't reached out either, pride or fear anchoring my fingers away from the phone. I knew which it was, but I just didn't want to admit it.

Climbing the stairs, I held on to the banister for support, the emotional exhaustion clinging to each limb. As I reached the landing, an unexpected light pulled my gaze toward the parlor. There, beneath the warm embrace of an antique table lamp, sat Nona. Her unbound white hair caught hints of gold in the light, her eyes squinted in focus over a crossword puzzle sprawled on the table before her.

"Nona?" I approached, curiosity briefly overshadowing my thoughts. "What are you doing up so late?"

She looked up, her glasses perched precariously on the bridge of her nose, and offered me a wry smile. "Stella, my dear, when you get to my age, sleep becomes more of a suggestion than a requirement. And these old bones..." She gestured vaguely toward her limbs with the end of her pencil. "They don't take kindly to lying idle for too long."

I smiled, despite the tightness in my chest. "And the crossword?"

"Ah, this rascal is my latest conquest." She tapped the paper, leaving a small graphite mark among the boxes. "Keeps the mind sharp, and less sleep means more puzzles to solve."

I watched her fill in another answer with confidence. It was a simple moment, yet there was something soothing about the domesticity of it—the steady tick of the clock, the soft hum of the night, and Nona, our unwavering matriarch, finding peace in wordplay while the world slept.

"Mind if I join you?" I asked, my voice weary but seeking the solace of normalcy.

"Have a seat, child." Nona patted the empty chair beside her, and I obliged, lowering myself into it with a soft exhale. I read a clue and picked up a pencil, slowly writing in the answer. We worked in silence for several minutes, though I spent more time gazing into empty space and thinking about Aiden than working on the puzzle.

Nona scanned a clue with a gnarled finger, peering at the letters already in place. "What's an eight-letter word for perturbed?"

"Agitated," I said, my voice distant, fingers tracing the embossed patterns on the tablecloth as I spoke.

"Seems you're quite agitated yourself, Stella." Nona's voice was gentle, probing. "Something on your mind?"

I hesitated, then confessed. "Aiden and I had an argument. I might've... well, I jumped down his throat and got defensive. And things haven't been the same between us since."

"Is that so?" Nona placed her pencil down, her posture straightening. "Tell me. What sparked this fiery exchange?"

"Expectations, misunderstandings..." I sighed, feeling the weight of my own stubbornness. "I guess we both have strong opinions on how things should be done and what we are to each other."

"Ah, a clash of titans." Nona smiled, folding her hands atop the puzzle. "But there is a lot of history between you two and now a reconnection. Are you in love with him?"

My heart skipped, and I nodded silently, acknowledging the truth even as it frightened me. "Yes. Maybe that's why I acted the way I did. I'm not sure I'm ready for this."

"Love can be terrifying," she agreed, her voice soft and understanding. "But it sounds like this tiff isn't insurmountable. Perhaps it's time for you to give a little, show him he matters to you."

I shifted uncomfortably in my seat, memories of the fight swirling in my mind. "Even after I practically shut him out?"

Nona leaned forward, her gaze sage and knowing. "Especially after," she said firmly. "Think about it—if you reach out to him now, after pushing him away, won't that show him how much he means to you? That you're willing to put your pride aside and fight for your relationship?"

Her words struck a chord within me, stirring up

conflicting emotions. Was I ready to apologize and admit my fault? My fear? Had he really changed over the years?

Nona must have sensed my hesitation because she continued gently, "You don't want to lose him, do you? Stella, you have worked for so long at being strong and unassailable, you've built a shield around yourself. Don't let fear stop you from loving and being loved." Nona's faded blue eyes twinkled as she squeezed my hand. "Trust me, sometimes, a little vulnerability is exactly what a relationship needs."

I bit my lower lip, considering her words. She had a point. Maybe it was time for me to swallow my fear—and my pride—and make things right. "You always give good advice. Thanks. I've got a lot to think about."

"And I might remind you that the two of you have been seeing each other for quite some time now. And yet you've never invited him over for lunch or dinner."

I straightened, frowning. "Not true! I invited him to the pool party, but he had an emergency to deal with."

She stared at me with that unrelenting gaze. "And since?"

I swallowed, unable to refute that. Why hadn't I included him more? Aiden was a warm, successful man who got along with anyone. And I was proud of him, to be seen with him. Why was I so afraid?

Her gaze softened, that wry sense of humor rising once again. "And let's not forget the practical side. Between your father and me aging and your siblings' penchant for getting in trouble, having a doctor in the family could come in handy."

I couldn't help but laugh, the tension easing from my shoulders. Her comment was classic Nona—wisdom delivered with a dose of humor.

"Thanks. Maybe I need to stop being so stubborn and focus more on people instead of my career... including Aiden."

"Good girl." Nona's approval warmed me more than the lamplight ever could. "Now, back to this puzzle—what do you think about teamwork for twelve across?"

"Perfect fit," I replied, but I wasn't just talking about the crossword anymore.

THE NEXT MORNING, sunlight cast stripes across the floor of my sitting area. Pilar lazily washed herself as the beams warmed her, pausing to stare at me with those inscrutable green eyes. Her sides were starting to bulge now, an indication of the kittens she carried. I was curled up with a glass of water I hadn't touched in fifteen minutes. My thoughts were still wrapped around Nona's words when my phone buzzed on the glass tabletop.

"Stella? You up yet?" Hunter's voice was sharp and alert. He'd always been one of those horrible morning people.

"Define *up*," I muttered, rubbing at my eyes. "Everything all right?"

"Yeah. I've been thinking a lot about the thefts. The first things stolen were orchids, right? So either our thief has a thing for exotic flowers or knows how to sell them."

I set my water down, instantly becoming more alert. "That makes sense. You already think it's someone with outside access, right?"

"I do. And I've got a plan to catch him."

"Tell me more."

"I'm thinking about setting a trap. What if we use some of your best orchids as bait?"

Reflexively, my heart skipped at the thought of losing more of my precious blooms and my eyes automatically zeroed in on the ones by my balcony door. "You want to use my orchids as... lures? Hunter, it takes years to grow them!"

"I know, and that's exactly why a really special one, or two, would be perfect. The thief won't be able to resist. You set a couple of them near the restaurant to entice him. Pick them carefully, okay? Put them near the others so they don't look out of place—we don't want it to look obvious. I'll come down and stake the place out. We'll see what happens."

I couldn't refute his logic, though the idea caused my stomach to drop. Pilar rose and rubbed against my legs. I reached over and absently scratched under her chin. "Should we loop in Evan or Gabe?"

"Not yet." His voice held a firmness that told me he'd thought this through. "Evan knows I'm working on something—we talked about it at the party. Plus, the fewer people involved, the better."

"Makes sense." I grinned. "So are we going to hide out together in a dusty old sedan, waiting for our creeping thief to abscond with the bait?" My bad mood was slipping away by the minute.

"Get real." He snorted. "You're not going to be anywhere near. Hopefully neither will anyone else. I've got a lot of experience with stakeouts, Stella. And catching bad guys."

My smile faded. I hadn't really expected him to let me tag along, but his answer was unsettling. I shifted in my seat, stroking Pilar's ears to cover my uneasiness. No one really knew what Hunter had done while in Special Forces, and he never went into details about it. "I know you do. I was just teasing."

"You're the only one I trust to pick out the right orchids." His voice softened. "I'm sorry, Stell. This is the best way."

"Well, if the first orchids tempted Ben to steal them, the new ones I choose should prove irresistible." I tried to sound confident. Then memories from the farmer's market flooded my mind—the day I'd reconnected with Aiden while picking out replacement orchids. I shook my head, forcing the recollection away. "When do you want me to pick out the flowers? The landscaping project is close to wrapping up."

They'd planted several new palm trees around the resort and updated underground sprinkler lines throughout. As much as I disliked Ben, I had to admit the crew had done a great job sprucing up the place.

"No time like the present," Hunter said. "I've got a few days off coming up. Can you choose the bait today?"

I blinked at how rapidly he was moving now that he'd decided on his plan. "Sure. I can do it tonight while I'm working."

"Call me when you find the right ones, and we'll go from there. Hopefully, tomorrow we'll discover who our thief is." Hunter's voice held a steel edge of determination.

"It's Ben, Hunter." I smirked.

"Maybe, maybe not. Not all Coleridges are terrible people, though he doesn't have a great track record. Call me later, okay?"

"Got it," I replied, resisting the urge to say over and out. After hanging up, a potent mix of concern and anticipation rose in me as I prepared to carry out Hunter's plan.

THE DINNER RUSH died down around 10:00 p.m., finally giving me the time I needed to stroll through Orchid's nearly deserted dining area. After a thorough perusal of my beautiful charges, I ended up in a section that fronted the beach but was secure within the restaurant. Some of our most beautiful orchids were kept here. My eye automatically darted to a bare area, one I was reserving for my long dreamed of monkey-face orchid. Rare and in great demand, I had never been able to get my hands on one. I examined several magnificent blooms before making my final selection.

I chose two stunning specimens of the Cattleya *Queen Sirikit*, known for its resilience and delicate lavender hue that reminded me of dawn skies over the beach. *Queen Sirikit* could survive outside with the proper care, making the two orchids perfect lures for our thief.

I called my brother, cradling the phone between my shoulder and ear as I carefully tended the plants one last time. "Okay, Hunter. I've found my blooms."

"Excellent. Place them outside by six a.m., no sooner. I'll be down by then."

"Six in the morning?" I grumbled, lifting my hand to prop it on my hip. "You know I work until after midnight, right?"

"Oh, cry me a river. I'm the one driving from South Beach, remember? I'll be up by two." He laughed, and it was good to hear the lightness in his voice. It only served to remind me how rare it was to hear his laugh.

"All right. You win." I managed a smile even though he couldn't see it. "I promise they'll be in place first thing."

After I hung up, I went back to finish my shift, which

passed quickly and without drama, thank God. Shooing out the rest of the staff, I collected my two beautiful orchids and set them on the counter next to the back entrance. Ready for tomorrow. I turned off the lights and locked up, the weight of the restaurant's keys in my hand a reminder of the responsibility I carried. But as I walked away, keys jingling in rhythm with my steps, my mind quickly diverted to my other conundrum. And the fact that the threat of our prowler wasn't what weighed heaviest on my mind.

It was the possibility of losing Aiden.

How could we overcome our differences? I needed to find a way to bridge the gulf between us—to navigate from the past to what we were trying to build now. Because I was coming to realize the thought of losing him felt far more daunting than any thief.

# Chapter Twenty-Nine

## Aiden

THE FIRST BIRDS were beginning their songs in the trees surrounding Dove Key Marina, the sky a pastel painting of pink and orange. With each careful stroke of the brush, I applied the final strokes of varnish to the wood before me. It shone under the growing light, smooth and clear—the finishing touch to my project.

For the thousandth time, my thoughts drifted to Stella. The memory of her smile mingled with the air, and I could almost feel the warmth of her skin under my touch. Each swipe of the brush seemed to echo my growing desire to win her back, to show her that we were worth another shot.

Luke's words came back to me, clearer now than when he'd said them last night. Maybe it was the quiet peace of the dawn or the rhythmic motion of the brush, but I got it now. I wanted—no, needed to prove to Stella that our careers didn't have to be at odds with our relationship. That we could thrive together, support each other, and build a life that didn't compromise on love or ambition.

Rocking back to sit on my heels, I took a moment to admire the finished project. I wasn't a flashy, over-the-top kind of guy. As grand gestures went, I wasn't sure it was all that grand. But it was me.

I capped the varnish and cleaned my brush. The scent of the sea mingled with the fresh tang of the wood treatment, a combination that had always felt like home. But as I descended the stairs to get ready for my day, I imagined the cabin through Stella's eyes, and the tight confines became more noticeable.

"Maybe she's right," I murmured to myself as I surveyed the cozy, lived-in cabin where every inch of space was utilized. "It is a little cramped."

My eyes traced the lines of the compact galley, the small table cluttered with coffee mugs and notes, and the narrow hallway that led to the even narrower bathroom. I pictured her here, imagined her laughter bouncing off the walls, her presence filling the space. The idea of a permanent place on land—a proper apartment or a bungalow—didn't seem so far-fetched anymore.

Stepping into the bathroom, I turned the shower knobs, wincing at the initial burst of cold before it warmed up to a more comfortable temperature. The water pressure was nothing to boast about, but it got the job done. I let the warm cascade wash away the remnants of varnish, uncertainty, and the last tendrils of sleep.

Refreshed from the shower, I stood in front of the mirror, swiping a hand across the fogged-up glass. My damp hair was sticking up in odd directions but smoothed under my fingers. I dressed quickly for work in slacks and a button-down shirt, the fabric feeling crisp and cool against my skin.

My mind shifted gears as I straightened my collar and

tucked in the shirt. My clinic would be bustling today, a schedule packed with patients who each carried their own stories, ailments, and hopes. It required a clear head, sharp focus, and empathy—the qualities I prided myself on. Yet underneath it all, my heart thrummed with an undercurrent of anticipation for the evening ahead.

By tonight, I'd have some answers. I'd either rekindle something beautiful with Stella or finally close a chapter that had never truly ended. The stakes were high, and the thought sent a shiver of nerves through me even as determination settled in my chest. I gave myself one final look in the mirror, a small nod of encouragement, then grabbed my bag and headed to the galley.

I pocketed my cell phone and climbed up the stairs, locking the cabin door behind me. By now, the sky was fully blue, and boats were slowly moving out of the marina, ready to start the day's work. Then familiar jingle rang out—I pulled my phone from my pocket to see the call was from Mom.

"Morning," I answered, settling into a camp chair and watching the seagulls compete for breakfast scraps. I was running ahead of schedule and had some time to spare.

"Good morning, honey. Did I catch you at a bad time?" Her voice was warm and carried the comforting lilt of home.

"Perfect timing. I'm ready for work but don't need to leave yet." I could picture her in the sunlit kitchen, sipping coffee by the window.

"Oh, good. I woke up wanting to hear your voice."

"How's life in Michigan?"

"Good! I just started a new volunteer project. We're setting up a community garden, and I'm really getting into the planning."

I smiled, enjoying our much more easygoing rapport. "That's fantastic, Mom. You've always had a green thumb, and a garden will really bring people together—something fresh and vibrant."

She laughed. "It keeps me busy. Speaking of fresh and vibrant, how's Stella?"

The question hung in the air, a gentle reminder of the one thing that wasn't as bright as it should be in my life. "Things with her aren't so great at the moment."

"I'm sorry to hear that." The concern in her voice was clear, even as she tried to keep it light.

"I'm trying to show her I'm not the same guy who left all those years ago—that I'm here to stay. But I can't seem to get through to her." The words tumbled out, heavy with the weight of my fears.

"Oh, sweetheart, I know you are. And I'm sure she'll see it too. You just have to give it time."

"Time," I replied, gazing out across the water where the horizon blurred into the sky. "That's what I'm afraid we're running out of."

"I'm sorry, Aiden. It shouldn't be this way." Her voice softened with a hint of regret. "You shouldn't have to prove yourself. And it's our fault that you're in this position."

I propped my feet on the gleaming railing, glad to finally be resolving this issue with my parents. "It's okay, Mom. I love my medical practice, and I love being back on Dove Key. I've come to believe I'm right where I'm supposed to be." The words were more for myself than for her, an affirmation as the first rays of daylight spilled across my boat. "And if things are meant to be with Stella, I'll know soon enough."

There was a brief silence on the line, one filled with understanding and the unspoken guilt of what could happen if Stella and I didn't reconcile. Just the thought of that made my stomach twist, an uncomfortable knot of anxiety and longing.

"Your father and I are so proud of you, Aiden," she continued, tactfully changing the subject. "You know, I've been talking to Pam Bryant a lot lately. Does that name ring a bell?"

"Of course." I smiled, pushing away the conflict with Stella to picture one of Mom's oldest friends in Dove Key. A friend who had also become one of my favorite patients. "I've seen her around a few times. How is she?"

"Thrilled with her new doctor." Mom laughed heartily. "A few months ago, Pam called me up just to sing your praises, and we've rekindled our friendship. She said you changed all her medications, and she feels better than she has in years."

I smiled at the compliment, feeling a swell of pride. "Well, Dr. Nelson had his medical philosophy, and I have mine."

"You're not going to tell me a thing, are you?" she teased.

"Nope." I grinned.

"You're very good at what you do, Aiden. Dove Key is lucky to have you."

Her words wrapped around me like a comforting hug. "Thanks, Mom. The longer I'm here, the more I love being a small-town doctor. The sense of doing my best for the people here."

"Which is precisely why you're so special. We should have realized that sooner." She paused, the kind filled with unspoken apologies and old regrets. "We didn't give you enough credit, honey. You've proved us wrong time and again."

"Hey, no need to get into all that now." I wanted to put the awkward regret in the past forever. Where it belonged. "Why don't you and Dad come visit sometime? The island's more beautiful than ever."

"Really?" Her surprise was evident, a smile audible in her voice. "We'd love to visit you, wouldn't we, George?" I heard some muffled assent from my dad in the background.

"Absolutely, but fair warning—the quarters are a little tight here on the boat. Unless you like the idea of sleeping on deck."

"No, thanks! We'll find a nice place to stay. Calypso Key is a lovely resort, you know..."

My smile widened at the leading tease in her voice. "Yeah, it's just about perfect."

"And of course, I've heard nothing but praise about their fine-dining restaurant."

I laughed out loud. "Okay, now you're laying it on a little thick."

"I know. We'll make plans to come down soon. Oh, Aiden, we're so excited!"

"Can't wait to show you both around. Just be ready to meet the two sides I have now—Aiden and Dr. Mitchell."

She laughed, that hearty, infectious laugh that used to echo throughout our house. "We wouldn't expect anything less. You've made quite the impact, son."

"Let's hope the impact lasts," I murmured, more to myself than to her. "I gotta go, Mom. Patients to see and all that."

"Of course, darling. Take care."

"Will do. Bye, Mom."

The line went dead, and I pocketed my phone, feeling a curious mixture of pride and yearning. The latter, no doubt, tied to the fluttering image of Stella on a Calypso Key beach, sun-kissed and carefree. Or manning the booth at the Sea and Sand Festival. Shaking my head to dispel the thoughts, I turned to face the day, knowing it would take more than a successful career to fill the void she left.

I stepped off the boat with a sense of resolve that was as clear and sharp as the morning air. I was headed toward a full day, yet all I could think about was Stella and the conversation we were long overdue to have. I was willing to give her a gesture of my love, my dedication. But I needed one back if this relationship was going to work.

Tonight. I'd call her tonight.

The thought alone made my heart race, but it was a risk I had to take. I turned for one last look at my boat—the vessel that had been both my sanctuary and the symbol of my freedom. It had seen me through some of the loneliest nights, cradling me in solitude while my thoughts churned with memories of Stella. Now, it bore witness to the determination to make those memories real. It was time to shed the shell of the past and reach for what I wanted most.

Taking a deep breath, I squared my shoulders and strode toward my car. I clung to that courage like a lifeline. After work, I was either going to win back the love of my life or make a complete fool of myself. But no matter the outcome, I'd know I had given it my all.

For Stella.

For us.

And for the future I wanted more than anything.

# Chapter Thirty

## Stella

THE WARMTH of the sun soaked through my skin as I sat on the pool patio, sipping coffee that had lost its steam long ago. The Big House was quiet except for the occasional chirp of a bird hidden in the trees above. It was late morning, but the day felt like it had already stretched much further.

My alarm had gone off much too early, but I'd trudged down the hill with bleary eyes. The dark pre-dawn air had seemed thick with anticipation as I placed the two orchids on the patio outside Orchid's dark entrance. They would be noticeable when the area became fully light, but not so obvious the thief would realize they were a lure. At least I hoped so. My heart was hammering.

True to form, sleep evaded me once I crawled back into bed, leaving me tossing and turning in a tangle of sheets. My phone vibrated at seven, tearing me from my restless thoughts. Hunter's message on the screen was terse, a stark contrast to the chaos in my head.

Hunter: In position. Don't go near Orchid.
I'll handle it.

His words were meant to be reassuring, but they only fueled my impatience. I wanted to be there, in the thick of the action, not sidelined. But I also knew when to follow orders like a good soldier. With a snort, I dragged myself out of bed, foregoing any attempt at further sleep.

I'd been camped out on the patio ever since, my breakfast picked over and each sip of coffee an attempt to drown the turmoil inside me. A run on the treadmill in Evan's gym would have probably been a good idea, but I seemed stuck in this weird limbo like I was frozen on the patio. In a bid for distraction, I indulged in a delicious fantasy of Ben Coleridge in handcuffs. It was petty, maybe, but imagining his downfall made me think all this work might be worth it.

I took another sip, letting the liquid slide down my throat, and forced my attention away from the churning thoughts of Ben and onto the other major issue ahead. Aiden. My chest tightened at the mere idea of bridging the gap between us. The silence from his end was still deafening, a reminder that if things were going to change, it would have to start with me. And maybe not an undeserved reminder.

"Stella, up and about already?" Evan's voice interrupted my musings as he approached, his tone light but tinged with surprise.

I glanced up to find him dressed in crisply pressed slacks and a staff polo shirt, Calypso Key's logo stitched over his heart. Mr. General Manager in action.

"Couldn't sleep," I said, offering a tight-lipped smile. "Apparently, my body thought the morning was just too beautiful to sleep through."

He nodded, then tilted his head, examining me with those perceptive eyes that missed nothing. "You sure everything's okay?"

"I've got some things going on," I said, the qualm of guilt for keeping him in the dark about Hunter's plan twisting uncomfortably in my stomach. "We'll talk more later. I don't want to keep you."

"Things to do with Aiden?"

"Some of them, yes."

He nodded. "Aaah. This must be the day for the big sting. That what's got you worked up?"

My mouth hinged open. "Hunter told me not to tell anyone! You know?"

"He got on a conference call with me and Gabe to give us a heads-up but was vague on the *when*."

I relaxed in my chair. "Good. I didn't like the idea of keeping it from you guys." Then my gaze sharpened on Evan. "And apparently neither did Hunter."

His face was impassive. "As he should be. I'd be mad as hell if he'd kept something this big from me that involved my own resort."

I smiled. "I'm really glad you two are talking again."

Evan stuffed his hands in his back pockets. "We're both walking on eggshells around each other. But I guess that's better than throwing punches."

"Yes, it is. Much better."

"Heard anything from Hunter?"

"No. He's around somewhere, watching. But we have no way of knowing when the thief will strike. Or if he will."

"All right then." He flashed a brief smile, then gestured toward the resort. "I better get going. Lots to sort out at the office."

"See you later, Evan." I watched his hitching gait as he retreated with purposeful strides, leaving me alone again.

Another hour passed. And, of course, my thoughts inevitably drifted back to Aiden—his ocean-blue eyes, the way they could be so warm and yet so guarded. His cautious nature had always been a puzzle, each piece meticulously placed, revealing only what he chose. Like his single-minded focus on becoming a doctor. But I understood ambition, and I understood being driven. It was fear that held us back, fear that carved the gulf between us. And most of that fear was on my side.

In my chest, something heavy shifted. Hopefully, all this thief business would get sorted out today. As soon as Ben was arrested, I'd surprise Aiden with a visit. We needed to talk and get everything out in the open. Could he convince me he had changed? I still wasn't sure.

My phone buzzed with a text.

Hunter: It's done. Police arriving now.

My heart lurched into a gallop. My fingers barely managed to clutch the phone as I rocketed to my feet, adrenaline surging through me. The porcelain mug slipped in my hand, coffee splashing onto the stone tiles before I rushed it to the table. I bolted down the hill, my pace reckless. As I neared the lobby building, two police cruisers came into view. No lights were flashing, but their silent presence was more ominous than any siren could be.

Reaching Orchid, my breaths came out in short, sharp gasps. A crowd had gathered by the entrance, a tangle of curious faces and hushed murmurs. Hunter stood among them, his tall and easily recognizable frame a beacon of calm authority amidst the chaos.

Skidding to a stop, I scanned the scene. Then looked it over again. It didn't make sense, and my mouth dropped open. Matt, our prep worker who usually moved with such quiet efficiency, was now the center of attention—his wrists secured in handcuffs, his face a mask of defeat and shock.

"Matt?" I whispered, disbelief clouding my thoughts. Where was Ben?

Movement caught my eye. Ben Coleridge and his coworkers were pruning one of the palms they'd planted months ago, the same ones we'd argued next to. Now he was keeping one eye on the tree and the other on the hubbub, a hint of curiosity etched across his features as he continued working, shears snipping away methodically.

My feet carried me toward Hunter, the ground beneath them feeling strangely soft and buoyant, as if the earth itself had turned to waves.

"Matt?" My voice was quiet, but it cut through the morning air like the sail of a boat slicing through calm waters. I looked him over and noted a swelling around his left eye, the skin darkening.

Hunter's gaze met mine, and for a moment, I saw the weight of the ordeal etching lines into his usually unflappable demeanor. "Caught him red-handed," he confirmed, nodding gravely toward Matt. "Both orchids in his arms." His large hands mimed the act of holding someone, a silent testament to the struggle that must have ensued. And where Matt's black eye came from. "I restrained him until the cops showed up. He confessed as soon as he saw them."

I followed his gesture to where the remnants of my prized plants lay scattered on the ground, their once-perfect blooms now crushed underfoot. My heart twisted at the shards of broken pottery glistening like tears. Matt stood there, the image of defeat, his shoulders slumped as the handcuffs glinted in the sunlight.

"How could you do this to us?" The question burst from me before I could rein in the hurt lacing my words. It was more than the loss of the stolen items. It was the betrayal, the trust shattered of someone I'd personally worked with. Mentored.

Matt's eyes flickered to mine, holding a mixture of shame and defiance. He swallowed, visibly struggling to find his voice. "My mother had a greenhouse in Key Largo. She specialized in orchids and exotic flowers. She taught me how to care for them, which ones were valuable." A bitter laugh escaped him. "I needed money. And stealing here was easy."

"Easy?" I gasped the word, my heart thrumming painfully against my ribs.

Matt's gaze hardened even as a sly smile rose on his lips. "Especially when everyone is so eager to blame someone else."

His declaration hung heavy in the air, a force that seemed to push against my chest. The feeling was almost physical. Two police officers stepped forward, gripping Matt by the elbows to lead him away. He bowed his head, accepting his fate with a resignation that made my fist clench.

For a long moment, I stood there frozen as my mind worked to face the obvious. I'd been wrong—so utterly wrong about Ben. And Matt. The realization struck like a sudden, fierce storm, whipping through my thoughts and leaving clarity in its wake.

The world tilted on its axis, sending my senses spinning as I stood rooted to the spot, absorbing the revelation. Ben Coleridge, the man I had been so quick to judge, was innocent. He'd been watching Matt trudge away and now turned back to the palm tree, applying the final touches. Ben was exactly what he'd tried to tell me—a hard worker trying to start over. The taste of regret was a bitter brew that settled heavily in my stomach.

"Never ceases to amaze me," Hunter mused next to me, his gaze fixed on the retreating figure of Matt. "It's always the ones you least expect."

I whipped my head back to glance at him, seeing the grave set of his jaw. "You knew?"

"Not specifically, but I learned a long time ago to keep an open mind about suspects." He turned toward Evan and Gabe, who had joined us, their faces lined with concern and relief. "I'm sorry about not telling you this was going down today, but I couldn't risk spooking that guy." His gaze narrowed on Evan. "You're damn good at what you do, Evan. So am I."

Their gazes locked in a silent exchange, laden with history. Then, after what felt like an eternity, Evan nodded. "You made the right call. Well played, Hunter."

"Thanks." Hunter's voice was rough around the edges, betraying the tension he'd held at bay.

I watched the moment unfold, feeling oddly detached, as if observing strangers through a fogged glass. My own folly loomed larger, the shadow it cast darkening my thoughts. How had I missed the truth?

"Stella?" Evan's voice cut into my thoughts.

"Sorry, I... I need some air." With legs that seemed to move of their own accord, I walked to the short bluff in front of the restaurant. The breeze off the sea was a cool caress against my flushed skin. Gulls wheeled overhead, their cries echoing the confusion that swirled within me.

Alone, I stared out at the horizon where sky met water

in an endless embrace. My fingers dug into my elbows as my mind raced. If I could misjudge Ben and Matt so completely, what did that say about how I'd treated Aiden? His face materialized in my mind, his blue eyes that had only tried to reassure me. Until I'd finally pushed him too far. Catching Matt brought it all home—the rush to judge Ben paralleled my reluctance to trust Aiden.

A sharp laugh escaped my lips, tinged with irony and self-reproach. How had I allowed my fears to color my judgment? I saw Ben's culpability where there was none, yet veiled Aiden's strengths in fear. My intuition, once a trusted ally, was now completely unreliable. I closed my eyes and let out a long breath. I needed to bridge the chasm my doubts had created and work to repair the damage.

"Hey, sis." Evan's large hand settled on my shoulder, gentle yet firm.

"Hey." I turned to look at him, trying to focus the whirlwind in my mind.

"Are you okay?"

"I'm not sure." I shot him a small smile. "Turns out I'm not the great judge of character I thought I was."

"Join the club." His tone was light, but I heard the truth underneath.

"Thanks for being here."

Evan's presence was always a comfort, even when I was grappling with internal chaos. He was solid and dependable, the one we all counted on.

"Always." He squeezed my shoulder before stepping back. "Hunter's got everything under control, so why don't you take tonight off? Luis can run the kitchen, and Rea can help. You've made sure they're ready."

"Thanks. I think that's a good idea."

After watching him walk back to the small crowd, I

turned back to the sea, letting the endless rhythm of the waves soothe my unease. It was time to confront my own shortcomings, to acknowledge the fear that had held me captive. Aiden deserved that much—a chance to be seen without the veil of our past clouding the view.

I stood at the edge of the bluff, arms folded over my stomach as Nona's words came back to me. What she'd warned me about had just become very clear. I needed to prove myself to Aiden. Ideas swirled inside me, darting in and out of the shadows of my mind.

I had an idea of what I wanted to do. But I needed help.

Determination filled me as I spun around. "Sorry, guys, but I have to go." I lifted my arm in a wave as I strode past where Hunter, Evan, and Gabe were still clustered around.

"Go?" Hunter looked up, his dark brows creasing. "What's got into you?"

"Shopping," I said, my voice breaking into a laugh. "For supplies to mend some fences. See you guys later. And good job, Hunter!" I called over my shoulder, my laughter trailing behind me like a kite tail in the breeze. I left them with questions dancing in their expressions, but I didn't give them a chance to ask. No time for that now.

The scent of motor oil and salt air mingled in the garage as I slipped behind the wheel of my car, the one that had seen all corners of the Lower Keys. The key turned, the engine rumbled to life, and I felt everything else fall away. As I drove north up the paved road, the Big House shrank in the rearview mirror. Mangroves blurred past, their green branches whispering secrets only the wind could under-stand. My hands trembled slightly on the steering wheel, not from fear, but from an eagerness that vibrated through every fiber of my being.

*I need him to know.* The thought was a mantra, and his name pulsed with each heartbeat. Aiden.

I had been blind. So achingly blind, but no more.

My mind still spun, so I dialed Grace on my car Bluetooth. "Are you doing anything right now? It's kind of a nine-one-one situation."

"That doesn't sound good. I was planning on a day of grading papers and watching sappy movies, but if you've got a better idea, I'm all ears."

"I need some help with a project, and I'm on my way to Key West. I could use a sympathetic ear too."

"I can definitely provide that. And a day in Key West beats any sappy movie. I'm in."

"Thanks, Grace. I'll pick you up in ten."

As I headed toward her apartment on Dove Key, my mind raced ahead to Key West. One of the funky shops there would undoubtedly hold what I was looking for. What I hoped would be the symbol I needed to convince Aiden I'd been terribly wrong about so many things. I would find a way to mend what was broken, to bridge the gulf between us.

This wasn't just about second chances. It was about seeing clearly for the first time.

# Chapter Thirty-One

## Aiden

THE SUN WAS a molten smear across the horizon as I pulled my Ranger into the marina parking lot, the sky painted with the kind of vibrant oranges and pinks that only seemed to exist in this part of the world. Even at the end of the day, my hands still felt the fatigue from my morning's work on the boat. My labor of love that doubled as a grand gesture for Stella now concerned me as being trite, too whimsical.

But it would have to be enough. I wasn't Casanova, dammit.

My mind briefly turned away from Stella as I remembered this afternoon's small victory. Kayla had returned to my clinic for a final goodbye appointment before transferring to an obstetrician. And she'd arrived alone, without her mother. She had thanked me for helping her decide to accept her boyfriend's marriage proposal and form her own family. Maybe it wasn't the biggest victory I'd have, but helping a young patient find her own voice had felt pretty damn good. I sighed.

*Now if I can just capture some of that magic with Stella.*

My anxiety had been building all day. Now, with every task crossed off my list, I was ready to call her. As much as I wanted her to reach out, I needed to bridge the gap between us—I couldn't stand the silence anymore. As I approached the dock, the soft clatter of halyards hitting masts created a familiar rhythm in the warm air.

Then I skidded to a halt as my heart thundered in my chest.

Stella stood stiffly on the deck of my boat, silhouetted against the fading light. For a moment, I could only stand there, the wish blooming in my chest a fierce contrast to the worry that had been nesting there all day.

"Stella?" As my feet stumbled forward once more, my voice barely carried over the gentle lap of water against hulls.

Her head swiveled toward me, and even from a distance, I could see how her brow furrowed and her lips pressed into a tight line as apprehension clouded her delicate features. She held a box about a foot long in both hands. What was she doing here? All this time, all this effort—it had been for her. Yet part of me feared she might retreat once more, leaving me with shadows of what could have been.

"Hi." Her voice was soft and held a hint of hesitation that was so unlike her.

I stepped onto the deck and felt the slight sway beneath my feet, an echo of the turmoil inside me. "I didn't expect to find you here." My words held more surprise than I intended but also an undercurrent of something else. Relief, maybe.

Or the first budding hints of hope.

"I needed to see you... to explain."

"Explain what?" I stopped myself from saying more, swallowing the rush of emotions threatening to spill over.

Her eyes searched mine, and resolve flickered within them. We both stood on a precipice, each needing the other to take that final step closer.

She wet her lips. "How sorry I am. For everything."

"Sorry?" I asked, apparently unable to do anything but parrot back her words. I watched as she clutched the box tighter in her hands, and a part of me—the doctor trained to observe—registered the tremor in her grip.

"Can we sit?" Stella gestured toward the built-in bench near the stern, and I nodded, unable to find words just yet. We settled onto the cushioned surface, the setting sun casting an amber glow over us and enhancing the gravity of the moment.

"Today," she said, then stopped to swallow, her throat moving. "This morning. Hunter came down and caught the thief who's been stealing from the resort. The police took him away to be charged." She paused to bite her lip, as if gathering the courage to continue. "Aiden, I was so incredibly wrong about all of it."

"The thief wasn't Ben Coleridge?"

She shook her head, the movement more like a jerk from side to side. "No. It was a prep worker from my restaurant— one I've been working with for months! I've been completely blinded to the truth. I just assumed I understood what was happening. Except I didn't have a clue."

The weight of her gaze held me captive, the intensity unlike any I'd seen on her face before. "And Nona gave me some advice. She made me realize how terrified I've been. How I let my career ambitions shield me from fear... from really living. To become an excuse to avoid taking any risks."

Inside, my heart began to mend with each word she spoke. After all the risks I'd avoided, all the past failures that still haunted me, this woman was the one risk that mattered most—and it was worth everything.

"Stella," I said gently, reaching out to take her trembling hands in mine. "It's okay. You built those walls for a reason. And there's nothing wrong with being ambitious."

She looked down at our joined hands, a smile touching her lips, but her eyes shimmered with unshed tears. "I know. But what I missed is that... I wasn't the only one trying to avoid pain. You were too, and yet you reached out over and over. Took what I was willing to give, even when I hid behind my walls. I was so wrapped up in myself I didn't see it."

"Hey." I tilted her chin up so she'd meet my eyes again. "We both have our scars. It doesn't mean we can't heal together."

"Really?" Her voice was a whisper, fragile as sea foam on the tide. "Will you forgive me? It isn't too late?"

"Really." My heart soared as I saw the walls she'd meticulously constructed around herself crumble. "Stella, nothing would make me happier than facing the future—with all its risks and rewards—with you. That is all I've ever wanted."

The sincerity in her eyes was my answer before she even spoke. "I want that too. More than anything."

Her eyes held a newfound clarity, like the blue sky after a storm. "I brought something for you. I didn't have time to wrap it. I came straight here." She reached for the unwrapped box sitting next to her and handed it to me, a mixture of hope and trepidation flickering through her brown eyes.

The wooden box was heavy, much more solid than I'd expected. Setting it on my lap, I carefully lifted the lid, revealing a treasure within. A chill danced down my spine as I stroked it with my finger.

The antique brass compass gleamed in the dim light, its surface etched with intricate designs that spoke of centuries past and countless journeys taken. Each line and curve held a story, whispering secrets of distant lands and adventures yet to come. My fingers traced the patterns with awe and wonder, imagining the hands that had once held this very compass on their own journeys through life.

"It's beautiful," I murmured, awestruck as I lifted it out. The compass felt heavy and significant in my hands, a tangible symbol of direction and purpose.

"Right after Matt was arrested, I knew what I had to do. I called Grace and we drove to Key West and searched through all the little shops. She helped me sort through what I was feeling so I could see clearly. We rummaged through half a dozen shops without finding anything that spoke to me. Then we went into this little cupboard of a nautical antique shop. When I saw this, I knew it was perfect. It was exactly what I'd been searching for." The corners of her mouth lifted fleetingly as her eyes became shimmering. "A compass. I wanted to give you something that would always guide you back. Back home, back to... me. Us."

"I don't know what to say." I paused, emotion clogging my throat. "It's stunning." Once again, I traced the smooth surface of the compass, feeling the connection. It was a promise, a commitment, and a reminder rolled into one beautiful artifact.

"Every time I look at this," I continued, meeting her gaze, "I'll be reminded of you and how you've changed my world. How you've given me a reason to always come back."

Acknowledgment flickered in her eyes, and I could tell she understood—that this wasn't just about a physical return, but about finding my way back to her heart, no matter what storms we might weather.

"Thank you," I said, the words inadequate for the swell of gratitude filling me. "For this, for coming here, for giving us another chance."

"Thank you for not giving up on me."

Our eyes locked, and something shifted between us—a recognition that whatever had held us back before was now behind us. We were two people, imperfect and scarred, choosing to navigate the uncertain waters ahead together.

A single tear rolled down her cheek. "I love you, Aiden. And I'm sorry it took me so long to figure that out. I'm so sorry I pushed you away."

My heart nearly stopped at hearing her say those words. A simple sentence I'd come to doubt I'd ever hear her say again. With my own eyes filling, I wiped her tear away with my thumb. "I love you too. And I'm not going anywhere."

Her eyes sparkled with tears, but her smile was radiant. "I know that now. We're a risk worth taking."

As my gaze returned to the compass, I realized where we were sitting and remembered what I'd been up to all morning. I burst into laughter, tipping my head back.

"What's so funny?" Tears drying, she arched a brow, and the Stella I knew and loved rose back to the surface.

"I've got something to show you too." Rising to my feet, I pulled her up. Guiding her by the wrist, I could feel the rhythm of her pulse as we moved together toward the very stern of the boat, the cool sea breeze playing with strands of her hair.

The sun was sinking, but enough light was left to illuminate the name I'd painted. The sound of the waves against the wooden hull was like a gentle whisper urging me on, encouraging me to unveil the piece of myself I'd embedded into this vessel.

"I finally named the boat." My voice held a mixture of pride and hesitation as I gestured toward the freshly painted name on the stern: *Catch of the Day*. Fear that compared to her generous gesture, mine was stupid.

Stella's eyes widened with surprise and curiosity, her lips parting into a smile as she took in the bold letters. "*Catch of the Day*?" She turned from the name to me, questioning.

"Luke and I were discussing it last night, and I wanted to make a gesture to show you I *get* you, Stella. A very wise chef told me not too long ago how important this phrase was. What it represented." I leaned against the rail, watching her face for a reaction. "She said that the catch of the day wasn't just a menu item. It was the dish you put your soul into, the one that proved your worth."

Her gaze lingered on the name, her smile widening, and I could see her mind piecing together the metaphor. "So this boat... it's your catch of the day?"

I laughed, my grin lingering. "Not even close. The name is solely to remind me of what the real catch is. The real prize." I stepped closer and took her hands in mine. "You. Maybe it's a little sappy, but it works as a name for a boat. It's whimsical and yet there's real meaning behind it. Deep meaning. And now that I have a compass too, it's just additional proof that I will navigate any storm to find my beautiful Stella."

She reached down, her fingers brushing over the painted letters as if to confirm their reality. "It's the perfect name for a boat!" She straightened back up and slid her arms around my waist and drew me close as her face sobered. "I'm so sorry I accused you of living on a boat so you could sail away at any moment. I don't even know why I said that. I love your boat."

I grinned. "It is a little small, but it's given us some great memories, hasn't it? We've both been through some rough seas. But look at us now, finding our way back to each other."

She nodded, her smile slowly returning, radiant and full of promise. "I guess sometimes you have to get a little lost to really appreciate being found."

"Or to recognize what you've caught," I added, feeling the weight of our journey settle into a peaceful anchor in my chest. Stella, here before me, fully accepting the love I'd never stopped feeling. And me, ready to prove every day that she was my greatest catch.

Drawing her tight against me, I felt the final pieces of the barrier between us crumble, leaving nothing but raw honesty. As our lips melted in a searching kiss, the world around us blurred into nothingness.

"I love you," Stella murmured against my lips, her tone strained as if she needed to say it again. Her hands cradled my face as she pulled back to look into my eyes. "Now that I've allowed myself to finally feel it, to say it... I don't ever want to stop."

A rumble of desire reverberated through my chest as I drank in her tousled hair and flushed cheeks. This woman rendered me undone in the best possible way. "Then don't stop," I rasped out, slanting my mouth over hers again. "Say it as much as you need. I can't get enough of hearing it... feeling how much you want me."

She moaned softly into our fevered kiss, her roaming hands plunging into my hair to tug and grip fistfuls, sending sparks of delicious pain lancing across my scalp. It only stoked the fire raging inside me as our need for each other reached a fever pitch.

"Oh, Aiden... I need you," she panted out between searing kisses trailed along my jaw. The urgency, the burning yearning we had both fought so hard against for too long was finally set free. We were two halves of a tormented puzzle that finally found their perfect fit, unlocking a wild passion we could not contain.

Rational thought fled as I slid my hands down to grip her ass and squeezed, pulling her body flush against the undeniable evidence of my arousal. "You have me, all of me. Always."

"Take me inside. Right now. Take me."

# Chapter Thirty-Two

## Aiden

THE ONLY SOUND I could hear was the blood roaring in my ears. My grip firm, I held Stella's hand, guiding her down into the cabin. The narrow confines of the stairwell were close, intimate, and heat radiated from her body like a beacon drawing me in.

As soon as we stumbled into the relative openness of the galley kitchen, restraint became a memory. My hands acted of their own volition, and I slammed Stella against the counter with a force that echoed through the small space. Her breath hitched, eyes wide with a mix of shock and unmistakable desire. This was more than just a kiss. This was years of pent-up yearning crashing down around us.

"Stella..." It was all I could manage before our lips crashed together in a collision of past and present. A storm of emotion swirled between us as I pulled her waist tight against mine, wanting no space, no air to separate us. Our mouths moved in desperate harmony, a clash of tongues and teeth and everything unsaid that we'd been holding back for too long.

"God, I've missed you," I breathed against her lips, each word punctuated with another urgent press of my mouth to hers. I wanted every inch of her. My hands roamed over her back, pressing her even closer.

"Me too... so much," she panted when our lips parted for the briefest of moments, her voice thick with the same raw need that was consuming me.

This wasn't gentle. It wasn't the soft rekindling of an old flame—it was a wildfire, uncontrolled and all-consuming. And I wouldn't have it any other way. Stella was here, in my arms, and I burned for her. My hands found her breasts, and I cupped them hard through her shirt. Stella's gasp was swallowed by my mouth as she moaned, her body arching into my touch. My thumbs rubbed the peaks, feeling them harden even below her shirt and bra.

Stella reached under my shirt and clawed up my chest, leaving trails of fire in her wake. The sting from her nails sent a jolt shuddering through me, and it only made me hotter for her. My pulse roared, my need for her eclipsing all rational thought. She was mine, here and now, and nothing else mattered.

I broke the kiss, panting heavily, our foreheads resting against each other's as I tried to find my bearings in the storm. As I pulled my head back, our eyes locked and oceans of emotion crashed into one another. I saw my own longing reflected back at me, magnified in her gaze.

"Oh, Stella." My voice was quiet with the weight of what I needed to say. "I'm so sorry for leaving, for all the lost years. I wish I could take it all back. All I had were memories. Of you. Of us. So many—"

Stella's finger pressed against my lips, silencing the

storm of apologies threatening to overwhelm the space between us. "No," she said fiercely, her voice thick with emotion. "No regrets. Not anymore." Her eyes were alight with fire, a signal to leave the past where it belonged. "From this moment on, we live in the present. We look to the future. Our future."

My heart swelled beyond what my chest could hold. Her words were a balm to my own wounds. If she was ready to leave the past behind, then I sure as hell was. Starting right now. My eyes dropped to her mouth, and raw desire overtook me again. My mouth found hers in a crushing kiss, our teeth smashing as I raked my lips over hers. I plunged my tongue into her mouth. A groan escaped me when I felt her respond with equal fervor, her body pressing against mine, urging me on.

I tangled my fingers in her hair, grabbing a handful and yanking her head back to deepen the kiss, to claim her as I'd dreamed of for years. A growl rumbled in my throat, raw and unfiltered—the sound of desire and possession.

With urgency propelling us forward, I led her from the galley kitchen, our footsteps thundering across the wooden floor in a hurried rhythm. We reached the doorway of my bedroom, and the air was thick with want, charged with electricity. I spun to her, pinning her with my eyes. In them, she would see all the hunger, the need to consume her, protect her, love her, and devour her all at once.

"I've dreamed of this," I said, my voice low and throaty. "I've dreamed of you. I want you more than I've ever wanted anything in my life."

My hands, shaking with raw desire, found the hem of Stella's shirt. I peeled the fabric away from her skin, revealing inch by tantalizing inch of her. She mirrored my actions, her fingers deftly undoing each button of my shirt.

"God, you're so gorgeous," I whispered. The sight of her, half-undressed before me, was more intoxicating than any liquor.

"Yes," she breathed out, a single word that was both a plea and a command.

Clothes became a memory as we clawed them off and let them drop to the floor. Our bare skin came together, setting off sparks where we touched, every nerve in my body firing at once. I traced the curve of her waist, committing the softness of her flesh to memory, while she explored the hard planes of my chest and abdomen with a rough, trembling desire that matched my own.

We stumbled toward the bed, a tangle of limbs and lips. I was so hard, I felt about to burst. I needed to be within her, consumed by her, and I couldn't wait.

"Take me, Aiden. Hard and fast." Her voice was demanding, laced with boldness as she stared at me.

A jerked nod was all I could manage as I climbed onto the bed. The heat of body beneath me drowned out my senses. I reached for the nightstand drawer, my movements almost frantic, fumbling for the little foil packet. With hands that shook, I rolled on the condom, my body poised at the brink.

I slid on top of her, skin to skin, heat to heat. I positioned myself at her entrance, our gazes locked. Then, with one furious thrust full of pent-up longing, I buried myself deep within her. The sensation was beyond thought, a primal instinct taking over as I moved within her, each stroke fueled by years of dreams becoming vivid reality. She arched and cried my name, fueling me even more. Heat coursed through my veins, my heart a drumbeat echoing hers. This wasn't making love.

This was claiming and being claimed, a storm of emotion and flesh entwined.

She wrapped her legs around me, pulling me deeper, and I obliged with a strength and fury that left no room for anything less than total surrender. For either of us. We moved together, a rhythm born of old familiarity and new discovery, building toward an inevitable release.

Stella pushed against my chest, fierce determination in her eyes. Her hands were firm on my shoulders, and with a swift movement, she flipped our positions, leaving me staring up at her. She perched above me like some wild goddess, her back arching in an arc of pure seduction, hair cascading like a dark waterfall, catching the light that slipped through the open doorway.

"Oh my God," I gasped, my voice ragged. The sight of her sent a rush of heat to every nerve ending, nearly sending me over the edge before we'd barely begun. Our bodies entwined fluidly, a dance as natural as the ebb and flow of the tide outside, pulling and pushing with a rhythm that was all our own.

Our kisses deepened, becoming even hungrier and more demanding. Our sighs and groans filled the room, melding with the creak of bedsprings, the whisper of skin against skin. We moved together in a primal dance, raw and unfiltered, the years apart only fueling the fire that now consumed us.

"Yes! God, Aiden," Stella breathed out, her voice laced with the intensity of our connection. "Don't stop. Never stop."

Her words stoked the flames, and I felt myself spiraling toward a climax that had been building for what seemed like a lifetime. With every roll of her hips, every clench of her around me, I was drawn closer to the brink. She rode me with a fervor that matched my own, her body a vision of ecstasy that would be seared into my memory.

"Stella!" The name erupted from me, torn from the depths of my soul. Pleasure exploded within me, a release so monumental it was as if every pent-up regret, every moment of longing, burst from me in a deluge. My body shuddered violently, gripping her tight as if I could hold on to this moment and never let go. The world narrowed to the beat of our hearts, pounding in perfect unison, two lost souls finally aligned.

My fingers traced patterns across the small of her back as we clung to each other, riding out the waves of our shared oblivion. There was no past, no future, just the eternal present of Stella and me, united. This was where I belonged.

This was home.

Slowly, the sweat that beaded our skin began to cool in the evening air, yet the warmth between us only grew stronger. As I lay with Stella nestled in the crook of my arm, I felt a peace that had eluded me for years. Her breath against my neck was a soothing rhythm.

"Please tell me I'm not dreaming this," I murmured, pressing my lips to her soft hair.

Her gentle laugh vibrated against my chest. "Believe it, Aiden."

My fingertips traced the curve of her spine, savoring the smoothness of her skin. "I'm never letting you go again."

Stella lifted her head, her brown eyes glinting. "Then don't."

And she sealed that promise with a kiss that tasted of desire and love. As her lips slanted over mine, each gentle press a reaffirmation, my heart sang. This woman, entwined with me in heart and body, was my anchor.

Contentment settled over us like a warm, comforting blanket. Our conversation dwindled to nothing more than shared breaths and the occasional brush of lips, a silent language that was louder than words. In the quiet harmony of our embrace, sleep crept upon us, a gentle tide pulling us into its depths. Stella's breathing deepened, and her body relaxed fully against mine. I tightened my hold and wrapped her in my love. Finally, a smile stretched my lips and I followed her lead, letting the peaceful darkness take me.

# Chapter Thirty-Three

## Stella

THE NEXT AFTERNOON, my stomach fluttered and flitted as I dragged my feet across the resort grounds, my sandals leaving fleeting impressions in the soft grass. The emotion felt so foreign compared to what I had been basking in—willingly drowning in—since Aiden and I had collided yesterday. I took a deep breath, trying to exhale the tight energy building at the task I was about to accomplish. Orchid's rose-colored walls blushed in the sunlight, but that wasn't my destination.

My gaze drifted over to where Ben Coleridge was working, the muscles in his back flexing as he gathered tools into his wheelbarrow. The landscaping crew was wrapping up their duties, their last day of transforming the resort coming to an end.

I hesitated for a moment, taking in the changes—the new flower beds bursting with color, the meticulously trimmed hedges. The palm trees were soaring and healthy, croton plants provided pops of color, and our new underground irrigation was hidden and invisible. I couldn't fault the work Ben and the rest of the crew had done, even if it had been carried out under a cloud of misunderstandings and resentment. With a steadying breath, I approached him.

"Ben," I called out softly, not wanting to startle him.

He turned, dirt smudged across his brow, and for a long moment, his movements paused. His eyes locked onto mine, and his guarded expression brought an embarrassed flush to my face. I watched as he straightened up, wiping his hands on his jeans, trying to brush away the soil that clung to his skin.

"Stella," he acknowledged, his voice careful.

"I owe you an apology. I judged you unfairly... about everything that happened with the thefts." I swallowed hard, my words laced with regret. "You didn't deserve what I accused you of. And you didn't deserve how I treated you."

His face was a closely guarded fortress, shadows of emotions flickering behind his blue eyes. There was hurt there, etched deep, but also something resolute. As if he was used to accusations and adding more bricks to the walls he'd built to protect himself.

"Thanks for saying that," Ben finally said after a heavy silence. His nod was slow, deliberate. "I've made my fair share of mistakes. I'm only trying to make things right now."

I could see the weight of the past resting on his shoulders, not unlike the weight I had been carrying around until Aiden helped me set it down. "I hope you find what you're looking for. Again, I'm sorry."

He nodded, but his face remained inscrutable. Then his expression softened slightly. Not a smile, but the hard cast of his face relaxed. "Good luck, Stella."

As he bent to pick up more tools, I turned to leave, feeling a new lightness in my chest. An apology was a small step, but it was a step forward nonetheless. With the weight of destructive patterns lifting from my heart, I wandered toward the Big House. I had so much to look forward to, so much to be grateful for.

My mind drifted to Aiden, and an involuntary smirk tugged at my lips. Our incredible night together—and this morning too—replayed like a favorite song that you can't help but put on repeat. And how many more could we look forward to now?

The expanse of lawn where the festival had been held stretched out before me. It seemed different now, like a stage after the performance that still hinted at the sounds of laughter and music. But for me, the echoes were also whispers of newfound perspective, eyes no longer afraid to see what was directly in front of them—a chance at love, at happiness, that I had almost let slip by.

Approaching the house I'd grown up in and now called home again, my gaze narrowed at the sleek black SUV parked out front. Hunter's car. I hadn't realized he was visiting today, but then again, I'd taken off immediately after Matt's arrest.

I pushed open the kitchen door, the familiar creak a comforting welcome, and was greeted by a sight that warmed me more than the sultry Keys air ever could. Dad, Evan, and Hunter were gathered next to the sink. The sight of these two brothers casually leaning against the counter, *together*, sent a surge of deep emotion through me. For a moment, I let myself indulge in the rare harmony before joining their huddle.

"Hello there, guys," I said, reaching for the pitcher on

the counter and pouring myself a glass of lemonade. "What's up?"

"We were just discussing the situation about Matt," Dad said.

"At least that's over now," I said, then glanced at the floor. "I just apologized to Ben Coleridge. He took it better than I thought he would."

Dad reached out to grip my shoulder. "People change, and it takes courage to admit you were wrong. I'm proud of you, sweetie."

Then he turned to Hunter. "I'm proud of you too. Your plan worked beautifully. I honestly couldn't believe someone was stealing from us." His brow furrowed with regret, adding, "Shame it had to be someone we trusted."

Hunter's jaw clenched ever so slightly, then he nodded. "Thanks, Dad. It's done now. But I don't care if you're sick of hearing me say it. You need a security team. More than just cameras. Calypso Key is growing, more guests, more events—more risks."

"You've mentioned that before," I added before taking a sip of tart lemonade.

"Absolutely," Hunter insisted, his eyes flickering with a passion I hadn't seen in a long time. He always did have a protective streak a mile wide.

"I agree, and I've been making calls all morning," Evan chimed in, pushing off from the counter and crossing his arms. "There aren't any agencies around here, and the ones in Key West and Marathon are booked solid. No one is accepting new clients. We're kind of at a dead end here."

"We can't exactly expect the guests to fend for themselves," I added. The Markhams might have been known for many things, but poor hospitality wasn't one of them.

"Security isn't just about reacting. It's about anticipating and keeping your eyes open," Hunter said, as if he were addressing a prospective client instead of his family in a sunlit kitchen. "You don't wait for the storm to hit to start boarding up windows."

I leaned back against the cool granite of the kitchen island, letting the sharp sweetness of lemonade play on my tongue. Hunter was pacing now, a caged predator. I watched him, and the idea that came to me was so complete, and so perfect, I couldn't believe I hadn't thought of it earlier. I took in his towering, muscular physique, his short, trimmed beard, and that hushed, efficient way he moved with every step.

"You know, Hunter." My voice was steady despite the butterflies that had just alighted in my stomach. "Maybe it's time you put your money where your mouth is. Why don't you start your own security agency?"

He stopped mid-stride, turning to face me with a quizzical arch of his brow. "Excuse me?"

"Think about it," I pressed on, feeling the conviction in my words. "You've got the expertise, and you obviously have a passion for it. And it's clear there's a need here. From what Evan just said, it sounds like there's an opportunity in the Lower Keys just waiting for someone to grab it."

The room fell silent, Dad's and Evan's eyes bouncing between us like spectators at a tennis match. Hunter's gaze remained fixed on me.

"Start my own..." His voice trailed off, and for a moment, something flickered behind his guarded expression. Doubt? Excitement? Maybe both. His eyes slid to Evan, evaluating the reality of the two of them living near each other again.

"Stella might be on to something," Dad interjected.

"This resort is more than a business—it's our home. Who better to protect it than one of our own?"

"I don't know, Dad." Hunter ran a hand through his hair, a telltale sign of his mind racing. He looked out the window, where the ocean lay calm and inviting. "Starting a business, coming back home... it's not a decision to take lightly."

"Of course not." Offering a supportive smile, I kept from wringing my hands together. "But sometimes the biggest risks lead to the greatest rewards. And you've never been afraid of risk, have you?"

For a long, contemplative moment, he didn't respond. Then his eyes slowly traveled over the three of us, lingering on Evan. Evan gave a firm nod back.

"We'd all be here to support you," Dad added.

Hunter stood completely still, the wheels in his head almost visible. "Okay. I'll look into it."

A swell of pride filled me as I watched him embrace the idea. The spark in his eyes spoke of possibilities and new beginnings—a light that seemed to chase away the shadows that had lingered there for so long.

The room seemed to exhale, a collective release of tension as Hunter's decision hung in the air like a promise. I sensed it was the perfect moment to shift the atmosphere from serious to celebratory.

"Speaking of new beginnings. I have something to share myself." All eyes swiveled toward me, and a flutter of excitement danced in my chest. "Aiden and I are officially a couple. Again. For good this time."

"Is that so?" Evan's eyebrows shot up, his playful smirk betraying his feigned surprise. "I wondered if he was the reason you bolted out of here yesterday."

I nodded. "The situation with Ben made me realize I

was being blind with Aiden too. Fortunately, I wasn't too late. He put up with a lot from me, and we had some stuff to work out... but we did."

Dad gave me a one-armed hug. "I'm glad to hear that."

"And I'd love for him to be in on one of our family get-togethers," I said. "How about a family picnic at one of the deserted keys? I can't think of a more perfect way to introduce him. Again."

"Sounds like a great idea!" Dad said, his eyes crinkling at the corners.

"We could try for Sugar Beach," Evan added. "That place is pretty amazing if we can time it right."

"I love that idea!" My mind was already working on the possibilities.

As we basked in our plans, the kitchen door swung open with a gentle creak. Gabe strode in, wearing workout gear. He raised a brow, all easy confidence. "I was just on my way to work out in the gym." He wandered over to our little cluster. "What's going on here?"

"Perfect timing," Dad said. "We were just discussing a picnic for the whole family so Stella can officially show off Aiden. And there's one other big news item." He told Gabe about Hunter's decision to come home.

Gabe whirled to his little brother, who was several inches taller. "Seriously?"

Hunter tilted his head back and forth, equivocating. "Maybe. I'll look into it, but there could be an opportunity for a new security agency here. My boss is driving me up the wall and a couple of guys I work with would likely come with me. We'll see what happens."

Gabe embraced him, and they slapped each other's backs. Evan stayed out of it, but his posture was easy. I took comfort in that.

Dad grinned around the group. "I'm thinking we're going to need extra room for this get-together. Let's take *Shark Bait*."

"I'll drive if you want," Gabe offered.

Evan turned to me. "When were you thinking?"

"Probably not for a couple of weeks. It will take that long to clear all our schedules, and Gabe will need to check the marine forecast. I'm so excited!" I pressed my hands together and even Hunter smiled.

Gabe leaned against the counter, his gaze sliding over to Evan with a teasing glint. "Did you tell her yet?" he asked, nudging his head in my direction.

Evan's grin widened, and he shook his head. "Nope. Why don't you do the honors?"

That made my ears perk up. "Tell me what?"

"Let's just say," Gabe said, his smile growing sly, "that your next trip to Dove Key to see Aiden is going to have a little extra... scenery."

"Scenery?" My imagination ran wild with possibilities. "What are you talking about?"

"You'll see soon enough," Gabe teased. "Keep your eyes peeled when you cross from our island to Dove Key."

"Fine." I sighed, feigning annoyance while secretly delighted by the prospect of a surprise. "Keep your secrets. For now."

Gabe shrugged, refusing to tell me. Then pushed off the counter and headed toward the gym. "You'll know it when you see it. See you guys later."

Hunter straightened and set his empty glass of lemonade on the counter. "Well, I'd better start scouting locations if I'm going to open a new business." He shot me a smile when I couldn't contain my applause. He was really, *really* thinking about moving home!

"I need to split too," I added, placing my empty glass in the dishwasher. "There's a certain someone I need to see."

After a series of hugs, I dashed upstairs, the weight of the day lifting off my shoulders with each step. In my room, I changed into a sundress that fluttered against my skin—a splash of light red that brought out the warm tones in my complexion, according to Liv. My heart thrummed with anticipation.

Driving north, the familiar landmarks of Calypso Key blurred past my open window, the salty breeze playing with loose strands of my hair. As I approached the bridge that connected my world to Aiden's, something new caught my eye—a billboard on the other side of the road, its back turned toward me like a secret waiting to be unveiled. Curiosity tugged at me until I pulled over just beyond it. I stepped out of the car, the sun kissing my cheeks as I crossed the road to face the huge sign.

I stumbled to a halt, my jaw dropping open.

There I was, larger than life. My image was splashed across the billboard with a confident smile, Orchid's logo gleaming beside me. "Head Chef Stella Markham. Home of the Best Fresh Catch of the Day Specials in the Keys."

Laughter bubbled up from deep within, unrestrained and pure. It was perfect. Orchid wasn't just my workplace— it was my canvas, where I painted flavors and crafted experiences. Shaking my head, I hopped back into the car, the engine purring to life before I rejoined the road. The billboard shrank in the rearview mirror, but its image was imprinted on my mind, a reminder that sometimes, coming home could lead to the most unexpected of journeys.

The marina was still a busy hive of activity when I arrived. Aiden was already sitting on the deck of his boat, his hair ruffled by the sea breeze. He looked up from the bottle he was coaxing open, his warm eyes reflecting the sun's light.

"Hey, beautiful." The corners of his mouth tipped up in our shared secret smile.

"Hey, yourself." My voice was lighter than air as I stepped onto the deck, the gentle rock of the boat beneath me like a welcome embrace.

He popped the cork with a practiced twist, and the sound mingled with the soft lapping of water against the hull. Aiden filled two glasses with champagne, the bubbles rising eagerly to the surface as they tried to escape into the warm air. He handed me a glass, and our fingers brushed—a spark, an acknowledgment.

We clinked our glasses together, a toast to the unspoken but deeply felt. The cool liquid fizzed on my tongue, but it was the anticipation of his lips that had my heart racing. I set my glass down, drawn to him, and wrapped my arms around his neck. He responded, his hands finding the small of my back and pulling me closer. Our kiss was deep and searching, a tender exploration that promised more.

Always more.

When we finally parted, there was a shade of happiness in his eyes that surely matched the one in mine.

Aiden laughed, a deep, melodic sound that resonated through me. "What's got you so giddy?"

I shook my head, overwhelmed by the whirlwind of emotions—the surprise of Hunter coming home, the excitement of the billboard, and most of all, the contentment here in Aiden's presence. My heart swelled with the sheer wonder of it all. "I don't even know where to start! But if I had to pick the most important item... How would you like to join me and my family for a picnic?"

# Chapter Thirty-Four

Aiden

AS I TOOK A SIP, the frothy head of the beer tingled against my lips. The cool liquid was a welcome respite against the balmy September sun that draped over *Shark Bait*. Stella sat beside me on the side bench as we waited to leave the island, our arms and legs brushing. Whenever we were together, which could never be too often as far as I was concerned, I couldn't stand *not* to touch her. To convince myself that she was really here.

"Where are they?" Gabe muttered. His eyes searched the area near the canal, his brow creased beneath the brim of his worn baseball cap.

Hailey, with her sun-kissed cheeks and expectant gaze, tapped his shoulder. "I know what you said, but maybe we shouldn't wait..."

"Not yet, angel," he told her, his eyes softening.

I cocked my head, trying to figure out their exchange, then let it go, too happy and content to muse over mysteries. Around us, the deck of Calypso Key's dive boat played host to nearly the entire clan of Markhams. Maia and Wyatt stayed close to daughter Skye. Now over a year old, she toddled on legs made even more unsure by the boat's gentle movement, her bright pink life vest making her seem bigger. Stella's face was covered in a huge smile at seeing all of her family gathered. Even Nona was there, her spry form eager for the adventure.

As Stella and I savored the moment, Gabe's voice cut through the chatter, tinged with a note of impatience. "Here they are."

I turned to follow his line of sight. April and Liv approached *Shark Bait* with hurried steps. April, her long blonde hair catching the light, offered an athletic contrast to Liv's voluptuous figure crowned by a long tumble of curls. They climbed aboard amidst apologies for their tardiness, citing a friend in need of comfort.

"Let's go! Off to Sugar Beach," Gabe announced with the authority of a captain taking charge of his ship. He climbed up to the wheelhouse, and the motor thrummed to life. After Wyatt untied the boat, we motored out of the canal at a slow idle. Across from us, Liv and April grabbed soft drinks before settling next to Evan. Gabe smoothly throttled up as he steered us out to sea.

"What's up?" Stella's inquiry was gentle but edged with concern as she alternated her gaze between the two women.

"Brenna Coleridge," Liv said, tipping her head in a gesture of compassion. "We've become friends in our book club, and she just had a nasty breakup with her boyfriend. He didn't take it well, so April and I wanted to be there for her." Her voice held a note of apology, not for their lateness, but for bringing a shadow over the day.

"Everything okay?" I asked.

Liv confirmed with a nod, yet something in her tone

suggested it wasn't quite the end of the story. Beside me, Stella remained quiet, her attention drifting. Following her gaze, I noticed Hunter, rigid as if carved from stone, his stare fixed on Liv and April with burning intensity.

"What does 'he didn't take it well' mean, exactly?" His voice was a low growl as he leaned forward.

April hastened to reassure us. "Brenna's fine. Just shaken up. Her ex can be a jerk. But now he's in the past, right where he belongs." She raised her can of soda in a salute to end the conversation, and maybe trying to ease Hunter's blazing expression. "Enough drama, we're getting close!" With a bright smile that washed away any lingering tension, April redirected our focus to the horizon and pointed.

I stood and shaded my eyes with my hand, a smile stretching my lips. Stella had told me where we were going, but she didn't do it justice. A long strip of sand slowly appeared out of the turquoise water, a sandy shoal that only appeared at low tide. The tropical sun quickly dried the powdery white grains, making it the perfect setting for a picnic.

After safely dropping the anchor, Gabe handed me a dry backpack filled with picnic supplies while shrugging into one himself. Evan and Hunter did likewise, and we all eased into the water and waded to shore. I turned back to check on little Skye, but she squealed with delight as both parents held her hands and her life vest kept her easily afloat.

I laughed at the sight. "Guess I don't need to worry about water emergencies, considering both of that little one's parents are professionals."

Wyatt returned my grin. "Skye will be a water baby, for sure. But it's always reassuring to have a doctor nearby."

I took Stella's hand, and we emerged onto the warm, soft sand. We spread out a cluster of blankets, and my love took charge of setting up our delicious picnic. She'd cooked it herself, and her touches were obvious in the tropical ceviche, grilled fruit skewers, and blackened dorado wraps. Individual key lime pie tarts finished the spread. Plenty of soft drinks and beer were on offer, which Hunter had carried in his backpack.

"Hey, Evan!" Wyatt called out as we started eating. "Maia might need some baseball pointers from you."

"Why would that be?" Evan raised an eyebrow, and I zeroed in, intrigued by the unexpected turn in conversation.

"Yup," Maia chimed in, her eyes alight with excitement. "A new recreational baseball league is forming, and I've talked to several resort staff who are interested. We might have enough people for a Calypso Key team. Any chance you'd be interested?"

Conversation dimmed, and everyone's head turned to Evan, whose face was turning red. I remembered well from my high school days what a talented player he had been, even as a youngster.

Evan gave a shaky smile, rubbing the back of his neck. "Nah. Nobody wants a washed-up ball player on their team. I'd be a liability."

"That's not true, and you know it," Hunter said quietly. Echoes of agreement went around the crowd, but Evan's discomfort was obvious, so we let it slide.

"Are you joining, Hunter?" Maia prodded, undeterred.

He shrugged, a half-smile playing on his lips. "I suppose, as long as it doesn't start until after I get down here."

A few days ago, Stella was thrilled when Hunter had called to inform her that he'd found a business premises with an attached apartment. Though he'd tempered the news by telling her it would be several months before his arrival.

"Count me in too. I'd love to play!" The words were out of my mouth before I could second-guess them. But the idea of being part of something so communal, so unlike anything in my old life, was irresistible.

"Absolutely! The more, the merrier." Maia clapped her hands together, and a ripple of laughter spread across the group.

With Stella's warmth seeping into my skin, I watched the interplay of this family I had come to know again. The way they ribbed each other, the way they rallied to put the broken pieces back together, it was all so... real. Coming to Dove Key, I'd been a man charting an unknown course, alone. But now, here I was, surrounded by people who were fast becoming my own kind of kin. And Stella was the compass that had led me here.

"Happy?" I whispered to her, leaning in close enough to catch the scent of the sea in her hair.

"More than I've ever been. And to think, all it took was removing my blindfold to see what was right in front of me." Her hand reached up, fingers tracing the line of my jaw. I caught it and pressed a kiss to her palm.

Nine-year-old Hailey, practically vibrating with antici-pation, stood with a huff and called out to her father. "Dad! Come oooon. We're all done with lunch." Her waves of brown hair bounced on her shoulders.

Gabe responded with an easy smile, reaching out a hand to his daughter and drawing her to sit in front of him, while he cradled April with his other arm. They created a picture that warmed me to my core. "Okay, go ahead," Gabe said gently, nodding to his nearly bouncing daughter.

Hailey jumped back up to her feet, her voice pitching high as she screeched, "April's having a baby!"

The cheers that erupted were spontaneous, and I found myself clapping along, laughing at Hailey's enthusiasm. It was infectious, the kind of news that sent ripples of happiness through the gathered family. April and Gabe came together in a kiss, his hand reaching to brush the hair from her forehead. I looked around, catching sight of Evan and Liv sharing a smile that wasn't laced with surprise like the others. A knowing look passed between them, and it clicked —they were in on the secret.

April caught Liv's eye and arched a brow meaningfully in their direction. "But we're not the only ones with an announcement, are we? Last night there were some unexpected fireworks at the baseball game!"

Liv's cheeks reddened as she extended her left hand. On her finger, a diamond glittered under the sunny light of day. Next to me, Stella sprang to her feet, her movements quick with excitement as she wrapped Liv in an exuberant hug.

"Oh, don't fuss! I don't want to upstage April and Gabe," Liv protested. Her voice was muffled against Stella's shoulder, but the embarrassment did nothing to hide her radiant smile.

"Nonsense," Nona chimed in from where she sat on a padded cushion across from me, her tone dismissive of any such worry. She got up to give Liv a hug of her own, then Evan. Her wise eyes sparkled. "This family can handle two sets of wonderful news. In fact, I'd say we're brimming with it." She nodded to me, and I smiled in return.

Warren rose to stand next to his mother, his arm circling Nona in a gesture that spoke of their shared history and love. His grin matched the pride in his eyes as he swept them around the gathering.

Stella returned to me, her eyes gleaming with unshed tears of joy as she leaned close. "Can you believe it? My whole family is getting along—it's been over a decade since..."

"Since things felt right?" I offered, my arm snaking around her waist to pull her closer.

She leaned back into me, molding herself to my side. "Not completely right. Hunter and Evan aren't exactly best friends like they used to be. But they're coexisting and getting along. And look at me too. I've figured out that I can have both my dream career and love."

"Here's to new starts," I whispered, pressing a gentle kiss to her temple.

"Look at Hailey," she murmured with a laugh. "She's practically jumping with excitement."

"Can't blame her," I said, my laughter mingling with hers. "Becoming a big sister is huge news."

"Everything today feels that way."

I nodded before turning just enough to rest my cheek against her forehead, reveling in the softness there. Then, breaking away reluctantly, I moved toward Warren, who was standing with his feet in the water as he scanned the sea.

"Beautiful day for a picnic, isn't it?" I said as I approached him.

"Nothing like the open water to clear your mind," Warren replied, his voice seasoned with the salt of many years spent at sea.

"Stella tells me you're providing the fresh catch for Orchid. Must feel good to be out on the sea again."

He smiled. "I could fish every day and not tire of it.

You've been good for Stella, Aiden. You balance each other. I'm glad you returned to take over Dr. Nelson's practice."

Warmth filled me at the praise, which meant a lot from this man. "I love it here. I love what I do, and I love your daughter very much."

"Just don't let me hear otherwise and we'll get along fine." His laugh tempered the edge of his words, and I liked that he was protective of his children. "You'll fit right in with us, don't worry. Stella tells me you're quite the sailor. Do you enjoy fishing too?"

"Absolutely," I said with a nod. "There's something about the ocean—it's where I feel most alive."

"If you have a free morning, you should come out with me on *Real Deal* sometime."

I nodded eagerly. "I'm experimenting with flex hours at the clinic, moving our appointments to the afternoon and evening one day a week, which gives us the morning off. It's been a hit so far, and it helps Stella and me line up our schedules a little better. So I'll take you up on that offer soon." We stood side by side in comfortable silence, watching the waves dance in the shallows.

After Stella's father excused himself to talk to Gabe, I threaded my way through the clusters of family as warm sand stuck to my feet. The salty breeze carried laughter and snippets of conversation. I caught Stella's eye and hitched my head toward April and Liv, who were chatting as they packed up the remnants of our feast.

"Hey, congratulations to you both," I said as we approached. "An engagement and a baby announcement."

April beamed, the healthy radiance of impending motherhood already lighting her features. "Thanks. Gabe and I are very excited. Neither of us is getting younger, so we're thrilled I got pregnant so fast."

"Have you and Evan set a date?" Stella asked Liv, admiring her ring again.

"Oh no! I'm still getting my feet back under me with the two bakeries. It'll be a little while yet."

After a few more minutes of conversation, Liv and April excused themselves to fold the blankets. Soon we were back in the water, then climbing aboard the dive boat. Gabe pointed us back to Calypso Key and we left Sugar Beach behind, though I was sure the memories would stay.

As I stood at the bow, the wind whipping past, Stella slid into the space beside me. The boat gently rocked us, and without thinking, I stepped behind her and wrapped her in my arms, pulling her back against my chest. I rested my chin on the top of her head as we watched the island slowly grow larger before us. The water flew by in a stunning mixture of blue hues. This was more than just an end-of-summer celebration. It was the start of something new. Not just for Liv and Evan, or Gabe and April, or even Hunter. But for Stella and me too. It was hard to imagine a future any brighter than the one unfolding before us. A future I had hoped for and that she had been brave enough to embrace.

"Thank you," she said softly. "For not giving up on me. On us."

"I don't give up easily," I said, my voice holding a tinge of levity. Then I brushed a soft kiss over her temple. "You're worth it. *We're* worth it."

She turned in my arms, her gaze capturing mine. Her hand rose, fingers tender as they brushed my cheek. "I'm very lucky you sailed back into my life. And this is only the beginning."

"Only the beginning." I leaned in, my forehead

touching hers as we shared a breath, a moment, a silent vow. A second chance realized.

## Epilogue

Stella

## SIX MONTHS LATER

I CRADLED a delicate orchid in my palm, admiring the vibrant lavender petals thriving under my care. Setting it gently on the smooth wooden surface, I smiled. The special plant display Gabe had crafted was more than just woodwork—it was a symbol of new beginnings and deserved its place in front of the bright, sunny window. After Matt had been arrested, I bought two new specimens of the *Queen Sirikit* orchid to nurture myself before placing them in the restaurant. Matt had hurled both at Hunter in an effort to get away, which was how he got the black eye.

Note—do *not* mess with Hunter.

I returned the plant to the spot next to its twin before brushing my fingers over the empty space on the top shelf. This was reserved for really special orchids, ones I hardly dared to dream of owning. I sighed contentedly, maybe even hopefully.

Aiden's and my cottage, now peppered with unopened boxes and scattered belongings, felt like the most inviting place on Dove or Calypso Keys. Despite the continued chaos of moving in only a few days ago. Three of these cozy two-bedroom homes stood in a row like soldiers, slightly separated from the Big House. We took the one on the southern end, the cottage nearest the Big House itself housing Maia and her family.

The canal winked at me from the bottom of the meadow, where *Catch of the Day* swayed gently, her lines secured to the dock. Securely fastened to the console, Aiden's compass was a reminder of what was important for both of us. He and I could set sail at a moment's notice, chasing the horizon whenever we chose. It was freedom anchored right outside our window yet tied to home.

Turning away from the window, my gaze swept across the cottage. Aged but spotless wood floors held the history of countless footsteps that had tread upon them before us, while the stone and timber walls stood strong. Exposed beams crossed the ceiling, and their roughness contrasted with the gentle light filtering through the windows.

Aiden had left early this morning, tight-lipped about his mysterious errand. His absence stretched the day thin, leaving me adrift in thoughts of how much had shifted in our lives. Six months ago, we were picking up the pieces, and now, here we were, delicately piecing together a shared existence. Boxes and all, this cottage felt right—like a puzzle finding its missing piece.

The front door creaked open, and I spun around, a smile breaking across my face. Aiden stepped through, the afternoon sun casting a glow about him. His eyes were alight, a secret dancing behind their blue depths as he concealed something behind his back.

"What are you hiding?" Bending sideways at the waist, I tried to peer around his frame.

"Nothing," he replied, his voice thick with poorly disguised mischief. The corners of his mouth twitched upward as he held back a grin that threatened to betray his secret.

"Come on, show me," I urged, taking a step closer.

He laughed. "So impatient!"

"Only when it comes to you," I shot back. My heart skipped with anticipation.

"Are you sure? I don't want to interrupt if you were doing something important."

"Dammit, Aiden!"

I stomped my foot and he burst into laughter. With a dramatic flourish worthy of a stage actor, he revealed his hidden treasure. My hands flew to my mouth, holding in a gasp. It was an orchid.

But not just any orchid.

I recognized it at once. The orchid was covered with delicate cream-colored petals, each highlighted in the darker pink center by the very distinctive and enchanting face of a monkey. My breath caught in my throat as I reached out hesitantly to take it from him, afraid that somehow its delicate beauty would vanish if touched.

"Where on earth did you find this?" I murmured, my voice quiet as I cradled the plant like the rarest of jewels.

Aiden's smile softened. "Let's just say I have my ways."

I couldn't tear my gaze away from the orchid. Its unique petals stared back at me, each looking like it might wink at any moment. This was more than a flower. I had dreamed of this plant for years—this was what had caused me to become entranced with orchids in the first place. Aiden had given me not just an orchid, but a tangible piece of my deepest desires. And he had done it with such casual grace, as if gifting me the world was nothing out of the ordinary for him.

"Thank you," I managed to say, finally looking up at him. "It's perfect. How...?"

As Aiden's chest swelled with pride, his lips parted in a victorious grin. "I found an orchid specialist up in Homestead. I've been emailing with her for months, waiting for her to get one in stock. Last night, she told me she had it."

Homestead? My mind raced north along Highway One, the miles ticking away. I burst into laughter, the sound bouncing against the stone walls of our home. "That's three hours away!"

"Exactly." His eyes twinkled as he leaned against the doorframe. "Why do you think it took me so long?"

I shook my head, still cradling the monkey-face orchid, now nestled in my palm like a fragile secret. The room seemed to brighten, every sunbeam pointing toward the unique gift that had traveled such a distance just for me.

Gently, almost reverently, I placed the orchid atop the wooden stand Gabe had crafted. In the most prominent position, the orchid stood out, its quirky petals smiling at us both, a silent witness to Aiden's gesture.

"Welcome," I murmured, addressing the plant as though it understood my gratitude. "You're going to love it here."

I spun around then, propelled by a whirlwind of emotion, and flung myself into Aiden's waiting arms. He caught me with ease, his body a familiar landscape of strength and warmth.

"I love it." My voice was thick and I swallowed over the

lump in my throat. "But you didn't have to do all this, Aiden. One grand gesture was plenty."

"Hey," he whispered, his breath warm against my ear. "Seeing you like this, happy. That's all I need."

A deep laugh rumbled in Aiden's chest, a sound that always managed to make my own heart feel lighter. His arms were still wrapped around me, strong and sure, but I sensed a shift in his mood—a playful annoyance edged with affection.

"No thanks to Luke," he said, a snort punctuating his disbelief. "He told me women don't make big gestures, only the guys. He knew exactly what he was doing, the jerk."

"Maybe he realized we both needed to give a little. And trust a little more. But he's right—women make grand gestures too." I'd roared with laughter when Aiden told me the story of Luke's wise council. But now I was serious as a giant swell of emotion filled every cell of my body. "You're the only person on earth who understands why I want that orchid. What it means to me."

Completely serious now, his gaze held mine. He wanted to say something, and the gravity in his eyes caught my breath. "I wanted to give you something that would remind you every single day of us—of this unexpected, beautiful thing we've got. I wanted you to have a piece of my heart that you could see, touch... Something as rare and extraordinary as you are."

My throat tightened, and the room fell away until there was only Aiden, his warm eyes reflecting a truth so raw and real it made my own pulse quicken. This man, who had learned the language of my silences and the map of my inner scars, was offering me more than a flower or a gesture. He was offering me his world. Our world.

"Every time I look at that orchid," I said quietly, slowly,

"I'll think of you. Of how you drove three—no, six!—hours just to see me smile. Of how you never gave up on us, even when I didn't realize I needed you."

"Always," he vowed, the word as solid and enduring as the stone walls of the cottage that cradled our new life.

"Always," I repeated, sealing the promise with a kiss that tasted of hope.

Aiden's face shifted, the playful spark in his eyes giving way to something deeper and more profound, a flash of vulnerability. "I have one more thing."

My heart hitched as he reached into his jacket pocket, producing a small velvet box that seemed to absorb the room's warmth. He opened it slowly to reveal a diamond ring that caught the afternoon light like a prism.

"Look," he said softly, his gaze never leaving mine. "Don't get scared. I know you're not the white-picket-fence-married-with-two-point-five-kids type. So I'm holding onto this... Just in case you ever decide you want to put down roots in more than your orchid pots." The corner of his mouth twitched. "No pressure, though. I just want you to know I have this. Ring or no ring, I'm here. For good."

As I took in the glinting stone—a symbol of permanence in a world where everything felt as transient as shifting tides —something shifted within me. Then solidified. My past fears and uncertainties had already been nearly vanquished. Now the tiny remainder melted away under this symbol of his commitment.

"Well, you know..." I couldn't help the grin that spread across my face. "It would be downright irresponsible to leave such a beautiful piece of craftsmanship lying around inside a drawer. We're still moving in. What if it gets lost?"

Understanding flickered in Aiden's blue eyes, the same ones that had seen through every façade I'd ever tried to wear. With a sage nod, he gently took my hand and slipped the ring onto my finger—fitting as perfectly as if it had always been meant to be there.

"You're right. It's safer this way," he agreed, his words wrapped in the twinkling of his eyes.

The metal felt foreign yet destined on my finger, a circle of promise and a future I hadn't dared to dream of until now. Aiden's hopeful gaze held mine, his question hanging in the air between us.

"We aren't kids passing notes in class anymore," he said, the corners of his mouth lifting in that boyish grin that still made my heart skip beats. "But how about wearing my ring? A promise ring."

I laughed through the tears that welled up. Shaking my head, I pushed back strands of hair that had fallen loose from my ponytail. Joy filled me that was so intense it was nearly painful. "Absolutely not."

Aiden's smile faltered, his eyes widening with shock, and he took an involuntary step back. But there was no room for doubt, not here, not in the warmth of our cottage where every wooden beam and sunlit corner spoke of second chances.

Closing the gap between us, I reached out, my fingers finding the familiar strength of his neck as I laced them behind it. The silkiness of his hair, the warmth of his skin, it all spoke of home. "We're beyond school-age promise rings, aren't we? I might not care for tradition. But Aiden Mitchell, I want to be your wife very much. So what do you say? Let's get married."

His eyes searched mine, looking for the anchor in the storm of emotions. And he found it in the depths of my gaze. The certainty that whatever tides may come, we would navigate them together.

"Anywhere. Any way you want," he said quietly.

And I knew, with the certainty of the ground beneath my feet, that this was where I was meant to be. "Promise me something."

"Anything."

"Never stop making grand gestures." My heart in every word even as my lips twitched into a smile. "They suit you."

As we stood entwined in the golden light of our small cottage by the sea, he dipped his head to capture my lips in a kiss that tasted of unbreakable promises. A kiss as bright as every sunrise we'd witnessed together and all those yet to come.

---

THANK you for reading MEMORIES OF YOU! Second chance romance is one of my all-time favorite tropes, and I hope you loved Stella and Aiden. And there is one Markham story left... Get ready for Hunter and Brenna!

SHADES OF YOU: A Small Town Forbidden Romance
Calypso Key Series

**Over a century of bad blood. A woman worth fighting for.**
**And a past that refuses to let go**.

*Hunter:*
I returned to the Florida Keys to face my demons— to rebuild both my life and my shattered relationship with my brother. I'm starting my security business when Brenna Coleridge crashes back into my world.

She's everything I've ever wanted, but she's also a Coleridge. Our families have fought for generations, and the thought of us together is as unthinkable as it is forbidden. Yet, when her ex becomes a threat, I'll do anything to keep her safe—even if it means risking everything.

With every stolen kiss and illicit touch, the line between protector and partner blurs. Until we obliterate it altogether and our connection explodes into passion. But I'm a man with a dark past, and Brenna deserves the world. A world I lost when my brother nearly died because of me.

Can we overcome the odds stacked against us, or are we destined to be star-crossed lovers?

**Dive into Calypso Key in the final installment of this small-town series of steamy interconnected standalones. Can Romeo and Juliet be rewritten with a happy ending?**

SHADES OF YOU, the finale of the
Calypso Key Series

IF YOU WANT a glimpse into Stella and Aiden's future, sign up for my Beach Read Update!

As a thank you for subscribing, **I'll send you a bonus scene** that offers a peek at them several years in the future. Click below to sign up:

Beach Read Update
(www.erinbrockus.com/memories)

MY BEACH READ Update subscribers hear about all my free content, plus exclusive offers and sales. I'd love to have you along! Plus, you'll stay up to date with cover reveals, sneak peeks, and exclusive content about the Calypso Key books and my other beachy universes.

If you're already on my list, I've got you covered! At the bottom of each newsletter is a link to all my free content for subscribers. Just find your last email from me to read this bonus, as well as any others you might have missed. Or you can simply sign up again—you'll have your bonus in a flash.

**CALYPSO KEY SERIES:**

Main Novels:

*Visions of You:* A Small Town Single Dad Romance

*Because of You:* A Small Town Fake Relationship Romance

*Memories of You:* A Small Town Second Chance Romance

*Shades of You:* A Small Town Forbidden Romance

Associated Short Stories and Novellas:

*Traces of You:* A Small Town Rivals to Lovers Romance*

* Subscriber exclusive

**HALF MOON BAY SERIES:**

## Main Novels:

*Finding Hope*: Half Moon Bay Book 1

*Defending Hope*: Half Moon Bay Book 2

*Rising Hope*: Half Moon Bay Book 3

*Forever Hope*: Half Moon Bay Book 4

*Half Moon Whim*: Half Moon Bay Book 5 (Standalone)

*Half Moon Ember*: Half Moon Bay Book 6 (Standalone)

*Half Moon Aqua*: Half Moon Bay Book 7

*Crowning Hope*: Half Moon Bay Book 8

## Associated Short Stories and Novellas:

Tropical Dawn: A Half Moon Bay Prequel Novella

*Tropical Chance**: A Second Chance Half Moon Bay Novella

*Tropical Hope**: A Half Moon Bay Prequel Short Story

* Subscriber exclusives

## Standalone Books:

*In Too Deep*: A Second Chance Romance

*Beached in Bali*: A Friends to Lovers Romance

# About the Author

**Dive into steamy small-town romance, where passion meets paradise!**

Erin Brockus writes steamy small town romances that transport readers to exotic, tropical destinations, and provide a perfect beachy getaway from everyday life. Her mature, relatable characters are impossible not to root for, and she weaves breezy romantic adventure into her stories, emphasizing scuba diving and the ocean.

Drawing on her twin passions for diving and travel, Erin infuses her characters and narratives with a sense of excitement and passion. Her idea of the perfect day involves sipping a cocktail on the beach after exploring the ocean depths.

Erin lives in Washington wine country with her husband, who is also a scuba instructor. She is currently hard at work on her next island adventure. When she's not writing, you might find her out for a run or cycling through the countryside on the next quest for adventure.